SNAKE OIL:
IT ALL COMES AROUND

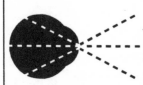

This Large Print Book carries the
Seal of Approval of N.A.V.H.

SNAKE OIL:
IT ALL COMES AROUND

BOOK THREE

MARCUS GALLOWAY

THORNDIKE PRESS

A part of Gale, a Cengage Company

Farmington Hills, Mich • San Francisco • New York • Waterville, Maine
Meriden, Conn • Mason, Ohio • Chicago

GALE
A Cengage Company

Copyright © 2019 by Marcus Pelegrimas.
Thorndike Press, a part of Gale, a Cengage Company.

ALL RIGHTS RESERVED
This novel is a work of fiction. Names, characters, places and incidents are either the product of the author's imagination, or, if real, used fictitiously.
The publisher bears no responsibility for the quality of information provided through author or third-party Web sites and does not have any control over, nor assume any responsibility for, information contained in these sites. Providing these sites should not be construed as an endorsement or approval by the publisher of these organizations or of the positions they may take on various issues.
Thorndike Press® Large Print Western.
The text of this Large Print edition is unabridged.
Other aspects of the book may vary from the original edition.
Set in 16 pt. Plantin.

LIBRARY OF CONGRESS CIP DATA ON FILE.
CATALOGUING IN PUBLICATION FOR THIS BOOK
IS AVAILABLE FROM THE LIBRARY OF CONGRESS

ISBN-13: 978-1-4104-8563-2 (hardcover alk. paper)

Published in 2019 by arrangement with Cherry Weiner Literary Agency

Printed in Mexico
1 2 3 4 5 6 7 23 22 21 20 19

SNAKE OIL:
IT ALL COMES AROUND

SPACE ONE
IT ALL COMES AROUND

CHAPTER ONE

Dakota Territories
1878

The town had a name, but it wasn't important enough to be committed to a sign. The scant amount of people who lived there knew the place's name but didn't travel far enough to feel the need to tell it to anyone they saw. And since most of the folks they saw were the same ones they'd seen the day before, none of that was much of a problem. The only problems they had were common to anyone who tried to make their living in the Badlands. Starvation, bear attacks, and the occasional Apache raiding party were common headaches for residents of those parts. At the moment, however, the folks in the small town had another problem. Its name was Dylan Garviss and he was extracting himself from the Dakota Broker & Exchange like a barbed arrow being pulled from a meaty thigh.

The Broker & Exchange was a long building taking up most of the town's second largest street. Being nestled in between the sheriff's office and a saloon was supposed to buy the business some measure of security. If the town's armed protectors couldn't be found in one of those two places, they were probably too far away to make much difference. When Garviss had ridden into town less than an hour ago, the sheriff was drinking in the saloon. When Garviss had decided to draw his .44 from the holster at his hip and announce his intentions to seize the stash of wealth kept in the Broker & Exchange's lockbox, the sheriff was walking to his office using a path that took him directly behind that very building. That way, within seconds after the first shots had been fired, the lawman was able to charge into the wide building to earn his pay.

Garviss's .44 spat two rounds into the counter dividing the small lobby of the building in half. Built much like the main room of a bank, the counter was just over waist-high and topped by an iron cage that stretched all the way to the ceiling. It would have been a formidable barrier if not for the rope tied to one of the bars near its base. The other end of the rope stretched all the way to the front door and outside where it

8

was tied securely out of sight.

"Open the damn door," Garviss snarled.

The man behind the counter on the other side of the bars nervously glanced at the small door leading to the public area of the lobby. He shook his head and lifted a shotgun in two trembling hands. "I can't do that," he said.

"You can and you will. Right now!"

"You should leave before the sheriff gets here," the clerk warned. "Or before I'm forced to shoot."

"Shoot me with what?" Garviss scoffed. "That scattergun? I got one better'n that!" As he spoke those words, Garviss holstered his .44 and reached over his shoulder to retrieve the weapon that was secured between his shoulder blades by a set of leather straps. The shotgun was sawed off on both ends, leaving a chipped wooden nub for a stock and two short, blackened barrels.

Before either man could pull his trigger, a shot was fired through the window behind the clerk. "That was just a warning," shouted a gruff voice from outside. "Come on out of there before things get worse!"

"Hear that?" the clerk said in a voice that was no longer so timid. "That's the sheriff. You're outgunned."

Shrugging, Garviss lowered his aim until

the shotgun was pointed at the top of the counter separating him from the clerk. He then fired both barrels at the counter, sending wood splinters and sparks into the air. He turned toward the building's front door and let out a short, harsh cry. Outside, a horse whinnied and stomped its hooves against the ground. The rope drew taut and, thanks to the damage done to the counter, yanked that bar straight out from its mooring to clatter noisily against the floor.

Garviss jumped over the bar as it was dragged from the room and climbed over the counter to land on the other side. His eyes were narrowed into slits when they met the clerk's startled gaze. Without a moment's hesitation nor a hint of fear, he pulled the shotgun from the other man's grasp and said, "Gimme the lockbox."

Any fire that had been in the clerk's soul was snuffed out by the outlaw's bold display. Even with the sheriff kicking in the back door to stomp into the building, the clerk didn't have enough gumption to do anything other than what Garviss had demanded. He kept his eyes on the shotgun that had so recently been in his possession while reaching down for the small iron box resting near his feet.

"And the others," Garviss said calmly.

Heavy footsteps thumped through the room, announcing the entrance of the man who'd busted in through the rear entrance. "What the hell is —" was all the sheriff managed to say before a blast from the clerk's shotgun ripped through the air to blow a hole in the wall at the back of the room.

Garviss didn't give a damn that his shot had only torn apart some wooden planks. He accepted the weight of the additional two lockboxes that were stacked on top of the one he already held. Balancing his prizes in one hand, Garviss dropped the empty shotgun and drew his .44 to fire in the general direction of the approaching lawman. That was enough to keep the sheriff back while Garviss climbed through the gap in the cage atop the counter. Once the outlaw's boots touched the floor on the other side, he wrapped both arms around the lockboxes to protect them like a swaddled infant.

Each box was the size of a large book. Once he made it back to his horse, Garviss stuffed them into his saddlebags before cutting the rope connecting the horse to the bar that had been pried from the Broker & Exchange. Several confused locals stood outside, carts and smaller buildings dotting the street, scratching their scruffy faces as they watched what was unfolding outside the wide building. A few of them were heeled and reached for their guns once the sheriff exploded through the front door.

"Stop that man!" the lawman hollered.

None of the locals were willing to draw any fire from Garviss now that he held his .44 at the ready and was looking for a target. Firing once toward the Broker & Exchange, he tapped his heels against his horse's sides to ride for the edge of town. The sheriff fired and missed, prompting the men in the immediate vicinity to do the same. By the time the gunshots built to a crackling storm, Garviss was on the outer edge of their range.

Only the first few bullets came close enough to cause Garviss much concern. He could hear the flying lead rip through the air all around him, but as he continued to ride down the street, they just became noise. He grinned at the thought of those frightened locals pulling their triggers in a panic, unable to hit anything other than the side of a building. His only concern had been the lawman and that eased once he rounded a corner to gallop down a narrower street.

There were still a few faces gawking at him from windows or behind cracked doors as Garviss raced for the edge of town. By

12

the time he got there, the sound of hooves beating against the ground echoed behind him. He'd reached the open trail, which was a short stretch of gravel-covered path leading into a range of sharp-edged hills. Garviss snapped his reins to coax some more speed from his horse. The animal pumped its head in time to its quickening steps while kicking up a cloud of dust in its wake.

More shots were fired from the town but were only wild displays of force from men eager to make up for their cowardice and failure.

Riding along a path he'd already scouted before entering town, Garviss tore through the Badlands and quickly left the trail behind. The terrain became rough in a hurry, but he knew it well enough to navigate the slopes and crags without endangering himself or his horse. The wind rushed through his ears along with the pounding of his excited heart. Before long, his breaths had become so heavy that it seemed he'd run all that way without the benefit of four able legs beneath him.

Before he spotted the glimmer of sunlight reflecting off of a watery surface, he pulled back on his reins and steered to the left. His horse broke through a thorny mess of branches to emerge quickly within a stone's throw of a good-sized pond. Still breathing heavily, Garviss climbed down from his saddle and landed heavily on his feet. He grunted while tensing one side of his body, all the while reaching for his saddlebag.

The lockbox he grabbed was like all of the others; heavy and cool to the touch. Garviss's fingers closed around it until his knuckles turned white. His eyes widened and his tongue flicked out to touch his parched lips. First, he tried to open it like he would any other box. When it didn't give way, he turned it over until he got a better look at the lock keeping it shut.

"Damn it," he snarled as though the lockbox was enforcing a personal vendetta by remaining locked.

Garviss fought the simple mechanism with growing impatience as sweat broke out on his brow. Wiping his pale cheek, he angrily threw the box to the ground and drew his .44 once again.

"Damn fool, Jack," he muttered while thumbing back the pistol's hammer. "Tryin' to sell me some damn key. I don't need no damned key." He punctuated his statement by pulling his trigger. Although the lockbox jumped a foot or so off the ground, it was still closed tight when it landed.

Garviss tried to steady his hand, which

was becoming increasingly difficult. His breathing was becoming shallow and salty perspiration dripped into his eyes. All of those things only served to anger him more. He fired again and again before eventually hitting his mark. Sparks flew from the front of the box and the lock shattered into several pieces.

Letting out a long, quaking breath, Garviss said, "Just what I thought. No key. No problem. Just gotta have brains."

The pistol was growing heavier in his hand, so he let it slip from his fingers instead of holstering it properly. Dropping to one knee, he swept aside the broken pieces of the lock so he could grab hold of the box and ease its lid all the way up. Garviss took his time, peering anxiously inside like a young boy getting his first glimpse at the soft wonders beneath a young woman's skirts.

Within the box, there was a small bundle of cash and a good amount of silver dollars. Garviss started to whoop happily but held his tongue and picked up his pistol instead. He picked up another lockbox, this time setting it gently on the ground before taking a few steps back. Swearing under his breath as he nearly tripped over a rock embedded in the dirt, he took a few moments to steady his aim. The next shot split the second box's lock in half. Rather than pick it up to examine its contents, Garviss dropped down to sit on the ground amid the boxes and metal remains of broken locks.

Garviss was panting now, opening the box so he could get a look inside. This one's contents put a broad smile on his face. He reached in with one hand to remove a few shiny pebbles and some gritty, glittering dust. As he manipulated the pebbles and rubbed the dust between his fingers, he nodded and expelled a wheezing laugh.

"I knew there'd be gold. I knew it! This should set me up for a good while."

Before he could get too excited, Garviss heard the rumble of horses approaching from the trail he'd left behind. He clamped his mouth shut and hastily closed the boxes before shoving them back into his saddle-bags. Garviss took hold of his reins to lead his horse further away from the thorny wall obscuring the pond from anyone passing by. He hunkered down and tugged hard on the reins until his horse bent its knees to lay on the ground beside him.

As the hoof beats drew closer, voices became more discernible.

"He went this way!" shouted someone who sounded several years younger than

Garviss.

"Course he did," replied another man Garviss recognized as the town's sheriff. "Only way he could've gone without us seein' him. Them shots we heard came from this way, too."

"Son of a bitch was tryin' to ambush us," the younger man said.

Garviss held on to his pistol with one hand while his other hand fished fresh rounds from the loops in his gun belt. As his eyes strained to catch a glimpse of his pursuers, his fingers went through the familiar motions of replacing the spent rounds from his cylinder.

"Wasn't no ambush," the sheriff said.

"Then what was all that shootin'?"

"Wasn't more than three or four shots. Trust me, boy," the lawman added. "When someone fires a shot at you, you'll know it for certain."

Now that his .44 was fully loaded, Garviss eased the cylinder shut. His arm jerked unexpectedly, nearly causing him to squeeze the trigger or drop the pistol altogether. He swore softly to himself while struggling to pull in a slow breath.

"So he went up into the hills?" the younger man asked.

"Either that or he's hiding somewhere."

17

Those words caused Garviss to hold on to his next breath. Part of him wanted to move further away from the leafy wall between him and the trail. Another part only wanted to stretch out and rest his eyes until the lawmen found somewhere else to conduct their search. Garviss snapped his eyes open, knowing that plenty of strange things could pass through a man's head when the blood was racing through his veins.

"I doubt he's hiding anywhere near here," the young man said.

"Why?" the sheriff replied. "You think you know so much more than me after spending a month or two with a deputy badge pinned to your chest?"

"This is too close to town, is what I meant. He was all fired up when he robbed the Exchange and then tore away like his ass was on fire. Seems like he'd go a lot further before running out of steam."

The two lawmen had been riding slower, their voices carrying through the space between the hills rising on either side of the trail. Garviss only needed to close his eyes to picture exactly where they were. Part of his preparations for the day's escape was riding back and forth along the trail several times to make certain a good amount of tracks had been laid down in the rocky soil.

That way, his detour through the wall of thorny trees and bushes would be at least partially concealed.

Garviss had planned on that being enough to buy him some valuable time to get across the pond, down a steep slope, and back onto another section of the winding trail that circled around the other side of town to take him south. Suddenly, that portion of the plan hit him like a fist to the stomach. He hadn't quite forgotten the strategy, but it had somehow drifted to the back of his mind where it seemed less important.

The lawmen's horses were moving even slower now. Their steps carried them closer to the outlaw's detour as one or both of them examined the tracks that had brought them this far in their pursuit.

"Looks like there was more than one of them," the deputy said. "Them tracks are fresh and there ain't this many folks riding this stretch of trail in such a short time."

"I only saw one man rob the Exchange," the sheriff said.

"That don't mean there weren't more of them about. Most robbers ride with at least one lookout to back him up."

The sheriff grunted under his breath.

Garviss reached out to place a hand on his horse's neck to soothe him before he started to fidget.

The lawmen started moving again, this time heading further down the trail and away from Garviss's hiding spot.

"The tracks keep going this way," the deputy pointed out. "We could probably get moving a bit faster."

"No need to go too fast. He won't be covering a whole lot of ground."

"Why? What are you looking for?"

"Blood," the sheriff said. "I know I hit that thieving bastard at least once on his way out of town."

"Then we should definitely be able to pick him up before long," the deputy said enthusiastically.

The sheriff said something else, but Garviss was no longer straining his ears to listen. In fact, every one of his senses were growing duller by the second. That's when he made sense of it. He'd been growing weak, sweating, shaking. He could barely stay upright. He'd written off all of those things to the excitement of the robbery or nervousness at getting caught. Instead, he now knew the dull pain he'd been feeling was from a bullet wound he'd picked up along the way. If he hadn't been partly delirious from shock or loss of blood, he would've figured it out sooner.

Garviss patted himself down. For a moment, he thought the sheriff had been wrong in his proclamation. Then, Garviss found a spot on his side in the meat around his waist where he couldn't feel anything at all. The flesh there was numb, which at least explained why he hadn't been alerted to the wound. When he thought back to his ride out of town, he could recall a pinch in his side during the shooting. It was during a getaway, though, which meant the only thing on his mind was getting away. After that came the gold and escaping a posse.

Now that those things were in the past, Garviss's main concern was the blood covering his hand and soaked into his shirt.

"Aw shit," he sighed as his vision started to blur around the edges.

Chapter Two

There were many mining camps scattered throughout the Dakota Territories. Some were rougher than others and they all varied in size. Some were almost large enough to be considered towns in their own right and others were meant to be bundled up and packed away at a moment's notice. Dugan's Find wasn't exactly sure which kind it wanted to be.

Most of the camp consisted of weathered tents flapping in the wind, while a few of its more important spots were encased in somewhat more permanent wooden walls. Slightly too large to be moved but too small to be well organized, Dugan's Find was a mess that was barely valuable enough to keep around. Like most everything else in the Black Hills, much of its commerce revolved around mining or anything that catered to those who scrounged for one more speck of mineral that was shiny or strong enough to be valuable.

Several of the camp's stores were in carts or small tents. A few of the camp's more respectable citizens resided in one of the rare wooden buildings in the center of Dugan's Find. There were plenty of distractions to be found within the camp, one of which had only rolled into Dugan's Find less than a week ago. While the man who owned the garishly painted wagon carried himself like one of the county's founding members, he'd recently been a stranger to many of the people who lived there. And, like most strangers who set themselves up near the busiest section of camp, he had something to sell.

"And you, sir! Yes, you!"

The man who spoke loud enough to be heard over the rest of the camp's commotion wore a dark blue suit that shone in silken splendor like a proverbial gem embedded within a wall of stone. His sleeves were impeccably cut to showcase the finely polished cufflinks attached to them and the cut of his jacket was tailor-made to keep the pistols holstered under his arms from creating an unsightly bulge.

The man to whom the dandy had been speaking had been walking away from one of the many gold traders in the camp. Upon hearing the finely dressed gentleman's words, he stopped, looked around, and then pointed quizzically to himself.

"Yes!" the dandy said. "Come over here."

"Why?" the man asked.

"I have presented a challenge to all of these good folks." Although the folks indicated by the dandy's outstretched arms numbered less than a dozen, he treated them as if they were a crowd large enough to fill a coliseum. "Did you have any business with that broker?" he asked while pointing to the tent from which the other man had come.

"Yeah."

"Then you probably are a miner, am I correct?"

"Most everyone here's a miner of some sort," the man said.

"Very true, very true. And I suppose you have been tricked by the wiles of these treacherous hills and the bounty she has offered?"

After a pause, the man grunted, "Huh?"

"You've tirelessly slaved, only to discover a kernel, a pebble, a few flakes, or perhaps even a small nugget of that which we all hold dear only to find you've been deceived!"

"Huh?"

"Fool's gold, sir," the dandy declared. "I speak of fool's gold, the dormant trickster that wastes our precious time and effort for no discernible profit."

"Any miner worth his salt knows how to tell fool's gold from the real thing."

"Perhaps, but would your life be considerably easier if you could tell you were about to unearth nothing but fool's gold before you started digging? Before you waded into the cold waters of an uncaring stream and panned through pounds of silt? Or, what if you could have a quick and easy test to save you time when you did make a find? Rather than gamble on a somewhat educated guess as to what you hold in your hand or take the word of a chemist with ulterior motives, wouldn't it be far more preferable to know for certain whether or not you hold trash or treasure in your hands?"

Some of the men gathered around the dandy were seasoned miners who wore their experience on gnarled faces. Some were smoother of skin with light in their eyes that had yet to be snuffed by the cruel turns of their chosen way of life. To those among them who weren't yet hooked by his pitch, the dandy added, "And wouldn't it be helpful to have a way to make certain those merchants and brokers were telling you the truth when they told you your gold was actually of the fool's variety?"

"What's that mean?" asked one of the younger men in the small crowd.

"Just what I said," the dandy replied. "I'm sure not every man to whom you sell your gold is crooked, but some among them certainly are. Haven't any of you brought what you thought was gold to one of them, only to be told it wasn't genuine?"

While none of the men surrounding him spoke up, more than a few of them were intrigued by the question.

"In those situations," the dandy continued, "did those same brokers offer to take that fool's gold off your hands for a paltry sum?"

The men who'd been interested before were even more so now.

"If that gold was genuine, then you, my good sirs, would have given away a small fortune. Even if this sort of thing happens to you once in your entire careers, I say that's one too many."

"What would you do about it?"

The dandy brightened even more, snapped his fingers, and said, "So glad you asked. What I have here is a device that can keep such a travesty from happening. Some of you are already familiar with it while the rest will no doubt be just as interested."

Over half of the men in the crowd looked anxious while the others were undeniably curious. "Get on with it," said one of the anxious ones. "We already seen this before."

"Patience, patience. Not all of you have been introduced to . . . Professor Henry Whiteoak's Mineralogical Purity Detector!"

As he spoke, the dandy stepped to one side to reveal a small table that had been set up directly behind him. On it was a flat wooden box with two brass plates perched upon slender rods that were connected to the top of the box. Between the plates was a polished needle that was currently poised in the middle of a placard upon which were written several sets of numbers, symbols, and decimal points.

The crowd stepped forward to get a closer look. One of the other anxious fellows declared, "That's just a damn scale!"

"It most certainly is not just a scale!"

"Says who?"

The dandy straightened up, took hold of his lapel, and declared, "I, Professor Henry Whiteoak, attest to that since it is also I who created this very device!"

Since nobody seemed to be particularly impressed by those words, Whiteoak relaxed his posture a bit. "Did you gentlemen provide the samples I requested or not?"

The men who'd appeared more anxious than curious all glanced around at each other before stepping forward.

"Excellent," Whiteoak said. "And, for the benefit of my ever-growing audience, assure me that you have all brought samples which represent a varied mixture of gold that is both true and bogus." Upon seeing the confused look on many of the faces around him, the professor added, "Some of the gold you've brought is real and some is fool's gold."

"Oh," one of the anxious men said. "Right."

"Perfect. Now, you, sir, approach my device so that I may tell you what sample you have brought to this wondrous demonstration."

If the professor was correct about anything, it was that the crowd around him had been growing. The number of men gathered around his spot had nearly doubled in the last couple of minutes. And, as the tension grew into a crackle of energy throughout the miners and prospectors, even more folks trickled in from other tents and a few of the smaller pathways winding through the camp to witness whatever miracle would happen next.

When the first volunteer approached the professor's device, he split his time equally between reaching toward one side of the scale and eyeing its creator apprehensively.

"Go on," Whiteoak urged. "Place your sample on the left plate."

The volunteer did as he was asked, surrendering his small bit of gold to rest upon the polished metallic surface before quickly pulling his hand back as though he was afraid it might get snapped off at the wrist.

Whiteoak raised his right arm, until he was pointing up at the heavens. After less than two seconds of his vaguely divine beckoning, he lowered that arm so he could place his extended fingers onto the plate set into the device's right side. The crowd was hushed as it leaned forward to get a better look at the device supporting the miner's meager offering.

Since the people in the immediate area had held their collective breath to become almost perfectly silent, the sounds coming from within the professor's machine could be heard. Within the walls of the box, there came a rattle as something inside moved through a series of unseen trials. Metal clacked against metal before knocking into wood. Hidden pieces moved, causing both plates of the device to tremble. Finally, the plate dropped an inch or so downward, which caused the needle between them to lean in that direction.

"According to my purity detector," the professor declared in a booming voice, "this sample is indeed pure gold. Is that correct, sir?"

The volunteer nodded shakily.

"Will the next man step forward to witness the amazing accuracy of my meticulously articulated device?"

The next man stepped forward once the first retrieved his gold and placed it on the metal plate. After a short series of similar noises from within the box, the plate once again sank downward to move the needle.

"Another fine specimen of genuine gold," Whiteoak said. "Congratulations, sir."

Members of the crowd were murmuring to each other as the third man stepped forward. He placed some shiny pebbles onto the plate, causing the machine to rattle and clank some more. This time, however, the plate clattered a bit before rising up an inch or so from where it had previously been.

"Oh, dear," Whiteoak said. "It seems we have a spoiled sample amongst the true pearls."

"Pearls?" someone in the audience said. "I thought we was testing gold."

"Shut the hell up, idiot!" the man beside him snapped. To Whiteoak, he asked, "What the hell's that supposed to mean? Why'd the scale go up instead o' down?"

Raising his eyebrows into a near-perfect representation of innocent wonder, Professor Whiteoak replied, "Just look at the meter for yourself. The readings are quite clear to those of us who know how to read them."

"What if you don't know how to read 'em?"

"I assure you, there are complete and easy to understand instructions included with every purchase of my detector. For the sake of this demonstration, however, I will decipher the findings for you." Pointing to the symbols etched into the polished surface behind the vertical needle, Whiteoak said, "This indicates, beyond any semblance of doubt, that the sample provided by this gentleman is not true gold."

Suddenly, almost every eye in that crowd was focused upon the man who'd brought that sample forward.

"Well?" asked someone from the crowd. "That true?"

The volunteer nodded, snatched his rocks from the top of the machine, and skulked away. As he tried to shove through the crowd, he was accosted by several of its members. All of them asked for verification of the professor's claims and all of them were told the same thing.

"It's true, all right!" the harried man finally said. "Just ask Winslow."

Winslow was the name of one of the most reputable gold brokers in the camp. Upon hearing that name, Whiteoak smiled. "Yes," he said. "Let's ask Winslow."

CHAPTER THREE

Professor Whiteoak may have drawn a sizable crowd for his demonstration, but it paled in comparison to the amount of folks who shoved their way into the large tent forming the front of Winslow's Mineral Exchange within moments after the demonstration concluded. Winslow's was one of the larger structures in Dugan's Find and had taken on some of the camp's eccentricities. Like the camp itself, Winslow's place was part wooden structure and part canvas tent. The former was a cabin that was attached to the latter which was nailed to the front of the cabin's entrance like a crude approximation of a porch. From the street, only the canvas awning and flapping walls could be seen. Inside the canvas shelter was a long table held down by several heavy scales.

As the crowd drew closer to the tent, Winslow himself placed his hands on the edge of the table so he could lean forward. He was a rotund man with dark skin and hair that looked to have been scribbled onto portions of his scalp with a stick of charcoal. Sweat glistened on his brow and his mouth gaped open to form a string of words that only he could hear. Kicking aside the chair he'd been using only moments ago, Winslow picked up the walking stick that had been leaning against the table and plastered a welcoming smile onto his face.

"Well, now," Winslow said. "What brings you all here on such a —"

"Tell us if this gold is the genuine article!" barked a man with a long beard and one lazy eye. His hand slammed down onto the table, causing all of the trays of Winslow's scales to rattle against the chains from which they were dangling.

Winslow looked down at the small nuggets hesitantly. "Is there a problem? If anyone doubts me as a broker, I can produce several men who can stand by what I say."

"We're not doubting you, Winslow. We're doubting him."

After straining his eyes to see all the men gathering around the canvas front of his shop, Winslow asked, "Who?"

"Me," Whiteoak said as he slid through

the crowd like greasy meat through a digestive tract. "I've informed them of the veracity of their gold and they want you to confirm it."

Winslow looked at a few of the men standing closest to his table. "I've worked with you before, Bill. You too, Cal. I've already told you what you need to know."

"That's why we trust you," Cal replied. He was a slender fellow with long, gray hair and a beard that hung well past the collar of his wrinkled shirt. "We're checking to see if what you say matches up with what he says."

"You're that Whiteoak person," Winslow said. "The salesman."

"Salesman, scientist, pontificator, and prophet," Whiteoak mused. "I am more than willing to stand by my wares."

"Well I'm not about to act like some kind of partner to a fast-talking New Yorker!"

"I beg your pardon!" Whiteoak exclaimed. His hands shot to his hips, causing his jacket to flare out and expose more of the expensive waistcoat beneath it. "I am not from New York, sir."

Winslow snorted in the professor's direction and looked away from him.

"Forget about that fella," Cal insisted.

"Tell us whether that there gold is real or not."

"I can run my usual tests."

"That's all we ask. And when you're done there, we got some more for you to test as well."

"That could take some time," Winslow said.

"We got plenty of that."

"I'm sure you do, but I'm not a part of whatever it is you've got going on here," Winslow said as he waved an impatient hand at the group huddling around the front of his tent. "And the longer you block off my place of business, the less profit I make. So, unless you've got real business to conduct, I'll have to ask you to find somewhere else to be."

Seeing that he was about to lose his potential customers, Whiteoak strode forward. "Do you charge a fee for your tests, sir?"

"Sometimes," Winslow replied. "But not if I do 'em before I make a trade if the customer wants it or if I got a question about what I'm about to buy."

"There is only a small handful of samples to be tested, sir. Perhaps you could just perform them so that these good people can put their minds to rest?"

Winslow locked eyes with the professor and hitched up his pants that somehow managed to sag in the front despite the ample amount of belly to fill them. "You're worried about backing whatever claim you've made? You perform the tests. This ain't my affair."

"Quite the reasonable request," Whiteoak said to the men gathering around the table. "I believe I made that offer before we got here."

"No, no," Cal snapped. "He ain't about to test his own claim. Of course, he'll say he's right! What do you think we are? Stupid?"

"Christ almighty," Winslow groaned. "You really got these men riled up."

"Wasn't my intention," the professor assured him.

"We all been listenin' to that windbag spout off about elixirs, tonics, magic rocks, and science gadgets ever since he drove that goddamn wagon into Dugan's Find," Cal said. "Half the time it works, half the time it don't, and the rest of the time . . ."

"The rest of the time?" Whiteoak chuckled. "How many halves are in this whole of yours, anyway?" He was still smiling when the miner's callused fist thumped against his jaw. The professor reeled back a step but quickly recovered. Everyone around him

37

waited for a retaliatory swing but were disappointed to see the professor reach into his breast pocket for a handkerchief. Dabbing at the corner of his lower lip, Whiteoak said, "If you'd like help in controlling that temper, I have a tonic that should do you wonders. It's a simple tea that tastes like honey and cinnamon. Very soothing."

Cal was about to take another swing at the professor; one that would surely do more damage than the first. One raised eyebrow and a stern glare was all it took to stay his hand. The scruffy miner paused long enough to get a look at the dandy's eyes, which showed him a whole lot more than just a man in fancy clothes. There was a spark in there. One hinting at a fire that had remained hidden until that moment.

Shifting his attention back to Winslow, Cal said, "This asshole's been fleecing us ever since he got here. If we know for certain he's full of shit, then we can get all our money back!"

"Been fleecing *all of you*?" Winslow asked. "I'd reckon it's been some of you more than others."

Although Cal did avert his eyes at the implication, he wasn't the only one to do so. A small number of other men in the crowd seemed none too anxious to meet

38

the gaze of their friends and neighbors at that particular moment.

Winslow sighed and swiped a hand flat against his forehead to remove some of the sweat that had collected in the folds of his skin. "This fella ain't the first salesman to come along. All of you, do yourselves a favor and either buy what he's sellin' or don't. Stop embarrassing yerselves."

"What's your fee, sir?"

Stopping partway through a slow turn to put his back to the crowd, Winslow shifted around again to fix his eyes upon the well-dressed man who was now leaning directly against his table. "Fee for what?"

"The tests," Whiteoak replied. "You said we're wasting your time and as a business-man myself, I know a man's time is money. So how much would you charge to test this gold?"

"How much are we talking about?"

"Three samples." Almost as soon as Whiteoak said that, voices erupted from behind the professor.

"Mine, too!"

"Test mine! I know he got it wrong!"

"Test all of 'em that the salesman tested!" one man shouted. "That's the only way to be certain!"

"Now just wait a minute!" Whiteoak

roared. His voice was loud enough to be heard over the commotion and passionate enough to silence it. "I am a patient and fair man, but I will *not* stand here and be doubted so extensively. Also, if you think I will pay to test all of your samples than you are indeed a bunch of lunatics!"

"You're paying?" Winslow asked.

Straightening the silk tie around his neck, Whiteoak said, "I'll pay for nine of them. After all, those were the ones I tested. Any more than that would be taking advantage of my good nature."

"Test the rest of us," someone offered. "Then the professor can put it in his machine. That'll show if it works or not."

"What's so important about this damn machine, anyway?" Winslow asked.

"You wouldn't ask if you were a miner!" said one of the men who'd featured prominently in Whiteoak's demonstration.

"Ain't a one of us that haven't been cheated at one time or another by one of you blowhards!" said one of the men, who was all but buried in the middle of the group.

Hearing that raised the hackles on Winslow's back. He straightened up to his full height after being pushed down by the impending weight of the shouting match going on in front of him. "You calling me a blowhard?" he snarled.

Not so many of the men were quick to respond.

Nodding slowly, Winslow cast his eyes from one man to another. "The reason I'm still in Dugan's Find is because I deal fair with all of you. A man don't flourish in this line of work unless he offers a square deal to his customers. Anyone who wants to slap me in the face by calling me names best step forward and do it proper so he can get what's coming!"

There were no takers for that offer.

"No need for this to get any uglier than it already has," Whiteoak said.

Now Winslow directed his furious gaze to the professor. "You don't know a damn thing if you think this here is ugly. It can get a whole lot worse if half the camp is riled up like this. You should know, since you're the one that's been doing the riling."

Raising his hands to shoulder height, Whiteoak said, "I'm here to alleviate this situation. If you'd be so kind as to test these samples, we can all get the answers we're after and you can have enough profit to compensate you for your time."

"Hold on just a minute," Cal said. "If Whiteoak is payin' Winslow for the tests,

41

how can we be certain it ain't a bribe to make sure everything comes out his way?"

"Oh, for Christ's sake," Winslow snapped. "Give me the gold and I'll test it. It's my damn job so I'll do it. Just disperse yourselves somewhere other than where I can see you! My payment will be your word that when you want to sell this stuff, you come to me first."

Grudgingly, the members of the crowd with gold in their possession dealt with the broker while everyone else wandered away. Whiteoak stayed put and tugged the lapels of his jacket to straighten its lines. "I appreciate your cooperation in this matter, sir."

"What I said about getting away from me goes double for you, asshole," Winslow said.

"All right, then."

CHAPTER FOUR

Winslow's tests shouldn't have taken too long to perform, but the broker was still grouchy about the circumstances under which he'd been pulled into the job and consequently seemed to be dragging his feet. Either that, or he was slowing his pace in hopes that most of the overly anxious crowd outside his place of business would lose interest and drift away. As far as the latter was concerned, he got his wish. With the chances of a fight involving the professor and an angry mob dwindling by the minute, several of the more bloodthirsty onlookers found other things to do with their time.

The professor was more than happy to put some distance between himself and the crowd. The first place he went was the busiest saloon in Dugan's Find; a large tent thrown over a wooden frame called the Tin Panner. He started with a few beers, graduated to whiskey, and eventually found himself pulled into a game of Five Card Draw. The stakes were low, amounting to a total of no more than five or six dollars on the table. Spirits were high, however, and Whiteoak's was highest of them all.

"Seems like I can't lose in this camp!" the professor declared while raking in a modest pile of pennies and a few half dollars. "Perhaps I should buy some land and plant some roots around here."

"If we were playing for more money, I'd think you were cheating," said a man with a scruffy beard that covered most of his face.

"Haven't I been accused of enough for one day?" Whiteoak replied in an overly dramatic manner.

"Ain't accusin' you of nothin'," the bearded player said. "Except for havin' a lucky charm jammed up yer ass."

"Always an eloquent speaker, my friend. Just for that, I'll purchase the next round of beers."

Other than the fellow with the thick mask of whiskers sprouting from his face, there were two others sitting at the table with Whiteoak. One of them had been at the demonstration earlier, and the other, a gnarled Mexican with long black and gray hair, rarely left the saloon. "Better take him up on the offer real quick," said the former. "Kinda hard for a man to buy drinks when he's in jail."

"Now why would an upstanding entrepreneur like myself wind up behind bars?" Whiteoak asked.

"Depending on what Winslow says after he tests that gold."

"I can tell you what he'll say because my machine has already given the results."

"And if them results are wrong?"

Whiteoak shrugged as he handed over some money to the older woman who'd approached the table carrying a tray of beer mugs. "Then I'll personally apologize and refund any purchases that were made. Since nobody has purchased my machine just yet, an apology would have to suffice."

"That's right," the Mexican said. "Nobody's put someone in jail for building a piece of shit machine."

"That's correct!" Whiteoak declared. His face quickly darkened as he snatched the beer that had just been set down in front of the Mexican. "And nobody's purchased a drink for someone who defames his life's work."

"Eh, you know I'm only kidding," the Mexican said good-naturedly. "I'm sure your machine is just as good as anything else you've put together."

"I don't know if you mean that as a compliment, but I'll stand by my word and let you drink," the professor said while handing the Mexican his beer. "As long as you promise to keep playing with the same skill you've shown thus far," he added with a wink aimed at the rest of the table, "I'm sure to win my money back quickly enough."

As the cards were being dealt for the next hand, Whiteoak tipped back his beer and let his eyes wander among the many young ladies roaming the saloon. Some of them worked there and others were merely out for a drink, but they all offered plenty of distractions for the professor's attention.

After taking a large swig from his mug, the bearded player let out a gurgling belch and pressed the back of his sleeve to his chin. Despite the effort to clean himself, there still remained a liberal amount of beer soaked into his whiskers. "Might wanna sit this hand out, Professor," he said.

"Why's that?" Whiteoak replied. "Afraid of losing again?"

"No, but you could be in to lose something yourself. Namely, a few of them teeth."

"Calm down and enjoy the game. I

thought we were having a good time."

"We are, but that fella there sure don't look like the type to be havin' much of a good time."

"Trying to get me to look away from the table?" Whiteoak scoffed. "A paltry effort at best."

The bearded man shook his head and raised a hand to point behind the professor's seat. "Ain't trying to pull no wool over yer eyes. There's a fella just came in who looks to be in a foul mood."

"Even if that's so, I doubt it has anything at all to do with —" Whiteoak's next words were cut short when a pair of strong hands clamped down on his shoulders, grabbed hold of his collar, and hoisted him up off his chair. Whiteoak's skinny legs flailed beneath him for a few seconds before his feet managed to touch the floor. No sooner had he attempted to stand than he was jerked away from the table, knocking over the chair in which he'd been sitting.

"Henry Whiteoak," growled the man who'd snatched the professor from his seat. "You're coming outside with me."

"If this has anything to do with my purity detector, I'll have you know my findings are still being tested!"

"Don't know what that is and don't care."

47

"Then if you're reporting a problem with my virility tonic," Whiteoak quickly said, "I'll remind you to read the label for proper directions in use."

"Not that, either," the assailant said while dragging Whiteoak toward the saloon's front door.

"Collecting a gambling debt?"

"Nope."

"Tax assessment?" Whiteoak asked.

"Not even close."

Still doing his best to remain on his feet while being herded out of the saloon, Whiteoak gripped the hands that had found their way to his neck and squeezed their thumbs with a sharp flex of his fingers. The man who'd pulled him away from the card table finally let him go before his thumbs snapped painfully out of joint. The instant he was free, Whiteoak stepped away from his captor and spun around to face him.

He was an inch or so shorter than the professor but much stockier. Most of that additional bulk looked to be muscle and gave the young man the appearance of a dog that had been bred strictly for fighting. Dark eyes glared at Whiteoak beneath the rim of a battered hat and were set deep within a rounded face. He wore a simple white shirt with sleeves rolled up to expose thick forearms and a vest that was cut short enough to grant him easy access to the holster buckled high around his waist.

Whiteoak reached for one of the silver-handled .38s resting under his arm out of pure reflex and regretted it almost instantly. The man in front of him snapped his hand to his gun as well, pausing just shy of clearing leather.

"What's your business with me?" Whiteoak asked.

"This," the younger fellow replied as he used his free hand to peel back one half of his vest to show the badge pinned to his shirt.

Leaning forward a bit, Whiteoak squinted until he could read the lettering stamped into the tin circle. "Well now," he said while easing his hand away from his holster. "Why didn't you say so, Deputy?"

CHAPTER FIVE

The lawman shoved Whiteoak along without responding to any of the professor's questions or comments. Considering how much Whiteoak talked, ignoring him was like walking through a rainstorm without acknowledging the water in your boots. Before too long, Whiteoak was pushed off the path leading between the tents so he could step inside one of the smaller cabins near the middle of camp.

Inside the cabin was a short bar where drinks were served to customers who preferred a quieter atmosphere than the Tin Panner. Only a few working girls were in sight, any one of them being attractive enough to catch Whiteoak's eye. Before he could return a smile from one of those ladies, Whiteoak was pushed toward a table against the back wall.

"Easy," Whiteoak said. "Isn't it obvious I intend on going along with you?"

"That's right, Matt," said the man who approached the table to sit directly across from Whiteoak. "Give our friend here credit for coming along quietly."

"Thank you very much," Whiteoak huffed while straightening the line of his suit jacket.

"He looks like a smart fella."

"Thank you again, sir."

"In fact, he's plenty smart enough to put his guns on the table so we can have a nice little chat."

Whiteoak stopped primping himself so he could take a better look at the man in front of him. He had a lean, muscular build and close-cropped light brown hair. His mustache was thick, but trimmed impeccably, resting above a pointed patch of whiskers beneath his lower lip. Small scars were scattered about his face, which he wore like medals won in several hard-won fights.

"Do I know you, sir?" Whiteoak asked.

"You might," the man across from him replied. "Then again, with so many others out for your hide, it may be getting difficult to keep us all straight. Name's Travis Farell," he added while extending an arm across the table.

While reaching out to shake Travis's hand, Whiteoak said, "I presume my reputation has preceded me."

"Sure has, Professor Whiteoak."

Beaming, Whiteoak settled back into his seat. "So, are you a deputy as well or are you also here at the behest of this young man?"

Matt stood nearby. He drew his pistol and placed it on his knee as he sat down. That way, he could point the barrel at Whiteoak without it being seen by everyone else inside the little saloon.

"I'm no deputy," Travis said. He then pulled open his jacket to show the badge he wore. It was similar to Matt's in basic design, albeit slightly larger.

Whiteoak's eyes widened. "U.S. marshal?"

Travis nodded.

"So that would make him a deputy marshal?"

"Damn, Professor," Travis said with a chuckle. "You really are a smart one."

Quickly regaining his composure, Whiteoak cleared his throat and folded his hands on the table. "How can I help you, gentlemen?"

"You can start by telling me how you robbed that bank in Kansas."

"Why, I don't know what you're talking about."

"Really? And what about the still that blew up and burned a nice-sized patch of Montana? Know anything about that?"

Whiteoak scowled. "I heard something about that. The fire wasn't all that large. Of course, I could have been misinformed since I only heard about it secondhand."

Travis studied Whiteoak carefully, unable to find a chink in the professor's armor. "I suppose it wasn't all that bad. You're saying you don't have anything to offer where those instances are concerned?"

"That's what I'm saying," Whiteoak calmly replied.

"All right, then. Now what about the claims that someone's been smuggling stolen gold through the Badlands?"

The shift in the marshal's tone was slight but noticeable. To Whiteoak, the difference was much more extreme. He'd been watching everything from the lawman's posture to the movement of Travis's hands when he spoke, all in an effort to find signals that might have been given throughout the short questioning. Much as he would study an opponent at the card table, Whiteoak picked apart the other man's habits in a matter of seconds.

"Stolen gold?" Whiteoak asked.

"Don't bullshit me, Henry. I know damn well you were a part of that Kansas bank robbery as well as that fire in Montana."

"Watch what you say," Whiteoak warned. "A U.S. marshal making false accusations is a serious offense."

"Serious offense, huh?" Matt said. "You've committed more than enough serious offenses to put you in a cage for the rest of your damn life."

Travis motioned with one hand for his deputy to be quiet and Matt obeyed the order immediately. To Whiteoak, Travis said, "That bank you robbed in Kansas was run by a bunch of crooked judges and old politicians. Most of that money had blood on it. As for that still in Montana, it only took a little bit of investigating to figure out the world's better off without it and the men who were brewing whatever it was that was being bottled up in them mountains. That's why the only ones who still give a damn about hunting you down are the bounty hunters looking to cash in on the price that was put on your head."

"I have no idea what you're talking about. I am a man of science and commerce."

"If you were stupid enough to not know about the bounty hunters after you, you'd already be planted six feet underground," Travis said. "And if you had a brain in your head, you'd ask what you could do to earn a favor from a U.S. marshal."

Now it was Whiteoak's turn to chuckle. "If you're through with the jokes, I'd like to be on my way."

"Stay where you are, asshole," Matt snapped.

The deputy's rough tone wasn't enough to keep Whiteoak in his seat. One look from the marshal, on the other hand, sent the professor straight to his chair again. "You've been lucky so far, Whiteoak," Travis said. "Either your cons have been too small to attract much attention or you've pulled them on men who are bigger sons of bitches than you. Either way, it hasn't been worth our time to track you down. You've just been another lying salesman swindling idiots out of their money."

Whiteoak straightened his tie and shifted his face into a suitably offended expression.

"Smuggling gold, on the other hand," Travis continued. "That's an offense that'll draw some attention. Y'see, it's the sort of thing that hits too many deep pockets. Mining is a big part of the way this whole part of the country works, which means the law's gotta make certain it runs smoothly. Understand?"

"Of course," Whiteoak replied.

"Claims get jumped, gold gets taken, robbers rob, it's all a part of the way things happen out here in the uncivilized world," Travis said while holding his arms open as if to embrace all of the Badlands around him. "But folks have to know that there are punishments for such things and steps to be taken when they happen. And," he added with an edge to his voice, "if they happen to the wrong men, they won't be tolerated at all."

"What's this got to do with me?" Whiteoak asked.

"You recall speaking to a man named Vickery?"

Whiteoak furrowed his brow and rubbed his chin. "The name sounds familiar. I may be thinking of someone else. There was a dancer named Victoria performing in Tennessee who was quite delightfully flexible."

"I know you know this Vickery. He's a judge and an investor in a string of mines north of here. He was real interested in what you had to sell."

"I'm afraid that doesn't narrow it down. Nearly everyone in these parts have some connection to the mining trade and there are a vast number of folks who are interested in what I sell. My goods are actually quite remarkable."

"Judge Vickery also has connections to the federal government. Seems he was bilked out of some gold right after he spent some time with a certain medicine man traveling in a wagon with ugly paint spattered all over it."

"Still doesn't specifically mention me," Whiteoak pointed out.

"It was you and you know it," Matt said. "Vickery described you down to the pasty skin and greasy mustache."

Whiteoak ran the back of his hand against one pasty cheek to brush along the edge of his combed and waxed mustache. "If you were so certain I was the one who committed this vague crime, you would have arrested me by now."

"Judge Vickery is just one judge using his influence to get rich in gold country. He put us onto your scent and since you're a man who's dealt with him, I'm sure you've dealt with others like him. Certain members of the federal government would like to know who these crooked men are and how much they've stolen while falsifying claims, accepting bribes, and tipping off robbers to where gold shipments are being taken."

"Sounds like you've got quite a bunch of sinners in the federal government," Whiteoak said, using the last two words as an obvious mockery.

"The gold that was taken from Vickery

didn't belong to him," Travis continued. "It was meant to be deposited in a bank in Colorado where it would be put to use building train stations and paying soldiers who look after the interests of every citizen within these great United States."

"How very rousing and patriotic," Whiteoak said. "Sounds like this judge lost quite a bundle."

"He didn't lose all of that gold. The fact that he did lose some of it could be enough to make investors nervous enough to think twice about handing their money over to where it needs to go. They start to think their funds could also be lost or that they can't trust the men in charge of these sprawling projects."

Whiteoak steepled his fingers. "From what you've told me thus far, those men might have a point."

Travis leaned forward, much like a hawk that was moments away from dropping into a predatory dive. "If you value that dainty neck of yours, I'd suggest you listen to what I have to say."

"I have been listening," Whiteoak assured him. "Very carefully."

"Then you should know I'm not a man you want to cross. More importantly," Travis added while easing back into his seat, "you should recognize a potentially valuable friend when one presents itself."

"I haven't heard much to suggest you might be one of those, Marshal. In fact, any man in my line of work often finds himself needlessly accosted by those wearing a piece of rounded metal pinned to their chests."

"You gonna tell me crooks like you and any other double-talking salesmen don't deserve to get arrested for bilking innocent folks?"

Whiteoak smiled. "Usually, being put under arrest is merely the threat. More often than not, the harassment I get from lawmen like yourselves comes in the form of sniffing around for bribes to avoid such an inconvenience. And, on the rare occasions when I am forced behind bars, the sniffing continues until a bargain is struck where I am the one being bilked out of my hard-earned profits."

"You suggesting I'm crooked?" Travis asked through gritted teeth.

Holding his hands out like a preacher addressing his flock, Whiteoak replied, "I only speak from experience. And I can tell that such an accusation comes as no surprise to you. Even if you've never lowered yourself to any wrongdoings like your mortal associates, I'm sure you know about the transgressions of lesser men."

Travis's face twisted into a sneer, making it seem he was about to spit on the table. "You got a real smart mouth. If you're through with all your high and mighty talk, maybe you're ready to listen to some sense."

Reluctantly, Whiteoak reined in the smarmy edge his last few statements had lent to his features. Looking somewhat more civil, he cocked his head and asked, "So you brought me here because you think I took this judge's gold?"

"Damn right," Matt said, shooting the words out as though they'd been cocked and ready since the conversation had begun.

Travis waved one hand back at his deputy to keep him at bay. "You're the one selling these devices that have to do with measuring or detecting gold or whatever the hell else you're claiming."

"Nearly everything in the Dakota Territories has to do with mining something or other," Whiteoak said in his defense.

"That could also make you the one convincing rich men to test their gold so you could switch it out for the fake stuff. Perhaps, by putting their gold into that machine so you can give them back something less valuable."

"Preposterous," Whiteoak scoffed.

"And if you do happen to be innocent of the charges," Travis added warily, "then I'm sure you would know who the guilty party is or how I might find them."

"Again, I'm brought back to what I could gain in this proposition."

"This ain't a proposition, Whiteoak," Travis said sternly. "It's me giving you the courtesy of a talk before the hammer drops. You may not respect this," he said while tapping the badge he wore, "but it still holds more authority than you. If I ask you to do something, you do it. Otherwise, there's a price to pay."

"Consider your fangs appropriately bared," Whiteoak sighed. "Do I need to give you my answer now or can I sleep on it? This has been quite a trying day. Besides, we'll have much more privacy if we hold off until after Mister Winslow reveals his results."

Both lawmen looked around, where they discovered the truth in the professor's words. Sure enough, there were several locals peeking into the tent as they passed by while others loitered outside with impatient looks etched into their faces.

Lowering his voice to a whisper, Whiteoak added, "I'll be much freer to discuss certain matters if my every action isn't observed

61

and thereby reported by outside parties who might gain from me being cast in an unfavorable light."

"What the hell do we care about what folks think of you?" Matt grunted. "Whatever suspicions these people have where you're concerned, I'm sure they're warranted."

Travis stood up. "Fine. You want to hear what the broker has to say? You want to scurry off somewhere to think? Go right ahead. Just know one thing. We found you once and we can do it again."

"Of course," Whiteoak said as he stood up and shot his cuffs. "You should also know that I will use this time to thoroughly weigh the offer you've given me."

Both of the marshals glared at Whiteoak as they made their way from the tent. The growing crowd outside the place parted so they could pass and then promptly closed in again. Smiling like a man who was out for a leisurely stroll, Whiteoak filled his lungs with a deep breath of cool night air.

"Such a wonderful evening, wouldn't you agree?" Whiteoak mused as he strolled away. He maintained his jaunty demeanor until he walked past another tent and then around it. Since none of the others chose to follow him, he broke into a run and bolted into the nearest convenient shadows.

CHAPTER SIX

Whiteoak moved like a reptile a fraction of his size whenever he was fairly certain he wasn't being watched. His strides became quicker and his breathing sped up, only to slow down as soon as he had to cross a more populated street or pass in front of a saloon or restaurant that was still open for business. On those occasions, he strolled as casually as possible, even tipping his hat or whistling a few short bars of a merry song. As soon as he was between tents or in a more secluded area, he sped up to a run once again.

The peculiar stagger-step approach lasted until he got within sight of his wagon. Once he could see the colorful walls adorned with symbols and testimonials in a number of foreign languages, he didn't care who was watching. Whiteoak bolted across the last bit of space between him and the wagon, not stopping one second before his hand closed around the little knob of the wagon's rear door.

Whiteoak kept his composure as he unlocked the door and pulled it open. The interior of the wagon was crammed full of cabinets, shelves, boxes, and various implements hanging from hooks nailed into the ceiling. There was a narrow aisle down the middle, which the professor navigated without disturbing a single thing around him. He knew every irregular angle within that garishly painted box so well that he could find anything inside it in a matter of seconds. Even so, he reached for a small lantern hanging toward the back of the aisle and lit it using a match that he produced from a shirt pocket.

As a flame sprouted from the wick, its light was reflected in dozens of glassy surfaces within the confined space. The professor's hands placed the lantern back on its hook and went straight to a small cabinet with a narrow door consisting of a pane of glass within a wooden frame.

"They don't know yet," he whispered intently to himself. "They don't know, but they suspect. Don't be silly," he added in a sterner tone. "Of course, they know. That's why they came for you. They know and they're after you." In the calmer voice, he said, "If they were after you, you'd be in shackles. Don't panic and all will be well."

As he spoke, Whiteoak removed one little glass bottle after another. Each bottle contained a small amount of liquid that varied in color from pale yellow to jade green. They were all sealed with a cork and a small amount of wax to keep any of their contents from evaporating or spilling. Once the cabinet, was emptied, he fished a thin strip of metal from one of the drawers behind him.

"You're tired," he continued. "Tired and jittery after all of the nonsense of late. That's why you came to the Dakotas after all, wasn't it? Get some rest, settle into a profitable routine, and ride it out for a while. Just like the old days."

The smile that had drifted onto Whiteoak's face lasted until he looked up to spot his reflection in the small square pane of glass. Suddenly, his demeanor shifted into a cold, serious mask. The man he saw in that glass wasn't a friend. That much was also reflected in the tone of his voice when he said, "The old days were full of poverty. Don't forget, you were running just as much then as you are now. More, even."

He blinked several times, shaking his head and averting his eyes as though he'd suddenly become ashamed of his monologue. Taking a deep breath, he wiped away any outward hint of doubt and flipped a strip of metal along the base of the cabinet so one beveled edge was pointing outward.

"They are nothing but lawmen," he said easily. He fit the beveled end of the metal strip into an almost invisible crack inside the small cabinet at its base. "Federal lawmen, of course, but lawmen all the same. Nothing I haven't handled before."

After a bit of persuading, the bottom of the cabinet popped up. Whiteoak took it out and set it aside so he could reach into the compartment that had previously been hidden. The moment his fingers dipped into the secret space, the worry that had been in his eyes drifted away. A leather pouch had been flattened after being stuck away but regained its proper shape after Whiteoak coaxed it open.

Carefully, he poured some of the pouch's contents into the palm of his other hand. The small golden nuggets were still rough and some were even still partially covered in dirt. As his eyes darted to each little piece, Whiteoak counted quietly under his breath. When he'd tallied the nuggets in his hand, he shook the bag, looked inside, and counted some more.

"All right, then," he sighed. "I should be safe. But, just to be sure . . ."

Whiteoak refilled the pouch, put it back into the secret compartment, and then fit the false bottom back into place. After that, he worked his way around the interior of the wagon going from one cabinet to another. While visiting several of the cabinets that were scattered throughout the wagon, he opened secret compartments in each one. Some of the compartments were false bottoms like the first cabinet, while others were hidden doors that opened on the side of a shelf on interior hinges. There were even a few small drawers that were only revealed after Whiteoak pressed a button disguised as a knothole in the grain of the wood.

Among other treasures stored in those spots, Whiteoak found several other pouches filled with varying amounts of gold. He counted each nugget in a flurry of rushed whispers until he stood in the wagon with hands perched upon his hips.

"All accounted for," he announced softly. "And none of the compartments were tampered with. If that's the case, then there's no way those lawmen or anyone else could have gotten to what's inside. And if nobody could get to it, nobody knows it's there."

His brow furrowed as the wheels inside his ever-churning mind began to turn a little faster. "That isn't necessarily the case, but it's a near-certainty. Besides, even if anyone knows what I'm carrying, they can't possibly connect me to the crimes being investigated by those marshals. Can they?"

The professor's contemplation was interrupted by the crunch of footsteps against the gravel outside his wagon. After years of seeking refuge within the familiar walls, Whiteoak had become particularly attuned to the sounds in and around the wagon. He could tell when someone was approaching and he could tell when many someones were approaching. He could also tell when those steps were coming in from multiple angles. Unfortunately, this was the worst of those possibilities.

Whiteoak moved even faster as he stuck the pouches in the safest spot within the wagon along with the rest of his most valuable acquisitions. He then opened a drawer near his waist containing a pair of .32 caliber pistols. They weren't as ornate as the ones he carried in his shoulder holster but were well-oiled and fit in his hands like extensions of his gangly arms. By the time

the inevitable knock came at the wagon's
back door, Whiteoak was ready.

CHAPTER SEVEN

"Open up!" a rough voice outside the wagon demanded. "We know you're in there. We can see the light from your lantern."

Without much of a delay, the wagon door opened and Professor Whiteoak poked his head out. "Of course, I'm inside. Plenty of work to do, you know. What brings you good people out here at such a late hour?"

"We're here about the gold."

Whiteoak's eyes narrowed as he carefully studied the scene in front of him. There were ten people outside, most of which were men. The women stood at the back of the group where they could either observe or remain out of danger, depending on how the situation panned out. Whiteoak recognized most of the faces, which left the few strangers as his most pressing concern. Given the number of miners that passed through camp, however, the population there was in a constant state of fluctuation.

"Gold?" Whiteoak asked.

"You know goddamn well what we're talkin' about," said a man who stepped forward to separate himself from the crowd. He was one of the faces Whiteoak had recognized right away since he'd also been present at the demonstration earlier that evening. In fact, he was one of the men who'd volunteered to put his small offering of gold onto Whiteoak's purity detector. Unfortunately, his sample wasn't deemed to be very pure.

"I don't believe I caught your name when we last met," Whiteoak said cordially while stepping out of the wagon and extending a hand.

Rather than shake the hand that had been offered, the man slapped it away. "Name's Brooks. You told me my gold wasn't real."

"My apologies for your misfortune, sir, but isn't it preferable to know the truth than to operate under false pretenses?"

"You callin' me a liar?" Brooks snapped.

One of the others took hold of Brooks's shoulder before he could take another step toward the wagon. "Nobody's calling anyone a liar. Not yet, at least. Let's get over to Winslow's place to see what he came up with."

"So, his tests are concluded?" Whiteoak asked.

The man who'd reined Brooks in was a tall fellow with dark brown hair. He had the rough hands and weary eyes of a miner who'd seen more useless rocks in his bins than genuine profits. "They sure are. Now come along to hear what he has to say."

"So . . . you haven't heard from him yet?" Whiteoak inquired.

The miner smirked. "Why? Are you worried?"

"Of course not! I just don't like to be in the dark in important matters."

"Guess I can't blame you for that."

"Don't listen to him, Brooks!" one of the others groused. "He's fidgety because he's a damn cheat!"

"And you're fidgety because he told you that big strike you pulled out of the water was fake," Brooks replied.

The unhappy fellow's mouth twisted a bit but remained shut. Whatever else he had to say, he would keep it to himself for the moment.

Brooks slapped a hand onto Whiteoak's shoulder to move him along. "Come on, now. We're all anxious to hear what Winslow has to say and before you ask again . . . the answer is no. We don't know what it is."

Although he was more than capable of twisting out of Brooks's guiding hand, Whiteoak allowed himself to be herded away from his wagon. At least, he allowed it for a few steps before planting his feet. "Allow me to lock up, won't you?" he said in a convincingly meek tone. "After all, my livelihood is in that rolling work of art."

All of them glanced at the wagon. The reactions ran the gamut from admiration to visible disgust.

"Sure," Brooks replied. "But be quick about it."

Whiteoak didn't take three steps toward his wagon before he was blocked by a stout body. The man in front of him was the same one who'd spoken up a few moments earlier. "Now just hold it, mister," he grunted.

While the professor had been willing to let the others think they could shepherd him before, he wasn't about to let them stop him from sidestepping his current obstacle so he could get to the rear door of his wagon. The man who'd tried to block him attempted to keep up but was shoved aside by Brooks.

"Let the man lock up his wagon," Brooks said.

"Why should I? He's a damn cheat."

"We don't know that yet. Besides, would you want to leave all of your possessions just lying inside an open wagon so they could be taken by any thief who passes by?"

The disagreeable fellow looked around at those surrounding him. While most of the faces were anxious, some of them clearly backed Brooks's point of view. Reluctantly, he said, "I guess not. But if'n he proves to be one of them thieves . . ."

"Then he'll be treated like one," Brooks said.

"And that wagon? Plenty of us have purchased things from this hustler! He's got our money and lord only knows what else in there!"

"If I am proven to be incorrect in my findings," Whiteoak offered magnanimously, "then I will gladly offer a refund to anyone I might have inadvertently wronged." Seeing the befuddled expressions around him, the professor added, "I'll hand your money back."

"Of course, he will," Brooks said. Once the wagon had been properly locked, he clapped a hand around the back of Whiteoak's neck to keep him moving. This time, Whiteoak wasn't so sure he could break loose.

CHAPTER EIGHT

"Fool."

That word cut through the pensive silence that had befallen Winslow's place and was accompanied by a gnarled finger pointing at one of the men who'd come to pay him a late-night visit. The man on the receiving end of that finger blinked as if he'd just been smacked on the nose.

Shifting his finger to another face, Winslow said, "Genuine." He then pointed at three more men in turn, jabbing his finger at them like a child's pretend pistol shooting holes in the clouds. "Fool, genuine, genuine."

"What's that supposed to mean?" asked the man who'd been most vocal about his distrust of Whiteoak.

"It means just what I said," Winslow replied. "Those men's gold was either the fool's kind or it was genuine."

"What about me?" asked someone from the back of the group.

"I already indulged the lot of you more than enough," Winslow sighed. "You all can approach me in an orderly manner and I'll do more tests. You got any more questions, you can ask them in the morning. Now, who's next?"

The miners filed in to talk to the broker. Less than half of them bothered to look Whiteoak in the eyes as they left. None seemed interested in hitting the professor.

Hat in hand, Whiteoak rocked on his heels and nodded to all of the miners whether they seemed to be in good spirits or not. When all but two had left, Whiteoak nodded while addressing those who remained. "So it seems my machine came up with the same results as this camp's highest regarded expert!"

"Yes, it would," Brooks said. "Now, how about you tell us why that happened?"

Whiteoak's victorious smile faded a bit when he asked, "Weren't you at my presentation?"

"I was there. I was also one of the first to hand over my gold to be tested. I'd like to know how your machine does what it does. As far as I can see, it's nothing more than a fancy scale with a few extra bells and whistles."

"No whistles on my current model,"

Whiteoak chided. "But that's not a bad idea for future modifications."

"Take this outside, fer Christ's sake," Winslow said as he started closing up his shop. "Some of us have better things to do."

"Precisely," said the professor as he took the initiative by wrapping an arm around Brooks to lead him away from the broker's shop. "Why don't I address all of your concerns over a drink? And, just to show there's no hard feelings, I'll buy the first round!"

Brooks walked with Whiteoak for less than a dozen steps before shrugging out from under the professor's arm and saying, "Better yet, why don't we have that discussion back at your wagon? That way, you can show me that machine up close and explain how it works."

"That would take quite a bit more time, sir."

"You saying I'm too stupid to understand how your contraption works?"

"Stupidity isn't a factor, my noble fellow. It's a simple matter of being well versed in the facts and terminology of science." Gazing up at the stars, Whiteoak said, "In centuries past, what we now consider to be simple science used to be regarded as magic. I'd be more than happy to bring you up to speed, but our mutual friend, Mister Winslow, brought up two very important facts. My conclusions were right and it is very late."

"I'm not too stupid or ignorant to tell what time it is," Brooks said in a cold, unwavering voice. "A quick explanation will do."

"Please. After a good night's rest, I'm sure I will be much more capable of giving you a better explanation."

Rather than respond with more words, Brooks stood his ground like a slab of granite that had been dropped from the top of the camp's tallest structure.

"All right, then," the professor grunted. "You want to make this night drag on even longer? You'll have your wish. Come on."

Whiteoak stomped back to his wagon, fists clenched and lips pressed into an angry line. Every so often, he started to say something over his shoulder to the man who followed him but would just as quickly bite his tongue and continue storming onward. Upon reaching his wagon, he jammed his hand into one of his pockets to retrieve a small key. "I'd be more than happy to entertain this notion of yours at a more reasonable hour," he hissed. "After the indignity of being dragged to Mister Winslow's shop not once but twice and then having to face an angry mob, I'd say I've been more than accommodating."

Brooks said nothing.

Fitting his key into the wagon door's lock, Whiteoak fidgeted with the device that was much more complex than it appeared. After having his valuables plundered by more than a few overly zealous brigands, he'd taken it upon himself to fashion a lock that operated as something closer to a puzzle than a simple mechanism to keep a door shut. The key was a handcrafted masterpiece that would require an expert of the highest level to duplicate. Once inside the lock, the key would do nothing if simply turned. It needed to be manipulated in a subtle way for it to tap a set of interior pins in a specific order to make any progress. Even if an intruder knew what needed to be done in order to breach the wagon's first line of defense, finding the pins by touch alone was a task that required a good amount of practice.

"I'll retrieve one of my devices," Whiteoak said while manipulating the key within the lock. By now, he was an expert in making the movements look like nervous fidgeting instead of a calculated set of motions to unlock the door. "I can explain the basic mechanics to you, but I must insist on waiting until morning if you want me to disassemble it. A lantern or candle does not provide enough light for you to see the intricate inner workings."

Brooks started to say something in response. Less than a single syllable escaped his lips before the word was swallowed in a gurgling rush of blood filling his throat. Whiteoak snapped his head around in time to see the glint of a blade raking across Brooks's neck to send a spray of crimson fluid through the air.

CHAPTER NINE

It wasn't the first time death had snuck up on Professor Whiteoak. It wasn't even the first time he'd witnessed a man's throat getting cut. Even so, the sight of Brooks being opened up at that particular moment did a hell of a job of catching him off his guard. His shock only lasted until Brooks's eyes rolled up into their sockets, which was also when Whiteoak found the last pin inside his wagon's lock.

As soon as the door came open, Whiteoak stepped inside. His boots had barely touched the interior floorboards when he was grabbed by the coattail and yanked outside again. It was all he could do to keep from breaking a bone or two when he was thrown to the dirt. His ears jangled and his eyes rattled within his skull as the stench of blood filled his nose. Even before his vision cleared, Whiteoak knew he was only an inch or so away from the spot where

Brooks had landed.

All he could see of Brooks's killer was a pair of filthy boots with a tooth embedded on the side of one toe. It wasn't a likeness of a tooth carved in by a knife or leather smith, but a real tooth wedged more than halfway into the boot itself.

"Pick him up," snarled the man with the tooth in his boot.

A strong, bony hand clamped onto the back of Whiteoak's shirt and hauled him to his feet. Once he was upright, Whiteoak could get a better look at the man with the gruesomely decorated footwear. He was shorter than the professor by several inches. What he lacked in height, however, the killer more than made up for with a burly chest, thick arms, and squat neck. Less than half a cigar was stuck in the corner of his mouth, burning brightly as he drew a shallow breath.

"Make sure it's him, Wes," said the man with the cigar. "Wouldn't want to go through all this trouble for nothin'."

Wes was still holding on to Whiteoak's shirt, which he used to throw the professor against his wagon.

"Skinny dandy with expensive clothes," Wes grunted. "Looks like him all right."

Whiteoak plastered a twitchy smile onto

his face, taking a quick gander at the man closest to him. Wes was taller and thinner than the fellow with the cigar and toothy boot. He also wore three guns strapped to his waist; two in a double-rig holster and another tucked behind the buckle.

"What seems to be the problem, gentlemen?" Whiteoak asked.

"You know damn well what the problem is, Whiteoak. You messed up real good."

"I'm afraid you'll have to be more specific."

The stout man grinned before driving his fist into Whiteoak's gut. Not only did he thump the professor's midsection, but he dug his knuckles up and slightly under Whiteoak's rib cage with enough force to lift him to his toes. Using his other hand to stand the professor up straight again, he said, "After that shit you pulled in Kansas, you were damn lucky to get away with your life. How long's it been since you robbed that bank?"

Whiteoak tried to answer but couldn't drag enough air into his lungs to get the words out.

"Any robber worth his salt would know to keep his head down after a job like that," the man continued. "But not you. You just can't help yourself from dragging this here wagon around and drawing attention."

"I'm . . . not a robber," Whiteoak wheezed.

"Ain't that what all robbers say?" Grinning, the man reached out to flip open the professor's coat. "You sure ain't no gunman, that's for certain. Otherwise you would've skinned them fancy pistols by now."

When the silver-handled .38s were taken from him, Whiteoak brought his hand straight down and out to chop Wes in the throat. While Wes was gagging, Whiteoak snatched the .38 back and cracked it against the side of the younger man's head. Now that he'd bought some room to maneuver, Whiteoak put his back to his wagon so nobody else could get behind him.

"Step away," Whiteoak said.

Although still grinning, the stout man regarded Whiteoak with a little more respect. "See? I knew he was in there. The real outlaw that's got the price on his head. The killer."

"I'm no killer."

"That so? I hear you've used that fancy gun of yours as more than decoration."

"I've defended myself," Whiteoak said.

"By killing."

"Only when necessary."

"And when you live a life of cheating

85

folks, stealing money, and robbing, that becomes necessary a whole lot, don't it?"

Whiteoak's eyes darted down to the body lying in the bloody dirt. "You murder an innocent man and call me the killer?"

"There's more than one killer in this camp tonight," said the stout man.

Beside Whiteoak, Wes was recovering from the quick blow to the throat. His breathing was ragged but, like a good dog unwilling to test its leash, he refrained from making a move before being told. That order was coming, Whiteoak knew. He could tell as much by the cruel glint in the stout man's eyes.

Like a rattlesnake striking from the desert floor, Whiteoak snapped his gun hand out to push the barrel of his .38 into Wes's chest. As he grabbed the front of the skinny man's shirt with his left hand, Whiteoak pulled the .38's trigger to drill a hole through Wes's torso. Whiteoak fired again, making a second muffled thump as the pistol's barking voice was swallowed up by its target. At that close range, sparks from Whiteoak's barrel ignited a small fire on Wes's shirt. The professor let him drop and turned to face the man with the tooth in his boot.

"You've gotten bold, Henry, I'll give you

that much."

"We've managed to keep things relatively quiet thus far," Whiteoak said. "I'd suggest you move along before we draw too much attention."

"This ain't a proper town. These miners are used to folks shooting each other. I'd wager there ain't even a scrap of law around for miles in any direction."

"That's where you'd be wrong. There are two U.S. marshals within a stone's throw of here."

The stout man looked around. "I don't see 'em. And if I don't see 'em," he said while knocking the pistol from Whiteoak's hand, "then they won't do you one bit of good."

Whiteoak's mind raced. In less than a second, he'd figured angles, strategies, and the best path to set those plans into motion. Another blink and he was ready to move. By that time, however, it was already too late. The stout man had already drawn a gun from his holster and was preparing to use it.

Something whistled through the air and landed with the wet sound of a butcher's first stroke into a side of beef. The stout man winced and bared his teeth, reaching down behind one leg. The gun in his hand had been temporarily forgotten since he was now more interested in the slender knife protruding from his calf.

Whiteoak looked for whoever had thrown that knife. Judging from the angle at which the blade had been thrown, he quickly found the figure hunched over in the shadows behind a weather-beaten livery near the lot where Whiteoak's wagon was parked. As he squinted to try and make out a few more details, Whiteoak saw the glint of another blade spinning toward its target.

Fueled by equal parts of rage and pain, the stout man twisted around to knock the knife away using the side of his pistol. Metal clanged against metal and when the knife hit the ground, the stout man was thumbing back the hammer of his pistol. Before he could tighten a finger around his trigger, he was put down by a solid impact to his temple.

Whiteoak stood over the fallen man, still holding the piece of scrap wood he'd picked up to knock him out. "Whoever you are," he said to the figure in the shadows, "we need to get away from here."

CHAPTER TEN

The whorehouse wasn't much of a house and yet it was sturdier than most of the tents in camp. Part of the structure was composed of canvas walls supported by wooden frames while other parts were remnants of sturdier buildings that had been there before all the miners started to arrive. At the heart of it was a set of three small brick walls forming an office where a single woman ran the house's finances. Whiteoak was in a room sharing one of those walls, thanks to a bit of sweet talk and some money placed into the proper hands.

"Are you sure you boys don't want any company?" asked the girl in her early twenties who'd led them into the room. It had been her hand that had received Whiteoak's bribe. She had smooth skin and long chestnut brown hair that hinted at an ancestry tracing back to one of the western native tribes. Her eyes were jaded and the smile she wore was mostly sass.

"I'm sure," Whiteoak said. "Thank you very much."

"If you two are only interested in each other, you can get a room somewhere else a whole lot cheaper," she said.

"What? No! It's not that. We're more interested in shelter for the night."

"Right," she said through a laugh that had seen her through a great many strange times. "Whatever you say."

"Where's Danielle?"

"So now you do want a woman?" the girl asked. Placing one hand on the doorframe, she cocked her hip and arched her back enough to display her pert assets. "I'm right here and I don't mind taking the both of you."

"I'm sure you don't, honey, but I need Danielle," Whiteoak insisted.

"And bandages," the man with Whiteoak said. "Be damn quick about it!"

The girl flicked the threadbare shawl that had been wrapped around her shoulders back up so she was covered once again. Craning her neck forward, she asked, "What's wrong with him?"

"He's hurt," Whiteoak snapped. "Now, go fetch Danielle before you'll be forced to clean up a dead body instead of a bit of blood!"

Although the eye roll wasn't the reaction he'd been hoping to get from the girl, Whiteoak was grateful that she at least decided to start moving. Whether or not she would follow through on his request remained to be seen.

"You really are hurt," Whiteoak said as the flap covering the door to the room was flicked shut.

"Yeah," the other man grunted. "I know that already."

"I'm sorry about before."

"You mean when you hugged me?"

"It wasn't so much of a hug," Whiteoak sputtered. "I'd call it more of a joyful embrace. You know. Between two newfound friends." After a slight pause, he added, "All right. It may have been a hug. I was overcome by the moment, but I surely didn't know you were wounded when I exuberantly decided to show my appreciation."

"You hugged me," the man said with disgust. "Who the hell does that?"

"It was a spur of the moment thing. I was glad to be alive. Let's just put it behind us, all right? What happened to you? Were you attacked by the same men who were attacking me?"

"No. This happened a while ago."

As they'd been talking, the man was going through the painful motions of peeling off his jacket and shirt. While removing the jacket had been uncomfortable, the shirt was partly stuck to him by layers of dried blood on his rib cage. When the dirty cotton didn't come away from his torso, he gritted his teeth and ripped it away.

"Careful!" Whiteoak said. "Now you're bleeding even worse."

"Been bleeding for a while, Doc. That's why I'm here."

The room was scantly furnished, containing only a bed, a small table, and a stool that was better suited for use while milking a cow. On the table was a washbasin containing whatever had been wrung out of the last towel that had been used in that room. Grabbing the small square cloth lying beside the basin, Whiteoak dipped it into the water and used it to start cleaning the other man's wound.

"Who are you, mister?" the professor asked. "I generally like to know the names of the men who pull my fat from the fire."

"Dylan Garviss," the man replied. His words were strained and his body tensed the moment the cloth was applied to his wound. "What the hell is that? Saltwater?"

"Most likely this water is mixed with soap and perspiration. This isn't exactly a doctor's office."

"Then why'd you bring me here?"

"Because we needed to get out of sight and this was the best place I could think of. Also, I know some of the good people who run it."

"Henry's real friendly with the whores in camp," said the girl with the chestnut hair as she stepped once more into the doorway. "I hear he's friendly with whores in most camps and towns he visits."

"It always pays to have friends with —"

"With nice tits and loose morals?" the girl cut in.

"No!" Whiteoak said. "I was going to say it pays to have friends with good instincts and sharp survival skills. I've found that women in your line of work usually have both."

"But those other things I mentioned don't hurt, right?" she asked.

"Well . . ."

She smiled and stepped aside. "That's what I thought. You said you wanted to see Danielle?"

The woman who walked into the room was a few inches taller than the younger girl and had a curvier figure. Her dark blond hair hung in wavy curls that grew lighter in color at the tips. She had thin lips, a dusting of freckles on her cheeks, and a subtle southern drawl in her voice when she asked, "What kind of trouble have you brought me this time, Henry Whiteoak?"

"This man is injured," the professor replied. "He could use some medical attention."

Dylan stared up at Danielle and asked, "She your nurse?"

Already on her way to the narrow bed, Danielle said, "What happened to him?"

"That's a good question," Whiteoak said. Shifting his gaze to Dylan, he asked, "What happened to you?"

"I was shot," Dylan replied.

Danielle shook her head. "Obviously. How long ago did this happen?"

"Day or so."

"It seems you've already found a doctor somewhere," Whiteoak said as he pointed to the gash in Dylan's side. The skin was being held together by thick black thread forming a jagged line in his flesh. "These stitches seem to be holding up."

"They're probably doing more harm than good," Danielle said. "Who put those in?"

"Did 'em myself," Dylan said.

"Fine job," Whiteoak sighed while averting his eyes from the newly flowing blood. "What are you doing there, Danielle?"

She used her fingernails to loosen the thread at the top of Dylan's wound. "Removing some of these stitches. This wound looks bad. Might be septic."

"Why don't I just excuse myself, then," Whiteoak said as he stepped out of the room.

Dylan looked up at the woman looming over him. "I thought he was the best doctor in the Dakotas."

"Maybe if you ask him," she replied. "But there are a few others who'd have a different opinion."

CHAPTER ELEVEN

Whiteoak returned a short time later carrying a satchel over one shoulder and a wooden case in his hand. The case was flat and about half the size of the satchel. As soon as he rushed into the room, he pulled a stool up close to the bed and set his satchel down onto the floor near his feet.

"I didn't think you'd be back so soon," Danielle said.

"I just needed to collect a few things," Whiteoak told her. "I knew this man would be in good hands."

"What have you got there, Doc?" Dylan asked.

Setting the case down on the bed near the other man's knees, Whiteoak opened it and removed two glass vials. "This is a mixture of my own creation. It's designed to fight the inflammation of open wounds and eradicate any septic dangers that might occur therein."

"What's in it?" Danielle asked skeptically. "Laudanum?"

Whiteoak chuckled while mixing the contents of two vials together. "Do you think laudanum will fight the dangers of septic wounds?"

"You put it in about everything else you sell," she said.

"This little mixture has performed wonders. If you doubt my word, I can present to you the signed testimonials of a dozen customers who swear by its authenticity."

"Give someone enough laudanum and they'll swear to anything," Danielle grumbled under her breath.

"What was that?" Whiteoak snipped.

"Nothing."

To Dylan, Whiteoak said, "This will be applied to the wound several times throughout the night. By morning, I guarantee you'll feel a whole lot better."

"Thanks, Doc," Dylan said.

"He's not a doctor, you know," Danielle announced.

"That ain't what I heard," Dylan replied.

Whiteoak took one of the cloths Danielle was using and poured some of his mixture onto it. "Thank you for the vote of confidence."

"I was told he's one of the best doctors

there is."

"Who told you that?" Danielle asked.

"A fella from another camp west of here. He says Doctor Whiteoak saved his life."

Danielle looked over to the man sitting near her. "You're telling people you're a doctor now?"

"I'm more of a professor, really," Whiteoak said.

"Same difference," Dylan said as he lay back and closed his eyes. "Healin' is healin', which is what I need."

Whiteoak smiled broadly. "You see? It doesn't hurt to be courteous. Some people could learn from that."

"If you've got so much doctoring knowledge, why did you come running in here and ask for me?" Danielle challenged. Her hands had stopped what they were doing and her eyes fixed on Whiteoak.

Whiteoak looked down at what she'd been doing as well. The old stitches had been removed and were currently being replaced by new ones that were much straighter and formed from thinner thread. "You have experience with this sort of thing."

"And how do you know I have this kind of experience?" she asked.

"Because you used to be a nurse," Whiteoak replied. "You assisted doctors at several forts throughout these territories."

"I'm surprised you remember that."

Whiteoak pulled in a breath and let it out as he pressed his cloth down a bit harder out of frustration. "I remember all kinds of things."

"Do you recall how you got that gunshot wound?" she asked unflinchingly.

His jaw set into a tense line, Whiteoak said, "I was shot while running from a posse. Is that what you wanted to hear?"

"Actually, I wanted him to hear it," she said while nodding down at the man whose wound she was tending. "He seems to think you're a respectable doctor. A misconception like that could cost a man dearly."

"Says the nurse who's decided to work in a whorehouse." The words had come from an angry seed in the pit of Whiteoak's stomach. It burned the moment it flared up within him and hurt even worse when he'd let it slip past his lips.

Danielle didn't say anything. She merely continued her work until the stitches were done. Then, she carefully placed her needle and thread on the table next to the bed and stood up to leave.

At first, Whiteoak was going to let her go. The burning in his chest was similar to what he'd felt before and he wasn't about to mishandle it again. Once he jumped to his feet and chased after her, the discomfort inside him faded away.

"Danielle, wait," Whiteoak said.

There was plenty of activity inside the cathouse, most of it confined to the many rooms that were built like so many honeycombs in a perfumed hive. She navigated between them, her steps never losing their methodical cadence as they moved from wooden floorboards to canvas tarp to bare dirt and back to floorboards again. Whiteoak followed behind and put an extra bit of steam into his strides so he could catch up to her. Since he wasn't as familiar with the changing interior of the place, his toe caught on the edge of a floorboard and sent him straight down into a heap of tangled limbs.

Danielle stopped when she heard the sound of his fall followed by the string of obscenities following it. She then took another couple of steps but didn't go much farther before stopping again and turning back around. "Once again, you get hurt because you're stupid and rush in without looking."

Getting up and dusting himself off, Whiteoak replied, "I'll agree to the latter but not the former."

"Oh, that's right. Because you're so damn

smart. Professor Henry Whiteoak, medicine man and miracle healer."

"Some titles a man earns. Others are placed upon him by his fellows."

"And others are hidden away," she said. "Titles like outlaw, swindler, con man, and thief."

Reluctantly, Whiteoak nodded. "Yes. Those are some of the others. Perhaps I may have earned a few of those as well."

"Just a few?"

Since picking himself up after his tumble, Whiteoak fussed with his shirt and tried to remove the dirt from his knees. After having found a tear in the fabric of his pants, he attempted to straighten it, which was doing him no good whatsoever. Frustration from his entire evening, which culminated in his fall, exploded onto his face as he swatted the ripped fabric while angrily tearing it even more.

"What, exactly, do you want from me?" he asked.

"I want you to leave me alone," Danielle replied. "I thought I made that clear the last time we saw each other."

"I didn't choose to come back to these territories."

She shook her head slowly. "If you've taught me anything, it's that people do what they want to do. Whether it's good for them or not, they'll do what they want and when they want to do something else, they'll find a way."

"What does that even mean?"

"It means you could've been a great man! You could have been a real doctor. You could have made a real difference. Instead, you . . ." She trailed off and turned around in a sweep of curls.

"This is all I know, Danielle," Whiteoak said while slapping his hands flat against his chest and the fine silks covering it.

"No," she said while turning back around to gently place a single fingertip upon his chest between his hands. "This is all you've wanted. You wanted to leave the Army and so you did. You wanted to forge your own trail and so you did."

"I remember that," Whiteoak said with a nod.

When she spoke again, her voice was softer and gentler. "Then do you also remember telling me you wanted to do more than just find new ways to earn a few quick dollars?"

"Yes."

"Were you lying to me like you lie to your customers?"

Whiteoak straightened his posture to look

almost regal despite the tattered threads he wore. In a serene, unwavering voice, he said, "I would never lie to you the way I lie to my customers."

Danielle rolled her eyes, let out a tired sigh, and walked away.

CHAPTER TWELVE

"Jesus!" Dylan snarled. "Fucking . . . shit!"

"Might want to keep your voice down," Whiteoak said. "Otherwise, folks might get the wrong impression of what we're doing in here."

Whiteoak sat on the stool next to the bed. In his hands was a cloth and a small bowl in which he'd mixed the substance that had been retrieved from his wagon. When it was applied to Dylan's wound, the substance foamed and fizzed angrily. It wasn't as angry, however, as the patient who had to feel the mixture interact with his freshly opened wound.

Balling up a fist, Dylan swung at Whiteoak. The blow was easily dodged, which didn't keep Dylan from trying again. "That damned stuff hurts worse than when I was shot!"

The professor leaned back to avoid the next swing and soaked the rag in his bowl.

"That's the idea. It's killing off the disease inside your wound. Why weren't you so fussy when Danielle was stitching you back together?"

"Because she's got a smoother hand than you. What disease are you talkin' about?"

"The same disease that forces field surgeons to saw off the limbs of wounded soldiers. The disease that turns a common cough and sore throat into a fever threatening the lives of those afflicted."

Dylan gnashed his teeth together while staring straight up at the flimsy roof over his head. "I didn't have no fever."

"It's a generality. Doesn't matter if you understand it or not. I've had truly good results from this mixture."

"Every time?"

The fact of the matter was that Whiteoak had been working on the mixture for quite a while. It, like so many of his other concoctions, was created from healthy doses of experience gained from working with chemicals, skill in his craft, and fanciful musings about how he could address a well-known ailment. He'd experimented several times with various derivations of his formula with mixed results. To his current patient and potential customer, however, he said, "Yes. Every time."

Dylan steeled himself with a breath and balled his fists tighter. This time, he refrained from throwing those fists at the man beside him. "Hurts like a bastard, but it ain't as bad as before."

"That's a good sign." Whiteoak beamed. "Even so, it might help things along if you had a flask of something stronger than water. Helps to ease the discomfort."

"If I had whiskey, I'd be drinkin' it," Dylan said.

"Fortunately, I have a little something." Whiteoak reached into an inner pocket of his coat to retrieve a thin silver flask. Flipping open the top with his thumb, he tipped it back for a quick nip and then handed it over to Dylan. "Try not to take it all."

"How long were you gonna hold out on me, Doc?"

Whiteoak said nothing and continued with cleaning the wound.

One sip from the flask knocked the breath from Dylan's lungs. Another sip put a lazy smile on his face. "This something you made yourself, too?"

"Not me. That came from a mean little family in Kentucky. Truly terrible people, but they know how to brew their spirits."

"Yes, they do," Dylan said before taking another longer pull from the flask.

Danielle had done a good job of stitching the wound shut and now that it was cleaned so thoroughly, Whiteoak could get a better look at it. "So," he said while poking the tender flesh to see how it would react, "what brings you to this camp?"

"You do, Doc. I got hurt and did the best I could to fix up myself but that weren't enough. I started looking for a doctor and it's like I said before. Your name was brought up."

"I'm surprised you could make it this far after being shot."

"I've had worse. The bullet ripped into the meat and passed on through. Started feeling weak, though."

Finished with the cleansing mixture, Whiteoak set it aside and picked up another rag. He used this one to start dabbing the wound, which he did with at least some small amount of care to keep from causing any more discomfort to his patient. "I'd imagine you felt weak. You lost a fair amount of blood."

"I've bled before. Plenty of times."

"And you were able to patch yourself up?"

"Mostly," Dylan grunted. "And when I couldn't, I found me a doctor to do the job. Much like I did this time around."

"Do you get shot often?" Whiteoak asked

as a way to divert Dylan's attention from what was coming next.

"Sometimes, yeah."

"Then perhaps you should consider a new line of work."

"What's that supposed to . . . OW!"

Whiteoak's fingers were probing another spot on Dylan's side. After pressing down on that area, he pinched a small piece of flesh between thumb and forefinger. "There's a bit more lead in there," he explained.

"I was only shot once, goddammit. It hurts now because you're the one hurtin' me!"

"I'm afraid there's more to it than that."

"What . . . what's that supposed to mean?" Dylan asked through a clenched jaw. Bending at the waist, he twisted around to get a better look at his side. "There ain't even another wound there."

Whiteoak let go of the skin he'd been holding. "All right then," he said calmly while prodding another area of Dylan's torso. "Then tell me . . . does this hurt?"

Dylan's face turned red and fresh beads of sweat pushed out from his forehead. As those little rivulets of perspiration trickled down his face, Dylan blinked them away and said, "Not one bit."

"That's what I thought," Whiteoak chuckled. Giving the unstitched portion of Dylan's ribs a gentle pat, he added, "I guess I'm all through here, then."

While Dylan had been able to force himself through one short sentence, he couldn't make it one more second after that. His upper body twitched and he slammed his head back down onto the pillow. "For fuck's sake! What the hell's wrong with me? Is it that septic stuff you were talkin' about?"

"Not exactly," Whiteoak said as he resumed prodding Dylan's side. "As I already mentioned, it appears as though you've still got some lead in you."

"But I was only hit once. Or that's what I thought. Was I hit again? Did I not see a wound?" Dylan asked as panic began to gain momentum in his voice. "Aw, hell. I been riding around with another bullet in me. I'm a dead man. That's it, right? I'm dyin'."

"You are dying," Whiteoak told him. "But only in the greater sense that we're all dying. The Reaper will claim you as it does everyone on this earth but not tonight."

"That's it. I'm dead."

"Calm yourself." The professor squinted and turned his face upward as his fingers continued to poke and prod his squirming patient.

"I can hear Gabriel's trumpets blowing now," Dylan wheezed.

"If you insist on spouting nonsense, then I'll have to insist you keep your mouth shut. I'm trying to concentrate." Whiteoak took one hand away so he could reach for his left boot. When he brought it up again, that hand was gripping a knife with a slender blade.

Dylan saw the blade and clenched his eyes shut. "All right. Finish me off. Just be quick about it."

"You're delirious. Shut up."

Dylan did lower his voice but wouldn't stop mumbling to himself. His exact words were difficult to hear, although a few names as well as jumbled pieces of a few different prayers were among the mix.

"You weren't shot again," Whiteoak explained. "The bullet that got you must have cracked apart and the smaller piece of lead split off from the other one's trail."

"I don't understand what you're saying."

"I can't put it any simpler than that, but I need to get the rest of the lead out."

"I still can't understand," Dylan said in a fading voice. "I think my hearing's gone. I'm dyin'."

"Jesus Christ."

"Not yet, but he's on his way," Dylan moaned.

Whiteoak placed the tip of his boot knife against Dylan's side and made a small cut. Although the outlaw took the pain well, he couldn't help but holler when some of Whiteoak's mixture was dabbed into the fresh incision. Dylan tensed up, sucked in a deep breath, and held it until his entire body went limp.

Chapter Thirteen

About an hour later, Whiteoak stepped out of the room. He used a cloth to clean his hands and took a deep breath while making his way to the small bar at the front of the brothel. Several of the girls working there regarded him with tentative suspicion due to the blood on his hands, but they'd already seen a lot worse in their young lives and quickly moved along. The bar was composed of several stacks of crates situated in a short row covered by a tablecloth. Whiteoak stepped up and knocked on the uneven surface to get the attention of the woman behind it.

"Whiskey," he said to the barkeep.

She was probably somewhere in her late twenties but had the wariness and scars of someone who'd lived much more than double those years. The barkeep poured his drink and set it in front of him. "Are you a doctor?" she asked.

"You know who I am, Mary," Whiteoak replied before paying for his liquor and draining the glass.

"I thought I did. You always struck me as nothing more than a fast-talking salesman with a line of bullshit a mile long."

Whiteoak cocked his head slightly. "Some of that seems like a compliment. The rest . . . I believe I'll choose to ignore."

She smirked, showing some of the inner beauty that would remain untouched as long as Mary somehow managed to keep the world from breaking her spirit. "You acted like a doctor in there."

"Were you watching?"

"A bit. Mostly I could hear the screaming."

Wrapping his hand around his empty glass, Whiteoak stared down at the few drops of whiskey clinging to its sides and said, "Nothing more than a bunch of vaguely organized butchery is all that was."

Mary's hand came down to settle on top of his. "No," she told him. "You helped that man. If you're not a doctor, then what are you?"

He looked at the woman standing across from him for a few seconds before his eyes drifted elsewhere. "I'm just someone who's been a lot of places and paid attention well enough to pick up some tricks along the way."

"You've treated bullet wounds before?"

"Yes. In the Army."

Giving his hand one last squeeze, Mary said, "Well, you did a fine job this time around."

"How would you know?"

"Because you're not the only one who's seen men shot," she replied. "There have been lots of fights in this sorry excuse for a cathouse and plenty of men who had to be carried out. That one in there is a whole lot better because of you. That's saying a lot more than I can for some of the pathetic drunks who have come around here calling themselves doctors."

Whiteoak was about to order another whiskey but held off. His thirst must have been written in his eyes because Mary grinned and poured him one, anyway.

"That one's on the house," she said. "For doing such a good job."

"Thank you kindly," Whiteoak said. This time, he sipped his drink instead of throwing it down as if he wanted to douse a fire in his belly.

"Oh," Mary said. "There was someone coming around here looking for you."

"Really? Who?"

"I don't know, but he was a real asshole. When I told him you were busy tending to someone who was hurt, he pushed right past me. Didn't make it three steps before them two dragged him out on his heels," she added while nodding toward two burly young men standing near the door.

Whiteoak glanced over at the muscle-bound pair. He didn't need to be told they were there, since they were part of the reason why he'd brought Dylan to that tent. Men were always stepping out of line in cathouses, which was why toughs like those two were hired to keep them in line. The two young men seemed relaxed and watchful, which was good.

"Who was this fellow that came asking for me?" Whiteoak asked.

"Skinny guy," Mary said with a shrug. "About your height."

"What did he want?"

"I don't know. Why? Did you want to talk to him? Because he looked like he wanted to knock you on your ass."

"He'll have to get at the back of the line," Whiteoak grumbled.

"Aww, it's not so bad. Especially since Winslow said your gold machine worked all right."

"You heard about that?"

"Everyone heard about that," she said. "It's a small camp."

Something gnawed at Whiteoak's gut. He drummed his fingers on top of the bar while slowly turning his glass in his other hand. Finally, he stepped away and approached the two men guarding the door. By the time he'd caught their eye, Whiteoak was wearing a beaming smile. "I heard there was a bit of excitement a while ago," he said.

Both of the men were large but not equally so. One resembled a thick tree stump while the other looked as though he could easily push that stump over. The stump scowled at the professor and said, "Huh?"

"I heard someone was asking for me."

"Who?"

Fighting back his frustration, Whiteoak looked to the other one and asked, "Didn't you toss someone out of here not too long ago?"

"Yeah," the burly man replied.

"Do you know who he was?"

The guard shrugged his shoulders. "Don't give a damn."

Whiteoak struggled to find some words that might get through the stony layers surrounding the big men's heads. Before he could come up with anything, the smaller of the two said, "You wanna know who he is? Go ask him for yourself. He's right over there with Danielle."

At first, all Whiteoak could see was a man of average height and build standing beside and slightly behind Danielle. They were across the narrow street near a small cluster of wagons that were shuttered up for the night.

"Has that man caused trouble here before?" Whiteoak asked.

Neither of the guards seemed interested in replying.

Angry words churned at the back of the professor's throat. Before he unleashed them, he replaced them with a proposition dipped in just the right amount of honey. "Perhaps you'll recall more if properly motivated?"

When the men looked at him this time, their eyes were immediately drawn to the silver dollars in Whiteoak's hand. With speed that seemed uncanny for a man of his bulk, the larger of the two men snatched the money from the professor's grasp. "He hasn't been around here much, but he was real interested in you."

"Is he a friend of Danielle's?" Whiteoak asked.

"Nah."

"You said he's hasn't been around here

much. When was he here before?"

"Last time was a few weeks ago," the smaller guard said after his partner handed him one of the silver dollars. "Looking for a gunman named Bob."

"Bob?"

"That's the only name he gave. Robbed some stores down in Nebraska, I think. He's in jail now."

"No," the other guard said. "Bob's dead. Got found guilty and strung up."

"I see," Whiteoak said. "Any chance you could go see what he wants?"

The guards glanced out of the tent and turned right back around. "He ain't doing anything wrong."

"What about Danielle?"

"She ain't doing anything wrong, either."

"No!" Whiteoak snapped. "What is she doing with him?"

Both guards shrugged. "Don't care," the smaller one replied. "Long as she ain't in here, she can do what she likes. Same goes for that asshole we tossed out."

Whiteoak had already heard enough to know what he was dealing with. Only two kinds of men came searching for robbers to drag them back to a jail cell where they would eventually get their neck stretched by a short rope: lawmen and bounty hunters.

The professor wasn't very fond of either. Taking another look outside, he spotted the fellow who'd been looking for him earlier still standing next to Danielle. He wore a dusty coat over a black vest and holster strapped around his waist. Whiteoak's eyes immediately darted to the gun the man was carrying, but the holster was empty. He quickly spotted the pistol when the man stuck the barrel into Danielle's ribs.

"Damn bounty hunters," Whiteoak sneered.

CHAPTER FOURTEEN

Whiteoak stepped out of the cathouse to approach Danielle and her escort. Before he could get too close, the man with the gun pulled her back and shoved her behind the carts. Thinking he would need to pursue them, Whiteoak rushed over to those carts only to find the pair waiting for him in a small alcove formed by a wooden wall and a waist-high fence surrounding a corral.

"I hear you've been looking for me," Whiteoak said.

"You heard right," the man replied.

"What do you intend to do with her?"

"Draw you out and away from anyone you might've hired to watch your worthless back."

"Well, you succeeded. And from everything I've heard," Whiteoak added, "my back, along with all of my other sides, is far from worthless."

"You got that right. After all the rich men

you've pissed off, you're one of the most valuable scalps I'm likely to take."

"Well, now. Is it odd that I'm mildly proud of such an accomplishment?"

"You can feel any way you want about it," the bounty hunter said. "Just know that this lady here will feel pretty damn bad if you don't come along quietly with me."

Whiteoak lifted his hands in the air. "As you like."

The skinny man narrowed his eyes into a sharp scowl. "Just like that, huh?"

"You seem to have me at a great disadvantage, sir. What else am I supposed to do? Of course, my cooperation is contingent on the aforementioned lady being allowed to walk away."

"That depends on how well you behave. Toss your guns," the man said. Nodding slightly toward a patch of shrubs nearby, he added, "Over there."

"Henry, don't," Danielle said. "He'll kill you, anyway."

"No, he won't," Whiteoak replied with a wry grin. "I'm worth so much more alive than dead."

"How can you be sure about that?" she asked. "Have you been keeping track of how much money you're worth?" After a slight pause, Danielle sighed, "Of course you've been keeping track of that."

Whiteoak spread his hands out a bit more. "It's rare that a man has a true way to measure his worth. I must admit, including the bonus for capturing me alive, my bounty has become quite impressive."

Thumbing back the hammer of his pistol, the bounty hunter said, "I might forsake that bonus just to shut your damn mouth."

"Better than you have tried."

"Henry, please," Danielle said. "Don't provoke him."

"I'm not provoking anyone," Whiteoak said dismissively. "He's got the upper hand and knows it. Even if I was to draw my gun, he wouldn't be worried. Isn't that right, Mister McGurn?"

The bounty hunter's eyebrows twitched upward, revealing more than a slight interest in the professor's words. "You really have been keeping an eye on things."

"Imagine the bragging rights I will have earned by having none other than Rob McGurn hunting me down." Smirking again, Whiteoak added, "I expected you to catch up to me a whole lot sooner than this. That either means my skills are better than imagined or yours are worse."

McGurn shook his head. "I figured you'd try talking your way outta this, but, so far, you're not doing yourself any favors."

Whiteoak eased his coat open to show the holster he wore. Taking hold of each .38 by its silver handle, he daintily lifted them from their leather home and tossed the guns into the shrubs.

"Keep going," McGurn said.

Stooping to reach for his boot, Whiteoak said, "What about her?"

The pistol barrel was eased away from Danielle's ribs before McGurn shoved her toward the more populated area of the camp. "She can go," he said. "And I'm sure she's smart enough to know I can find her any damn time I want. Or," he added before licking the corner of his mouth, "if I just feel like paying her a visit. You give me a discount if'n I come around to that whore-house?"

"Sure," she replied while walking away. "I'd be overjoyed if you came to me in a room alone, stripped your clothes off, and let me get my hands on you. I'd have you bleeding in places you didn't even know you had."

"Just go, darling," Whiteoak said. "Don't make a fuss."

"Real sweet woman you got there, White-oak," McGurn said after Danielle had taken a few steps away.

The professor removed a knife and a smaller pistol from hiding spots in his boots. Once the weapons hit the dirt near his feet, he stood back up and kicked them toward the shrubs. "What now?" he asked.

Before the bounty hunter could issue his next order, Danielle broke into a run. The instant she'd gotten past the carts blocking the small clearing from view by the rest of the folks in the vicinity, she let out a scream that shattered the night like a rock through fine china.

"Help!" she screamed. "Someone tried to kidnap me!" Knowing that wouldn't be enough to rouse the miners as quickly as she wanted, she added, "He's stealing horses!"

Whether it was in response to a woman's cry for help or the prospect of losing good horses to a rustler, a trio of men rushed toward her. Not far behind them was a fourth man who took it upon himself to take charge of the other three. "You men get behind me," Matt said as he exposed his deputy U.S. marshal tin for all to see. "I hereby order any horse thieves or kidnappers to show themselves!"

"Dammit," Whiteoak hissed. "No!"

Two figures emerged from the shadows behind McGurn to move into place to cover him. Three more separated themselves from the growing crowd of people in the camp by drawing pistols or bringing shotguns to their shoulders and taking aim at the deputy lawman.

"No!" Whiteoak shouted. "I had this under control! Now this is all going to hell!"

He didn't.

And it did.

CHAPTER FIFTEEN

One of the men who'd been milling in the crowd near some of the few carts that were still open for business took it upon himself to fire first. He carried a rifle in his hands, which he used to take a shot at the deputy U.S. marshal. Since Matt dropped to the ground as soon as fire erupted from the rifle's barrel, it was unclear whether he'd been hit or if he was simply presenting a smaller target. Either way, he managed to shoot at the rifleman once he hit the dirt.

The lawman's shot didn't draw blood, but it got close enough to send the rifleman running for cover behind a cart selling pickaxes. The other two men who'd opened fire on the lawman took positions on either side of Matt and the small group who'd rallied around him.

"You men want to earn your money?" Matt shouted. "Kill these sons of bitches!"

Whiteoak hunkered down low and covered

his head with his hands to keep his hat from flying off as he ran. "They'll know better," he said quickly to himself. "They won't dive into a fight they can't win."

The men on either side of McGurn slowly walked toward the more populated area of camp. Every other step they took was announced by a shot from their weapons. The men with Matt stood their ground, firing as fast as they could in the hope of bringing down one of their targets.

When one of McGurn's men put a bullet through one of Matt's hastily formed posse, the group scattered. The fight was far from over, however, since the deputy's men resumed firing once they got to a better position. A few seconds later, the gunfire intensified as several miners joined the fight by pulling the triggers of their rusted Colts and hunting rifles. Whiteoak kept his head down and scurried toward the bushes where his weapons had been tossed. Since McGurn and his men had their hands full, he got to them without much trouble.

"What the hell is wrong with these people?" Whiteoak said in a harsh, hurried voice. "And where the hell did my guns go?"

A rustle of leaves brought his attention to the shrubs where he spotted the glint of torch light on silver. Someone was crawling behind the shrubs to pick up his guns and if the rest of the camp hadn't been engulfed in a firestorm of lead, Whiteoak might have thought twice about jumping in after them. As it was, he was more confident taking his chances against one gunhand than a dozen.

As soon as he saw the hand that had picked up his .38, Whiteoak grabbed it. Although smooth to the touch, the hand was strong enough to jerk him off balance as it tried to pull the gun away. When White-oak staggered forward, he saw an angry face framed in curly dark blond hair.

"What in the hell do you think you're doing?" Danielle shouted over the rolling waves of gunfire.

"I thought I was getting you out of harm's way. You're welcome for that!"

"I should thank you?" A stray shot hissed over their heads, followed by another and a scream from a wounded man. "You're the one who started all of this!"

"What are you saying? I don't even have a pistol in my hand! Speaking of which," Whiteoak said before snatching the .38 away from Danielle.

Now that her hands were empty, all Danielle could do was ball one up and punch Whiteoak's arm.

"What was that for?" the professor yelped.

"For being the sort of man who can burn down a camp just by talking too much."

"Burn down? Aren't you being slightly dramatic?"

She grabbed Whiteoak's chin and twisted his head several degrees to the side until he was looking straight at a tent that was currently aflame.

"Oh," he said. "Maybe you're not being dramatic. Good Lord! How did that happen?"

"I don't know! Plenty of bad things happen when people shoot their guns in the middle of a crowded camp! That's Marvin Winkle's place. His wife and him sell dresses out of there."

"It's also fairly close to where my wagon is parked," Whiteoak added. "We've got to get over there."

"That's not close to your wagon!" she said as she followed Whiteoak away from the shrubs. "Can't you think about anything other than yourself for a moment?"

"I was! Coming after you when you were being held at gunpoint was a brave and selfless act, thank you very much."

"Nothing you do is selfless."

Even though they were less than a few yards from the periphery of the raging gun battle, Whiteoak stopped and turned around to face her. "Nothing, you say? I take offense to that."

"Doesn't mean it's not true."

Most of the fighting was between McGurn's gunmen and the locals Matt had rallied to his aid. Several other locals had joined in out of some connection to one side or the other or for the sheer thrill of shooting at someone in the middle of the night. Another, and very likely, option was that the men who decided to draw their guns were too drunk to know any better.

Whiteoak wanted to keep talking but was cut short when a series of three quick shots were fired in his direction. One of them hissed through the air. The second knocked a chunk out of a wooden post to his left and the third hit a lantern hanging from that post to provide light for a nearby stall. The lantern shattered, spilling its oil onto the front of the stall and thereby setting a fire on the wares being displayed there.

"That's one question answered," he said while hastily swatting out the flames. "We now know how the fire was started."

"That wasn't a question," she said as she lent a hand in putting out the fire before it could grow into a real problem. "This camp is a damn tinderbox. Isn't a week goes by without something burning up."

Another shot was fired at Whiteoak, which was all the professor could bear. With one hand, he took hold of Danielle's arm and pulled her behind him. His other hand came up so he could sight along the top of his .38's barrel. Whiteoak squeezed off a round aimed at one of the men who stood at McGurn's side. That man had a rifle to his shoulder, which he was reloading by hastily working its lever. Before he could complete the task, a bullet from Whiteoak's pistol caught him in the chest.

"Come on," he said while hurrying away from the battle.

Despite her struggles to break loose of his grip, Danielle was dragged along behind Professor Whiteoak. "Wherever you're taking me, I don't want to go," she said.

"It'll be better than the place you were before," he said.

"Not if you're there."

"That's a fine way to talk to your savior."

"Saviors make a place better," Danielle reminded him. "They don't spark fights and burn them down."

"I didn't burn anything."

"Where are you going?"

"To make certain my wagon doesn't catch fire," he replied.

"It's always about you! Can't you see there

131

are other folks with fires to contend with?"

Another of McGurn's men fired a round that drilled a hole through one of Matt's remaining deputies. After that, he began running after Whiteoak and pulled his trigger again. The shot sailed less than a foot high of its target but still failed to catch Whiteoak's full attention.

"First of all," Whiteoak said as he pointed his .38 at the approaching killer and squeezed his trigger, "it's not always about me!" Whiteoak's bullet clipped the gunman's shoulder, sending him back a few staggering steps.

"And second," Whiteoak continued while firing another shot that put the killer down for good, "there's enough chemicals inside that wagon of mine to blow a hole in the middle of this camp!"

"There's not even any fire over there!" she said. "There's hardly any fire anywhere, anymore."

The shooting had died down a bit since several of the combatants had been put down and several more had lost interest and run away. Matt was hollering for everyone to throw down their guns, but nobody seemed interested in obeying him. Another shot was fired, which silenced the deputy's voice abruptly. The only light on the camp's

132

crooked streets came from the few sputtering torches and lanterns that hadn't been knocked over or broken in the commotion.

"Ah," Whiteoak said. "It seems you're correct. Very efficient fire brigade in this camp."

"You were going to ride out of here in the confusion, weren't you?"

"Don't be absurd! My horses aren't even hitched to the wagon and my things aren't packed."

"You meant to hide, then," she said. "Is that it?"

"You're asking a lot of questions for someone who was just rescued from certain death. I still have yet to receive any gratitude for that, you know."

Danielle stopped in her tracks, spun around, and marched straight up to the professor. He was still wearing an annoyed scowl when she took his face in her hands and pulled him close so she could plant a kiss on his lips that caused his eyes to widen with surprise. When she pulled back, Danielle whispered, "Thank you."

Whiteoak was speechless. It didn't last long, but she relished every second.

CHAPTER SIXTEEN

The wagon sat in the dark, quiet as the dead men lying nearby. Whiteoak raced up to it, opened his arms, and placed both hands flat upon its side. He then dropped to his knees, running his hands all the way down the wooden panels.

"Do you two want to be alone?" Danielle asked.

"Give me a hand," Whiteoak said as he reached underneath the edge of the wagon with both hands.

"Whatever it is you're doing, you're on your own."

Something clicked beneath the wagon. That sound was followed by the muffled sound of shutters opening on well-oiled hinges. "Don't be silly," he said. "Take this."

Danielle didn't know what to think until Whiteoak produced a double-barreled shotgun from beneath the wagon. He handed it up to her and immediately reached back under the wooden vehicle. "Is this why you came back here?" she asked.

"Partly. I did have to check on my wagon but considering all of the hired guns swarming into the camp it seemed a good idea to better equip myself. And you in the process, of course."

"There were plenty of guns to be found back there."

"And plenty of gunmen to go with them. Sometimes it is best to step away from a situation to better compose oneself, prepare, and reenter the situation from a fresh perspective." Whiteoak took another shotgun from beneath the wagon, along with a bundle tied together with twine.

"Is that dynamite?" Danielle asked.

"Indeed it is."

"Things weren't bad enough already? Now you want to see how much you can blow up as well?"

"When your opponents have you outnumbered, your best advantage is to have them outgunned."

"How do you intend on using that?" she asked while eyeing the sticks of explosives clutched in the professor's hand.

Whiteoak tucked the dynamite under his arm and strode past her. "That has yet to be determined." After checking to make sure his pistol was loaded, he turned around and looked her in the eye. "I'd prefer it if you stayed behind where you'd be safe."

"Next to the wagon that might explode into a cloud of chemicals?"

"I intend on guarding that wagon with my life. It's made to withstand any number of intrusions. You'd be safe locked up in there and if things do get . . . heated . . . there are ways for you to escape."

She kept her eyes locked on his while stepping closer to him. The shotgun she'd been given was kept with the stock under one arm and its barrel pointed downward, showing it wasn't the first of its kind she'd used. "I know how to take care of myself, Henry."

"That has always been quite apparent." He placed one hand gently beneath her chin and guided her face closer to his. Their lips met, parted slightly, and then pressed together again with more passion and intensity. The firestorm that had been raging in the camp had already been dying down, but its sounds faded completely away as the kiss lingered on.

Whiteoak opened his eyes and finally, grudgingly, broke away. "You should go now," he said.

"Why?"

Raising his voice, Whiteoak looked past

her and said, "Let her go. She's not a part of any of this."

Danielle spun around to look in the direction Whiteoak's eyes were pointed. Three men stood near the wagon, two of them had showed up with McGurn and the third was a local who'd been there since Whiteoak had first arrived in Dugan's Find. Looking at the third man, Danielle said, "You're not one of these killers, Samuel."

"Maybe not," the local man said through thick layers of grit and dirt stuck to his face by sweat and too many days without seeing the inside of a bathtub, "but they pay well enough."

"All I have to do," Whiteoak said, "is light this fuse and we all die."

One of McGurn's men, a short fellow with muscular arms protruding from rolled-up sleeves, shook his head. His hair was cropped close to his scalp as though he'd shaved it off with a hunting knife. "You wouldn't blow up that pretty wagon of yours or that pretty lady."

"If I'm dead, none of those things matter," Whiteoak said in a voice that was colder than a dark, desert night.

"You couldn't get to a match before we gunned you down. Come along with us and make it easier all around."

"Easier for who?" Whiteoak asked.

"Us and you," Samuel replied. "And especially her," he added while fixing his eyes on Danielle. His gaze wandered up and down the curves of her body. Even though she was covered by the clothes she wore, he stared at her as though he'd burst in on her when she'd been changing behind a locked door.

Whiteoak dropped the dynamite and took hold of his shotgun with both hands. "Men have already died tonight. No need to add three more to the list."

"Only other man to die tonight will be you, Professor," Samuel said. "Once you're out of this camp, the shooting stops. Now, whether you walk out or are carried out in a sack, that's up to you."

"And you can stop looking over that way," added McGurn's man with the shaved head. "Since that lawman was gunned down, ain't nobody else is interested in coming after us."

Whiteoak glanced over to Danielle. She was indeed looking elsewhere and when he followed her gaze, it led him to a single figure approaching the wagon. Since both of them were now looking in that direction, the three gunmen took a glance that way as well.

"Walk away, mister," said the man with the shaved head. "This ain't none of your concern."

The man approaching them moved with slow, trudging steps. He dragged one leg slightly more than the other and kept a hand close to his side. There wasn't much lighting in the lot where the wagon was stored, so it took a few more steps before Whiteoak could tell who was headed toward him.

"Mister Garviss?" Whiteoak said. "Shouldn't you be resting?"

"Ain't nobody here is resting, what with all the yelling and shooting and such," Dylan replied. "What's going on here?"

The third man in the group confronting Whiteoak and Danielle had yet to say a word. Suddenly, he lost all patience with the way things were going and snapped, "If you know what's good for you, you'll get your ass outta here!"

"See, that's always been my problem," Dylan said. "I ain't never known what's good for me. If I did, I probably woulda been a bookkeeper like my momma wanted."

Eager to please McGurn's men, Samuel was the first to make a move against Dylan. He swung his shotgun around to point it at Dylan while thumbing back the hammers to both barrels. Dylan responded with a set of movements that weren't the fastest Whiteoak had ever seen but were steady and sure. He closed his hand around the grip of his pistol and cleared leather while Samuel was still preparing his shotgun. Aiming from the hip, Dylan fired twice in quick succession. Samuel reeled back as each bullet punched into his chest.

McGurn's men took aim, but not before Dylan's pistol barked again to catch the man with the shaved head in the throat. As that one dropped to his knees and clutched the fresh hole in his neck, Dylan extended his arm and took careful aim.

The last of McGurn's men carried a pistol and fired hastily. His finger pulled back hard against his trigger, causing the gun to shift in his hand just enough to throw off his aim. Dylan squeezed his trigger with even pressure. His round went right where he wanted it to go and bored a hole clean through the killer's forehead.

"A bookkeeper or maybe a banker," Dylan said as he walked forward. "That's what momma wanted. Daddy, on the other hand, wanted me to be a farmer like my brothers."

The man with the shaved head was still on his knees, covering the hole in his throat with both hands as if that would somehow keep his life from slipping away. Dylan walked up to him, placed his gun barrel between his eyes, and pulled his trigger. The expression on the killer's face barely shifted as his brains exploded into a red mist behind him.

"I just don't think that woulda suited me," Dylan said while reloading his pistol using fresh rounds from his belt. "A farmer or bookkeeper or banker, that is."

"No," Whiteoak squeaked. "I . . . I do believe you've found your calling."

CHAPTER SEVENTEEN

A few minutes later, Whiteoak emerged from his wagon. The stench of burnt cordite still hung in the air, mingling with smoke from flames that had been recently doused. Other folks and even the animals were only just poking their noses out from wherever they'd been hiding, testing the night with darting eyes and cautious feet.

"You weren't in there long," said one of the few people in the vicinity who didn't seem to be affected by what had come before. "You sure you got what you needed?"

Whiteoak clutched a small bag under one arm. Once he was out of the wagon, he locked it up using a key and tapping a few hidden latches. "Yes, Dylan," he replied. "I got what I needed. Mainly I had to make certain my possessions were secure."

"What he means," Danielle said, "is that he needed to lock everything up inside so it

142

wouldn't be found."

"I don't want intruders trifling with my things," Whiteoak told her. "Is that so wrong?"

Dylan smoked a cigarette that he clenched between his teeth in the corner of his mouth. Removing the cigarette with one hand, he held it a few inches from his face so he could admire the glow when its tip was touched by the passing wind. "Not at all, Doc. Might wanna pack a few more things, though."

"Why's that?"

"Because it might be healthier if you moved on from here. In fact," he added while chomping down on the cigarette again, "it might be best to hitch up your horses to that thing and ride out now."

"There's a stagecoach station about a day's ride south of here," Whiteoak said. "There's also a post office with a telegraph, which means I'll be able to acquire some news about some issues that have become very important to me. After that, I'll know whether or not a lengthier departure will be necessary."

"Oh, I think it'll be necessary."

Danielle had been tending to some business of her own while the professor was in his wagon. She hadn't been gone long but came rushing back as though she was afraid she'd miss something if she didn't hurry faster with every step.

"I thought I told you to stay close," Whiteoak said. "I distinctly remember saying that before I opened my wagon again."

"Yes, you did," she replied with an off-handed wave. "I had to check in on the others."

"You mean the other whores?" Dylan asked. "Back at that whorehouse where you work?"

"They are women who work to earn money," Danielle said. "How they do it is no concern to you."

"I ain't criticizin'."

Scowling at the outlaw, Danielle leaned in closer and sniffed the smoke that had formed a small cloud around Dylan's head. "What's in that cigarette? It doesn't smell like tobacco."

"I know. It's sweeter."

"Is that opium?"

"Nope." Once again, Dylan removed the cigarette from his mouth so he could admire it from a slightly greater distance. "It's a mix I got from an old Norwegian fella in Deadwood. Really nice. Want some?"

Shifting her focus to Whiteoak, she said,

"I'm surprised it's not something you gave him."

Whiteoak shook his head while checking to make sure the cylinder in his .38 was loaded, as was every loop in his gun belt, which he'd put on while inside his wagon.

"This is what you've put your trust in," she said to Whiteoak. "A killer who intoxicates himself with peyote."

"It ain't peyote, either," Dylan chuckled.

Turning her back completely to Dylan, Danielle grabbed Whiteoak by the sleeve and attempted to pull him away from the wagon.

"Excuse me," Whiteoak said. "You'll wrinkle the fabric!"

"You've got a lot more to worry about than that."

"It doesn't do anyone any good to panic. We're quite fortunate that the violence has subsided and even more fortunate that the slight legal presence in this camp is currently too preoccupied with searching for any other gunmen to worry about us. I'll just have to ride a mile or two tonight to put some distance between myself and —"

"That deputy was shot," she cut in.

Whiteoak blinked a few times as though her statement irritated him more than the smoke being produced by Dylan's cigarette.

"Matt?"

"Yes. He was shot sometime after we got away from all that commotion."

"Was it one of the bounty hunters that killed him?"

"He's not dead," Danielle replied. "But most folks think you did it."

"They don't think," Dylan said. "They're pretty damn certain of it."

"So that deputy U.S. marshal is a damned liar," Whiteoak seethed.

"Or he just believes it when someone else says you shot him," Danielle offered. "In all the confusion, it got pretty hard to tell which bullets came from where."

"Whose side are you on here?" Whiteoak asked.

All she could offer to that was a shrug.

Looking to the outlaw, Whiteoak asked, "You knew about that?"

"Yep."

"Were you going to mention it?"

"I was tryin' to," Dylan said. "That's why I said you should probably leave this camp altogether."

"You had plenty of time to say something more helpful!"

"You were busy gettin' ready to go," Dylan said. "And that's just what you should've been doin'!"

Whiteoak's eyes started to waggle back and forth in their sockets as if they were following the paths of excited moths. "All right. This isn't so bad. No worse than things got in New Orleans. Maybe a little worse, actually, but not impossible."

"Why would anyone think Henry shot that deputy?" Danielle asked.

"One of the bounty hunters was sayin' so. I heard him when I was tryin' to get out of that cathouse. My head's still a little fuzzy. Could be from that medicine you put into my wound or all that stitchin'."

Whiteoak's hand came up and around so quickly that it could barely be seen before it slapped the cigarette out of Dylan's mouth. Since he didn't so much as touch Dylan's face, Whiteoak caused the outlaw to stare in bemused wonder as his cigarette sailed through the air. "Think," the professor commanded. "Are you sure it was one of the bounty hunters making that accusation?"

"Yeah."

"Why?"

"I was gonna ask him more about it," Dylan said. "That's why I followed him out here. He kinda got ahead of me, though. Like I said," he added while tapping his forehead. "A little fuzzy."

"Oh, dear," Whiteoak said quietly. Then,

147

looking around at the men Dylan had left in his wake, Whiteoak added, "Not a lot of men left here to question. I don't suppose you saw where Rob McGurn went?"

"Not as such," Dylan replied.

"Oh, dear."

CHAPTER EIGHTEEN

A day and a half later, the camp was mostly back to normal. A few of the tents were scorched around the edges, a few were gone completely, but most of them moved right along with only a handful of colorful stories to mark what had happened on the last night when Professor Henry Whiteoak was in town. Nobody was certain where the professor went. Of course, nobody had gone looking for him, either. The majority of the locals and regulars weren't surprised that another salesman had chosen to move along in the dead of night. He would probably be back or he wouldn't. Such was the extent of their concern for the colorful dandy. The bodies that had been left behind drew some attention, but death wasn't much of a stranger to those parts, either. It would be left until the undertaker got around to cleaning it up and the carnage would be added to the rumors swirling around the camp like all the smoke from its fires.

Danielle, on the other hand, had commitments in Dugan's Find. When she didn't return right away, she was missed. Those who were concerned about her didn't get too worried, however, since she returned later that same night. She wasn't a working girl in the lewdest sense of the word. She acted as an assistant to the madam of the cathouse in which she worked. She helped the younger girls when they needed advice, cooked some of the meals, and patched up workers or customers alike when things got rough. Her most important duty was keeping the ledgers balanced, which she did every week on Wednesday night. Thursday afternoon, when she returned, she was greeted with a mixture of emotions.

"Ah, there you are!" said the woman who came to meet Danielle once she arrived in the cathouse tent. She was slightly taller than Danielle with an ample figure that was made to look even more so by the tightly cinched corset she wore. Dark brown hair was tied back in a braid during the day, giving her somewhat of a more professional appearance. After she'd wrapped Danielle in a friendly hug, she held the younger woman at arm's length and asked, "Where the hell have you been?"

"Why, Tara," Danielle replied. "I never thought you were the type to worry."

"I wasn't worried. The books need to be done and I'm not about to do them. There's other business to attend to. If you want to go off with some fancy man in the middle of the night, then you'd best be sure to come back here when there's work to do. Otherwise you can find someone else to pay you."

"Fancy man?" Danielle said as she pulled free of Tara's grasp. "What's that mean?"

"Spare me the innocent act. You were with that salesman. The same one you used to share your bed with when this camp was half the size it is now."

Some of the fire in Danielle's eyes was replaced by trepidation. "You know about that?"

"I was here then, too, you know," Tara said with a lazy wave over her shoulder as she turned her back to her. Knowing Danielle would follow her, she walked further into the tent and said, "I made it my business to know all I could about who was in who's bed and for what reasons. Love, lust, drunken mistakes, they all tie folks together in different ways. Someone in my line of work has to know that."

Being the one that kept Tara's books, Dan-

151

ielle was all too familiar with the various streams of income that filled the cathouse's coffers. Blackmail was one of the shadier methods, if not the darkest. "It's not like that anymore between Henry and me," she said.

Tara stopped momentarily so she could look at Danielle's face when she asked, "Is that so?"

Danielle did her best to nod sternly without giving anything away that might be used against her later. She couldn't read much of anything through the layers of powder and resolve covering Tara's face, leaving her unsure as to whether or not she'd succeeded.

"Whatever you say," Tara said with a shrug. "I'm glad you're back."

"Right," Danielle sneered. "Books need to be balanced."

"It's more than that. I like to think of you as a friend. After all, we've been working together for some time."

Tara stood in front of a sturdy wall in the rear portion of the cathouse that was composed mostly of wood instead of canvas. The framework provided a safe spot for a few of the cathouse's more closely guarded secrets. Tara opened one of the doors, exposing a room that was illuminated mostly by a window in the rear wall, which cast almost as many shadows as it dispelled.

"We have been working together for a while," Danielle said. "Long enough for me to know that's not the room where you keep your ledgers."

"The books still need balancing," Tara replied, "but that can wait until you're done in there."

"What's in there?"

"Not what. Who. Someone was asking for you. Came around this morning and requested some of your time."

Pain flickered behind the stoic mask Danielle tried to use to cover her face. The expression faltered for a moment and was quickly replaced by something much stronger. "I don't entertain men like that. Not anymore."

"I know, honey. It's not like that."

"Then what does he want?"

"Why don't you ask him?" Tara said as she motioned toward the open door.

The next room wasn't very big. In it, someone walked with heavy steps that thumped against the floorboards until a figure filled the doorframe. Danielle could see a rough-looking figure wearing a battered jacket and a holster strapped around his waist. His hand lingered over the gun kept there, almost as though it couldn't stray from the weapon even if the man wanted it to.

"His name is Ed Brudaker," Tara said. "Do you know him?"

"No," Danielle snapped.

Tara dropped her voice so it couldn't be heard past Danielle's ears. "Keep the door open a crack. I'll be able to hear you better that way. Me and some of the boys will be close by if you need us."

"Do you know this man?" Danielle asked in a matching whisper.

Tara shook her head slightly.

"Well, then," Danielle said as she straightened her posture and faced the next room. "It's good to know you're tossing me in there with him, anyway."

"Danielle, I . . ." When she reached out to touch the other woman's arm, Tara was immediately rebuffed and left behind as Danielle entered the next room.

CHAPTER NINETEEN

Whiteoak's horses were corralled nearby in a small lot behind a row of old shacks. He retrieved his animals, gathered his gear, and paid the old man running the livery in short order without making much noise. After dragging the bodies away, he hitched his horses to the wagon and climbing up into the driver's seat.

"Looks like you've had a lot of practice with that," Dylan said as he climbed up to sit beside the professor.

"A bit."

"Mind if I tag along?"

Without looking over at the man beside him, Whiteoak flicked his reins. "I'm too tired to stop you."

With the hour being as late as it was, there weren't many locals about to watch the professor leave camp. When they did draw the occasional glance, Whiteoak tipped his hat to them and moved along. Dylan sat with one foot propped on the board separating him from the horses. His pistol was in hand and resting upon his bent knee.

"Expecting trouble?" Whiteoak asked.

Slowly turning the pistol's cylinder to see that every chamber was filled, Dylan replied, "With you, it's good to be on your toes. I've gotten the impression that you're not just some doctor."

"I patched you up pretty well."

"Sure you did. What I meant was that you're a hell of a lot more. For one thing, you seem to know your way around the underbelly of a mining camp."

Whiteoak recoiled distastefully. "I beg your pardon?"

"Well, you could have taken me to a lot of places, but you chose a whorehouse."

"That was to keep you safe," Whiteoak reminded him.

"Oh, yes. So you told me." After a few moments of smug silence, Dylan said, "You could have also taken me to the doctor's tent at the edge of camp."

"There's no doctor's tent."

"It was put up a few days ago."

"And how do you know that?"

"Because I saw it on my way into Dugan's Find," Dylan said.

"Then why didn't you go there instead of

bothering me?"

"Because you were the one I'd heard about," Dylan told him. "And when I saw how you fixed me up, no questions asked, I knew I'd picked the right man for the job."

"No questions asked, huh?" Whiteoak chuckled. "And what questions was I supposed to ask?"

Dylan shrugged and looked at the trail ahead of them. "Eh, I don't know. Usually most doctors ask where I got all the other gunshot wounds and knife scars. They tend to get nervous about the pistols I'm wearing or the fact that I'm a wanted man in these parts."

"Doctors know that much about who's wanted and who isn't?" Whiteoak asked.

"In these territories? Yeah," Dylan replied. "There's a lot of wanted men in the Dakotas and the law don't take too kindly to them who patches them up. But I also have a hunch that you know a lot about that sort of thing, too."

"Do you, now?"

"Yep. I could see a thing or two while all those shots were being fired back there," Dylan said as he hooked a thumb toward the camp that was slowly being left behind the trundling wagon. "Didn't see the whole thing, of course, but I got a peek at how you reacted when them federal law dogs showed up."

"Things had already gotten well out of hand by then," Whiteoak said. "I was trying to keep from getting killed at that point."

Dylan shook his head. "Nah."

"Is your monosyllabic grunting supposed to mean something?"

"It means I don't believe you, Doc."

Giving his reins another flick, Whiteoak sighed. "And I can't begin to tell you how much that saddens me."

Dylan let out a laugh that cut through the dark silence surrounding the trail. As the wagon ambled further away from camp, the dim light cast by torches placed around Dugan's Find was also left behind. Not being able to see everything around him made Whiteoak nervous. Announcing his presence with such a boisterous display didn't help matters much.

"I don't give a damn about lawmen," Whiteoak hissed. "But there are plenty of other things to worry about out here, so keep your voice down!"

"I will, as soon as you tell me what you've got tucked away inside this rolling carnival of yours."

"You couldn't possibly comprehend what I've got in there. A description of the chemicals alone is enough to make your pea-sized brain ache."

"You know what's better than beating the tar out of a smart-ass?" Dylan asked. Figuring he wasn't going to get a response, he said, "Nothing at all. But I'll let that slide on account of you fixing me up."

"Goodness," Whiteoak sneered. "Thank you."

"And what the hell are you all worked up about anyhow? You're treating me like a goddamn leper."

"Perhaps that's because you brought a firestorm of calamitous proportions to a place where I was actually beginning to feel comfortable."

"You mean them gunmen?" Dylan asked.

"What else would I mean?"

"They was after you, not me. You know that."

"Do I?" Whiteoak snapped.

"Yer a smart fella so yes, you do."

Torn between basking in the compliment and continuing a perfectly good tirade, Whiteoak found himself flummoxed long enough for his ire to lose its steam. Eventually, he grunted, "I suppose that's true."

"Near as I can tell, you're angry about two things." Dylan held up his fingers to mark his points one by one. "You're upset about leaving that pretty blonde back at the cathouse, and you don't like folks getting too close to whatever it is you've got tucked away in this wagon."

"Again, I have *everything* of mine in this wagon."

"Nah."

"Again with that," Whiteoak groaned.

"There's something else. I been stealin' and hidin' for too long to be told any different."

"Stealing and hiding, huh?"

"Yep. Any thief worth his salt knows when someone is sitting on something valuable. He can smell it like fear pouring out of another person, only it's sweeter and goes deeper. Any man who's taken something he shouldn't have and wanted to keep hold of it knows how to hide it. Once he's hidden enough, he knows how to spot someone else who's hidin' something," Dylan explained while making a circular motion with his hands. "You know how that goes."

"The basic learning process? Yes. I'm familiar with it."

"And when a man who's hiding something feels that someone else is gettin' a bit too close to whatever it is he's hidin', he tends to get snippy for no good reason. His nerves fray like a cheap piece of rope, y'see. First, he wants to run. Then he wants to try and act like nothin's wrong. Then he gets hot under the collar. Next, he may even pull a gun or take a swing at that person who's closin' in on him. Kinda like a cornered dog."

Whiteoak steered the wagon off the trail. As the wheels left the ruts that had been put there by countless other travelers before him, the wagon jostled and rocked back and forth. Once he'd found a flat spot of even ground, he set the brake with his foot and set the reins down. "Tell me why you came to find me," he said.

Dylan's reply was short and confident. "Already did."

"Not that answer. The real one."

"The wound in my side wasn't real enough for ya?"

"That was a convenient device to get you to that camp and in my presence without raising suspicion."

"If you think gettin' shot was convenient, then you must never have been on the receiving end of a bullet."

"I've received plenty of bullets," Whiteoak said. "And I've spoken with plenty of liars."

"Then you must know I ain't one of 'em."

Whiteoak's eyes narrowed as if he was focusing on a specific spot behind Dylan's eyes. "I'm not a believer in coincidence and you meeting up with me at this particular time is too big of one for my liking."

"Weren't no coincidence, Doc. I was hurt and you've been riding all over these Badlands bragging about what an amazing healer you are. As for the rest of it, I'm thinking it's less of a coincidence and more of an opportunity."

"For what?"

"To make some money."

A smile broke across Whiteoak's face. It was a humorless expression that belonged on the face of an atheist hearing a passionate Catholic sermon. "Is this where I'm supposed to clap you on the back and tell you how right you are?"

"If you feel like it."

"I don't."

Dylan sat in a relaxed slouch with his legs apart and his arm resting at a seemingly lazy angle. Whiteoak immediately noticed, however, that he still clutched his gun in one hand. The other was pressed against his side to relieve some of the pressure from his stitches while protecting the wound that had so recently been dressed. "I sure as hell didn't mean to get shot, but since it happened, we might as well make the best of it."

"I had an obligation to do what I could for you," Whiteoak said.

"My ass."

"What?"

"Ain't nobody's obliged for anything unless it's to blood relatives and I ain't one of them to you. You could've turned me away, but you didn't. That shows the kind of man you are. Once I got my wits about me and could tell what was goin' on, I could see you had something else on yer plate other than doctor- in'."

"I'm a salesman as well and, for the last time, I'm not a doctor. I'm a professor."

"Why haven't you turned me away, then?"

"I've been asking myself that very same question."

"I'll tell you why," Dylan said. "Because I got a use. I proved as much by gettin' rid of them bounty hunters that were after you back there. They were another good hint that you ain't just some salesman, by the way."

"You did prove to be handy with a pistol," Whiteoak admitted. "And since there doesn't seem to be anyone coming after me any longer, now would be a good time for us to part ways." When nothing happened in the next few seconds, Whiteoak swept an arm toward the side of the wagon. "I said *now* would be a good time for us to part ways."

"I heard you."

"Then why are you still here?"

"Because there's still someone after you."

"I'm certain those marshals have things well in hand as far as that's concerned."

"With them bounty hunters back at camp, maybe," Dylan said, "but not the ones that followed you out here."

Whiteoak snapped his head around and leaned over so he could get a look at the stretch of trail behind his wagon. "Which ones?" Even as he asked that, he could see the pair of horses coming toward him from the camp.

Dylan reclined in his seat, idly picking something from between his teeth. "Two horses, right? I can hear 'em."

"Stay here," Whiteoak said.

"You sure about that, Doc?"

"Yes, I'm sure."

"And what happens if you get into trouble? Want me to step in or should I just take the wagon and run?"

"Where the hell do you intend on running with my wagon?" Whiteoak snapped.

Dylan shrugged and innocently replied, "Somewhere safer than here. Wouldn't want your stuff to get shot full'a holes, right?"

Whiteoak's face pinched into a stern, frustrated grimace. Keeping one hand on his holstered .38, he climbed down from his seat and walked toward the back of the wagon. Sure enough, there were two horses approaching from camp. One of the riders was slighter of build than the other and rode straight toward him.

"Henry!" That rider shouted.

Stopping in his tracks, Whiteoak replied, "Danielle?"

"Yes. It's me."

"Who's that with you?"

"He says his name is Ed Brudaker," she called back. "He says you know him."

"Ed Brudaker?" Whiteoak said, allowing the name to swirl around inside his head like milky tea in a porcelain cup. In seconds, his eyes widened and he said, "Ed Brudaker? Let's see him!"

The man riding beside Danielle came forward a few more paces, dismounted, and walked toward the wagon. Smiling to show a missing tooth, he laughed warily and said, "Henry Whiteoak. Don't you have a talent for staying alive?"

CHAPTER TWENTY

The closer Whiteoak and Brudaker got to one another, the more nervous Danielle became. Both men picked up speed as if they intended on locking horns like a pair of angered bulls.

"Now hold on," she said anxiously. "There's been enough trouble for one . . ." She stopped once the men got close enough to clap their arms around each other for a quick, rough hug.

"I was wondering if you'd remember that name," Brudaker said.

"Remember it? How could I forget such a mouthful? You never were very good at picking aliases," Whiteoak chided. "The point is to blend in, not stick out like a black sheep in a field of white wool."

"And you're one to talk about blending in? Laying low in the Badlands while pulling a damn circus tent behind you?"

Both men laughed for a short while until

they realized they were being watched. Danielle stood on one side of the pair while Dylan stood on the other. "Do you know what's happening here?" Danielle asked.

"Not a damn clue," Dylan replied.

"Sorry about that, folks," Whiteoak said in a tone of voice resembling what he used when first addressing an audience. "This is Corey Maynard, an old friend of mine."

"Corey Maynard?" Danielle asked. "What about Ed Brudaker?"

"That's just a name I've been using lately," Corey explained. "Seems some folks have been looking for me and I needed to throw them off the trail."

"Changing your name," Dylan mused. "Might wanna consider using that trick, Doc."

"Yes," Danielle said while sternly crossing her arms. "It's also a suggestion I've been making for some time."

Whiteoak waved off that suggestion like so much smoke before it got into his eyes. "In my business, a man's name carries a lot of weight. Besides, someone of my impressive physical attributes can't just stop standing out in a crowd. That would be like asking a diamond to stop glittering."

"Now there's something I haven't been missing," Corey sighed.

"Come along, all of you," Whiteoak said. "The spot I was intending on using isn't much farther from here. We'll make camp, have some coffee, and catch up on old times."

"It's late, Henry," Danielle said. "I have to sleep before I fall over."

"Me, too," Dylan said. "Getting shot at tends to take it out of ya."

"Perhaps we should pick this up in the morning," Whiteoak suggested.

Corey nodded. "I wasn't going to stay long tonight anyhow. Just wanted to make sure you were out of plain sight for a while. I've already got a place to sleep back in Dugan's Find. I'll come back in the morning."

"My wagon will be —"

"Don't worry," Corey interrupted. "I know how to find you."

Before Corey could turn away from him, Whiteoak grabbed his hand and shook it earnestly. "It's good to see you again, friend. I was beginning to think you'd been tossed into jail or worse."

"I was in Nebraska," Corey said, "so you weren't far off."

With that, Corey got back onto his horse and rode toward the dim glow of Dugan's Find. Danielle wasn't far behind him.

■ ■ ■ ■

The morning was filled with more talk from the professor as he cooked a breakfast of bacon and biscuits over a small fire. Coffee was brewed, which pleased Dylan very much but only served to sharpen his ears to hear more of Whiteoak's rambling stories. Finally, the gunman had to excuse himself to answer nature's call and then take a walk away from the wagon for a few minutes of blessed peace and quiet. When he returned, Whiteoak was even more excited.

"Good!" the professor exclaimed. "You're back! Come over and sit down with my good friend!"

Corey was approaching the wagon, leading his horse by the reins. Despite being well rested, he still looked as though he'd been dragged behind a steam engine. His hair was cropped close to his head in uneven clumps, exposing a scarred scalp and a portion of his left ear that had either been bitten off by an animal or severed in a very messy knife fight. He greeted Dylan with less than half a smirk and tied his horse off to the same trees where Whiteoak's team was grazing.

"Corey Maynard," Whiteoak said, "this is

Dylan Garviss."

Dylan extended a hand, which was enveloped by Corey's in a solid grip. "Yeah," Corey said. "I know who you are."

"You do?" Dylan replied. "Maybe we crossed paths somewhere in Missouri? You were wearing spectacles back then."

"Yeah," Corey replied with a nod. "Broke them some time back and I got used to seeing things a little blurry around the edges."

"Mind if I have a few minutes to catch up with the professor?"

"Have at it," Dylan said. "I was thinkin' of heading back into Dugan's Find to have me a bath and one of them ladies. Not your lady, though, Doc."

Whiteoak nodded, studying Corey's face. Once Dylan walked away, Whiteoak asked, "Something wrong?"

"Do you know who that is?" Corey asked while jabbing a finger in the direction Dylan had gone.

"Yes. I believe I was the one who introduced you to him."

"He's an outlaw."

"I know. Some might say the same about me. Although," Whiteoak added while straightening the collar of his shirt, "I'm more of a gentleman rogue."

"I've known about Dylan Garviss for a

170

while," Corey said. "He's more trouble than you want to be around. He's got more law after him than you and I combined."

"How is it that you know so much about him when Dylan didn't seem to recognize you? Perhaps you're mistaken. You might even be thinking of someone else."

"And why are you so quick to take his side?"

"Because he saved my life," Whiteoak told him. "He stepped into the middle of a fight when he could as easily have stayed out of it altogether. Not only that, but he put down a group of bounty hunters who were about to take me in."

"Why the hell haven't you given up this goddamn wagon?" Corey asked. "Lord knows you've made enough money to live off of for a while. Considering how much you probably haven't even told me about, I'll bet you've got enough to retire on for the rest of your life stuck away in all your little hidey-holes across this country."

"I have a profession and I am quite proud of it."

"You rob banks. You steal from greedy souls and trick others into snatching up whatever it is you're selling."

Whiteoak straightened his posture. "Those jobs aren't easy, my friend. Some of them bordered on impossible. If that's not something to be proud of, then you've lost your perspective."

Corey hooked his thumbs under his gun belt and paced a few steps. Taking a deep breath, he said, "You've almost been killed more times than you know, Henry."

"And what makes you say that?"

"The same reason I know all about Dylan Garviss. I'm a bounty hunter."

Professor Whiteoak's hand instinctively went to his pistol.

CHAPTER TWENTY-ONE

Tara Simms stepped into the smallest room of her cathouse, knocking on the doorframe to announce herself. She could have knocked using a hammer on an empty washtub with the same result. The woman sleeping facedown on a stack of open ledgers didn't budge. Gently, Tara approached the little table and placed a hand on the woman's shoulder.

"Wake up, Danny," she said. Shaking a bit harder, she added, "Rise and shine."

Still nothing.

Tara picked up one of the ledgers lying beside the woman's head, lifted it several inches above the table, and let it drop. When the woman snapped upright, wide-eyed and petrified, Tara said, "Good morning, Danielle."

"Oh. Good morning. What time is it?"

"Too early to be working on those books. I thought you were going to get some proper sleep. That's what you told me when you came stumbling in last night."

"I thought I was going to sleep," Danielle said, "but then I remembered the ledgers. Besides, I was too wound up to sleep."

"Wound up from what?" Tara said while idly touching one of the blond curls hanging near Danielle's eye. "Keeping company with that fancy professor?"

"Henry? No! Well . . . I was, but not like that."

"Why not? He thinks the world of you."

Danielle looked away and swatted at Tara's hand. Sometimes, she didn't mind when Tara treated her like a daughter. This wasn't one of them. "Did I miss anything while I was asleep?"

Tara stepped over to a small window cut into the wall at the back of the room. Through it, she could see a muddy patch of road behind the cathouse that was used mostly to carry garbage out of the place. It was also the direction of the rising sun, which made it easier to bear the sight of the squalid piles scattered everywhere outside. "There were a few drunks that got overeager with the Hovey twins, but that's nothing unusual."

"I meant anything strange."

"After that gunfight, things were pretty quiet."

"What about those marshals?" Danielle asked. "Did they come around again?"

"Why are you so worried about that? Afraid they'll set their sights on your silver-tongued professor?"

Danielle was going to protest, if only out of reflex. But Tara knew her too well and Whiteoak had visited Danielle's room too many times in the middle of the night for any protest to stick. "Sometimes it's best to know where everyone's at," Danielle said. "Especially when they're law."

There was a knowing glint in Tara's eye, which was overshadowed quickly by a hint of disgust. "U.S. marshals have no business here. They strut in, start giving orders, and think they can take over. I like this camp a whole lot better when we take care of our own affairs."

"I know someone who shares that opinion."

"Considering all of the swindling he does, it's no wonder Professor Whiteoak doesn't take kindly to the law." Patting Danielle on the cheek, Tara said, "You're going to have to choose, you know."

"Choose?"

"Between a life with him or a life here."

"He's not exactly the marrying kind. At least," Danielle added, "I don't think he is."

"Doesn't have to be marriage. Doesn't even have to be forever. That professor will pack up and leave this territory behind him sooner or later and I know he'd rather have you along for the ride. Or, you could try to go the other route."

"What's the other route?"

Tara grinned when the verbal bait she'd cast was so easily swallowed up. "You could convince him to stay. Probably won't be easy, but if anyone could pull it off, it'd be you."

"I think I might be the only one who'd want to do a thing like that," Danielle said.

"Not exactly. He's a useful sort to have around. Smart, handsome, knows how to mix up a good tonic."

"Don't tell me you've bought some of those tonics as well!"

"Some of them do a good job," Tara said in her defense. "The rest at least pack a solid punch."

Both of them laughed for a bit. When that subsided, Tara said, "The U.S. marshal was at Tacket's store last time I saw him. He's trying to find anyone who fired a shot at that fracas last night. Shouldn't be too much longer before he realizes that's a lost cause."

"Thanks," Danielle said before walking toward the front of the tent.

Stepping outside, Danielle had to take a moment for her eyes to adjust. Not only was the sun particularly glaring that morning, but it was always something of a shock to the system to see Dugan's Find bathed in sunlight. All the drunks, spent shell casings, and puddles of blood in the ditches festered like boils on the face of a sinner being forced into church on Sunday.

Bud Tacket sold bits and pieces of furniture, most of which he'd found discarded alongside several different trails leading through the Dakotas. Wagon trains were always desperate to lighten their loads and furniture was usually first to go. Bud gathered what he could find and sold it at the store he'd built between a row of clothes vendors and a stable. Considering how he'd acquired most of his goods, Bud wasn't the sort of man to welcome a lawman. To make the conversation as loud as it was one-sided, Matt was in a mood that made him want to shout every other word.

"Where's that young fella?" Matt asked in a raging voice.

Bud Tacket could barely be heard when

he asked, "Which one?"

"The one who was first to join my posse last night!"

"Was that a posse?"

"Course it was," Matt replied. "What do you think?"

Bud shrugged his shoulders. "There was shooting and a bunch of men wanted to join in. Happens all the time."

"I announced I was forming a posse."

"Must've missed that part. I know Sam Waverly and Jeremiah Bickings were shooting at each other because Jeremiah slept with Sam's wife."

"Oh, for Christ's sake. I caught some lead, too, but not that it matters none to the likes of you." Matt wheeled around so he wasn't looking at Bud any longer, which faced him toward Danielle.

Having just walked over, Danielle put on a smile and asked, "Is there anything I can do to help?"

"Help with what?" Matt grunted.

"It's good to see the law around here for a change," she said. "I thought maybe I could be of some assistance. I know plenty of people in this camp."

"Do you? What about the young fellow who was first to join my posse?"

"Posse?"

"Oh, for Christ's sake," Matt snarled. "What do you want?"

"I want to do what I can to make sure this camp doesn't turn into a slaughterhouse," she replied. "Some of us around here have been wanting the law to step in, but there are others who don't. Now that the U.S. marshals have arrived, things are finally looking up." Casting her gaze from side to side, she asked, "Weren't there two of you?"

"Marshal Farell isn't here. He left me in charge."

"Where did he go?"

"What's that matter?"

The angry defensiveness wasn't difficult to pick up in the deputy's voice. Softening her tone in reaction to it, Danielle said, "Folks have been asking about him, that's all. It's a comfort for us to know we're protected."

As expected, the deputy swelled with some small amount of pride in seeing her look at him as if he was to be respected and possibly even desired. That look in her eyes and subtle shift of her posture came from years of practice in turning men's emotions to her favor. And, like all those men who'd been so gently rebuffed or redirected to more willing girls inside Tara's cathouse,

179

Matt didn't have the foggiest notion he was being manipulated so easily.

"The killers who started the fight last night aren't far from here," Matt said while walking toward a small group of men gathering near a cart selling bottles of whiskey and other spirits. "The marshal is scouting them out so we can round them all up when the time comes."

"And when will that be?"

Matt's demeanor shifted back to how it had been when he'd last snapped at her. "Soon, honey," he said. He reached out for her, placing a hand on Danielle's soft cheek and brushing some of her hair back so he could sample the inviting texture of her curls. "Real soon. Don't you fret none. We came to keep you all safe and that's what we intend to do."

"But, what if there's another fight?"

"When there is, the shooting will be away from this camp. The next time you see those men, they'll be draped over the back of our horses."

"I thought you would take them into a jail somewhere."

Matt shook his head slightly and then smiled. "If they'll let us, sure."

Despite her good fortune thus far, Danielle knew she couldn't steer the deputy for too much longer before he either pulled away or would expect a whole lot more from her in return. When Matt eased his hand from her face, she reached up to touch his wrist. "I'm worried about the two of you," she said. "Will there be more marshals coming?"

"Don't you worry your pretty little head about it," Matt said while taking hold of her chin and tilting her head up to look directly at him.

Danielle pulled away out of pure reflex. That was the danger with giving a man like that an inch. They would always feel entitled to the rest. Trying to pass off her actions as coming from her general nervousness, she said, "We need more lawmen here. Or more deputies."

"This is a man's problem. How about I tell you about it later, though? You work at the whorehouse, right? Why don't you set some time aside for me and —"

"I work there, but I'm not a whore," she snapped.

"Well, what else do you do? Clean up the place?" Matt scoffed. "I can pay you a lot more and you'll like what I give you a whole lot better than washing dirty sheets."

"Maybe," she said with all the sweetness she could muster. It was just enough for her to part on vaguely good terms as she turned away from him and marched straight toward Tara's place. As soon as she was inside, she ducked into one of the smaller rooms and out through a flap in a canvas wall.

"Or maybe not," she sneered while using her hand to wipe the lingering feel of the deputy's touch from her cheek.

CHAPTER TWENTY-TWO

"Bounty hunter?" Whiteoak said through gritted teeth. "Is that what you just told me?"

Corey held both hands in front of him to show they were empty when he said, "Take it easy, Henry."

"Don't you address me like a friend!"

"What do you want me to call you, then? Professor?"

Whiteoak's eyes narrowed and his brow twitched, showing the turmoil that rolled through his head. "You were a bounty hunter all along? Is that why there were always men hunting us? Hunting *me*?"

"You were right the first time. They were hunting both of us."

"Why the hell would I believe that?"

"Because we were both getting shot at too many times for it to be a damn lie," Corey said. "And if I was gonna spring a trap on you, I would've sprung it before following

183

you into so many damn fool schemes to try and get out of 'em."

Some of the tension in Whiteoak's body lessened, but not by much. "When did you start taking money for hunting men down?"

"A few months ago."

"After we parted ways. Isn't that convenient."

Corey stepped toward the small fire that Whiteoak had built, only to be stopped by the metallic click of Whiteoak's pistol being cocked. "I just want to get some of that coffee," Corey said. "Or don't you trust me enough to let me sit down?"

"Toss your guns," Whiteoak said. "All of them."

Corey did as he was asked, tossing away a pair of .44s and a holdout .22.

"And the knife," Whiteoak demanded.

Once Corey's hunting knife landed in the dirt several feet away, he asked, "Can I sit down now?"

Whiteoak seemed torn by the simple decision. After a brief inner struggle, he nodded. When Corey moved toward the fire, the professor was sure to put himself on the opposite side of the flames. When Corey lowered himself to a seated position, Whiteoak did the same without once allowing his aim to falter.

"You always were the suspicious sort," Corey mused.

"Not suspicious enough, apparently."

"That's for certain. Can I have some coffee now?"

Whiteoak nodded.

"What the hell happened to you?" Whiteoak asked. "The last time I saw you, I thought we were friends."

"We were," Corey said while filling a tin cup from the pot that had been cooking over the fire. "Still are."

"Then why do I now find myself wanting to shoot you?"

"Perhaps it's irony?" Corey offered. "For once, you're the one that doesn't have all the answers." After a few moments, Corey started to laugh. "I'm sorry, Henry. This just feels too damn good."

"What does?"

"Me watching you flounder for a change. Do you know how many times I was the one in your position, wondering what the hell was happening and where it was gonna take me? You were always the one sitting back, working things out and putting things in motion."

"I never meant to deceive you," Whiteoak explained. "I was just . . . just . . ."

"Making it up as you went along," Corey

finished. "I know."

"Then why this?" His inner wheels still spinning, Whiteoak showed half a smirk when he asked, "Are you really a bounty hunter?"

"Yeah," Corey replied. Once Whiteoak's grin had been wiped away, he added, "But not one of the bastards that was hunting you down. Or, more specifically, hunting *us.*"

"I don't recall seeing you around when these killers were tearing after me!"

"Then you must have a real short goddamn memory!" Corey growled. "Because I was there with you plenty of times when the lead was flyin' and men were out to put us under the ground on account of some shit you pulled or some deal that went bad."

Whiteoak backed down a bit. "They weren't always my deals," he said.

"No, and they didn't always go bad. That's why I wanted to help you. I guess you could say I wanted to help the both of us."

"How? By becoming a bounty hunter?"

"Yeah," Corey replied through a predatory grin. "That's it exactly. After the last time we parted ways in Montana, I had assholes comin' outta the woodwork to take a shot at me. I doubt it was much better for you."

"It wasn't," Whiteoak said tiredly. "More than a few of them got close to accomplishing their task. There was even this one gunman in Wyoming who —"

"Wanna save the stories for later or don't you care to hear the rest of mine?" Corey interrupted.

"Oh, yes. Do go on."

Corey sipped his coffee and began swirling it around in his cup. "I spent a short while finding a good spot to hide, but that never suited me."

"I know how you feel," Whiteoak sighed.

Glancing over at the garishly pained wagon parked nearby, Corey said, "Yeah. I'll just bet you do."

Turning to see what Corey was looking at, Whiteoak huffed, "You know what I mean!"

"I do. When we parted ways, we both agreed it was better if we didn't travel together. That was supposed to make it more difficult for those bounty hunters to find us."

"Honestly, many of them have lost interest."

"Have they?" Corey chuckled. "Have they really? Sometimes I think you get dizzy from talking in circles so damn much. After you robbed that bank in Kansas, a price was put on your head that won't come off anytime soon."

"And after what we both pulled in Montana, there have been other prices put on our heads," Whiteoak said.

"Exactly! You just proved my point!"

Whiteoak blinked a few times while running over the conversation points in his head. Realizing he'd come back around to argue in Corey's favor, he thought about it some more and then let out a tired breath. "You're right. It's not as easy for some of us to hide."

"Some of us have been trying harder than others." Corey filled his lungs and exhaled, knowing that he'd already made the point he was about to beat into the ground yet again. "Why do you do this, Henry?"

"Argue or drive my wagon?"

"Both, but I'll settle for an explanation of the latter."

Whiteoak looked down and then quickly brought his eyes up again. "Don't try to change the subject. You're the one that needs to explain himself. Not me!"

"Simple," Corey said before taking another sip of coffee. "I tried laying low for a spell, but the bounty hunters kept coming. It looked like I'd have to run faster and farther, so that's what I did. I kept on runnin' until I started feeling like a damn coward so I decided to do something else. First, I stood and faced them bounty hunters whenever I could. The more of them I shot, the higher the price on my head got."

"Ah. You're probably worth more than me by now."

"Nope. Then there was this one bounty hunter who kept his face covered when he came after me. This was in a dusty old town in West Texas and the grit was so thick in the air that it caked your throat if you didn't cover your mouth with something. Since almost everyone had their faces covered, this killer was able to get in close to me. Damn near put me down, too. But I managed to get one over on him and left him dead in a back alley. I was certain he had some backup waiting for him, so I took the fella's bandanna, tied it around my face, and walked straight past them."

"Well played," Whiteoak said.

"I thought so. That got me to thinking how I might be able to slip past a whole lot more bounty hunters if they thought I was one of them. So, I started going by one of my other names I used to use and took jobs as a hunter."

"Ed Brudaker. That's a name you used

when you wanted to infiltrate a gang of rustlers, right?"

"Yep. I already knew some folks in West Texas as Ed Brudaker. Besides, I'm familiar enough with that name so it seems natural to answer to it. Worked out real well. I made some money here and there and whenever I had the opportunity to steer attention away from me or you, I could do that."

"How?"

"Passing along a few false rumors. Laying down some trails that didn't lead anywhere. Little things here and there that really added up."

Whiteoak grinned and nodded. "I'm impressed. It seems you learned something from me after all."

"When it comes to fast talking and spouting bullshit, there ain't no better teacher than you."

"Well, that's . . . touching."

"There's only one problem," Corey said. "You didn't uphold your end of the bargain. We were both supposed to lay low and instead you just moved your medicine show to a new audience."

"There's laying low," Whiteoak said distastefully, "and there's giving up on your life. I kept my head down for a while but decided not to put everything I am into the dark just to avoid a few well-armed savages."

"A few?" Corey challenged.

"However many there are," the professor said with a dismissive wave, "it's not enough to make me stop being me. Besides, my research has progressed recently in some very surprising ways."

"So has mine."

CHAPTER TWENTY-THREE

Danielle rode away from camp on a slope-backed horse normally used by Tara to run errands that were no more than a mile or two away. Since she was the one who did most of the errands in Tara's place, Danielle was more familiar with the mare than the rest of the girls and tried to take it easy on the old girl whenever possible.

Arriving at Whiteoak's camp, she tied the mare's reins to a tree near a patch of green grass and then fed her a cube of sugar from her pocket. "There you go," she said while patting the mare's head. "I won't be long. Stay in the shade until I get back."

"You should put that nag outta her misery," sneered a voice from nearby.

Danielle turned toward the voice and almost started reaching for the little .22 she kept hidden in one of the pockets of her skirt. "What did you say?"

Dylan stepped forward, wincing only

slightly from his wound. While he hadn't been hidden completely before, he'd been standing so motionless that he'd all but blended in with his surroundings. It also didn't hurt that the dirt covering his clothes and skin painted him in the same earthy hues as most of the rest of Dugan's Find.

"Looks like that horse is on its last legs," he said. "You'd be doin' her a favor by —"

"Just stop talking," Danielle snapped. "She's not in any pain and she's not being put down. If anyone is causing misery around here, it's you."

Dylan's eyebrows shot up. "Me? Last thing I did was save you and the doc from getting filled full'a holes."

"And the first thing you did was crawl in here, bringing those gunmen with you."

"You think they're here just 'cause of me? Darlin', you got some wrong ideas swirlin' around behind them pretty eyes."

The look on Danielle's face was sharp and cold as a blade when she said, "Don't try to pacify me with what you think are your rough charms. If it was up to me, Henry would have left you alone to . . ."

"To what? Die? Is that what you wanna say?"

She put her back to him and stomped away. "I was going to say alone to crawl somewhere else."

Dylan followed her for several steps before he was close enough to fall into step beside her. "I've only known the doc for a short spell and I can tell you he's a whole lot of trouble wrapped up in a fancy suit."

"I've spent a lot more time with him than you have. I know what I'm dealing with."

"That's funny, because it don't seem like you do."

"You got what you wanted from him," she said brusquely. "Why don't you just go about your business?"

"You ever hear an old Indian saying about what happens when one man saves another man's life? Them two men are linked by blood."

Stopping abruptly, Danielle pivoted around to face him with her hands propped on her hips. "Are you trying to tell me you're bound to Henry by *honor*?"

It took a few seconds for Dylan to stop and reposition himself so he was directly in front of her again, but he got there. Standing up straight with arms crossed, he replied, "What's so hard to believe about that? Is it because I don't live by the letter of the law?"

"I've known plenty of outlaws, Mister Garviss. A man isn't honorable just because

194

he follows the law or not."

"Exactly."

"You're a killer," she stated.

"If you don't think your friend the professor has killed . . ."

"No. It's different. When a man defends himself, he may have to kill," she said. "When a hunter gets food for his family, he kills. When a man goes against others who might hurt him or someone else, he might have to kill. Killers, on the other hand, just . . . kill."

Dylan's eyes narrowed. "You think I like it?"

"Do you?"

Whatever Dylan was going to say to that didn't make it to his lips. Instead, he ground the bitter words between his back teeth and swallowed them where they formed a pit in his stomach.

"That's what I thought," Danielle said. "If you truly do think you owe Henry anything for what he did, or if you might think the same about me, then leave. There's enough trouble around here without you."

"And if you don't want that trouble to rip all of you apart," Dylan shot back, "you'd best keep me real close."

CHAPTER TWENTY-FOUR

Danielle walked tentatively toward the wagon parked a bit off the trail. Each step she took was carefully measured so as not to attract attention. Mostly, she didn't want to startle anyone near the wagon since nerves already seemed to be on edge. What she found once she moved past a few trees, however, was far from what she'd been expecting.

"There you are!" Whiteoak said cheerfully. "I didn't think I'd see you again so soon!"

Walking a few steps behind her, Dylan approached the clearing with an expression on his face mirroring the confusion that was so evident on Danielle's. "What's goin' on here?" he asked.

"We're two friends catching up," the professor replied. "Why?"

"Because it seemed like one of you was about to throw a punch at the other," Dylan replied. "Or worse."

Whiteoak furrowed his brow. "Corey and I go way back. What's the matter? Are you disappointed one of us hasn't split the other one's lip by now?"

"No . . . it's just . . ."

"He was hoping that the two of you would at least soften each other up," Danielle said. "That way he could swoop in to save you again."

Corey grinned. "Guess it only takes one quick look to tell which of us would need saving."

"No!" Whiteoak said. "I'm sure that's not the case. Is it, Danielle?"

In response to that, she merely cocked an eyebrow and walked over to the wagon so she could remove a small, flat bundle of wooden slats from a compartment built into the side of the frame. The wooden slats, when snapped open, formed a simple chair, which she placed on the ground so she could sit on it.

"Is it?" Whiteoak prodded.

She glanced back and forth between the professor and the man standing closest to him. "Who is this man, exactly?"

"This is Corey Maynard," Whiteoak said quickly. "He's a bounty hunter."

Both Danielle and Dylan tensed when they heard that.

"Not to worry," Whiteoak assured them. "It was all a ruse. We've been talking and, while there have been a few rough patches between us, things like that can be set aside by a couple of amicable gentlemen such as us."

"When you speak in so many trite sayings," Danielle pointed out, "it means you're hiding something."

Corey smirked at Whiteoak. "I see she's been watching you pretty good."

Dylan planted his feet in a stance that kept him squared off with Corey. Inching his hand closer to the pistol at his side, he growled, "All I wanna hear is why I shouldn't burn down this bounty hunter son of a bitch right here and now."

"Because I can vouch for him," Whiteoak said.

"That ain't enough."

"It damn well better be."

Despite the fact that he was looking directly at a man who was eager to draw on him, Corey seemed more relaxed now than ever. He angled his head back slightly as though he'd suddenly grown bored with the situation and was doing his best not to nod off. "What's the matter, Garviss? Worried I'm coming to bring you in for those bodies you left behind in San Juan?"

"What bodies?" Danielle asked.

"Yeah," Corey said through a leering smile. "Tell her about the bodies."

"No need for any of that," Whiteoak said curtly. "Corey was a bounty hunter in name only. Isn't that right?"

Corey shrugged. "Nah. I've tracked and killed more than a few idiot outlaws. You'd be amazed how easy it is when the man you're after is dumber than a sack of rocks."

"Spoken just like a piece of shit manhunter," Dylan said. "You're worse than the Injuns who kill women and children."

"Depends on who you ask. If you ask Nate Rockwell, then, yeah, I'm a whole lot worse."

The fire in Dylan's eyes grew to a blaze. "You killed Nate Rockwell?"

Corey nodded.

"Who's Nate Rockwell?" Whiteoak asked.

"Just another stupid outlaw," Corey replied. "One of the dead ones."

Dylan's hand flashed to his holster. His weapon cleared leather in less time than it took a heart to beat and when he took aim at his target, Corey had already plucked a little .22 from a hidden pocket near his belt to point right back at him.

Whiteoak jumped to stand between the two men, interrupting both of their lines of fire. "That'll be quite enough!" he bellowed. "This is all just a miscommunication. Corey, this man stepped in to take my part when lead was flying. And Dylan," he said while shifting his pointing finger toward Corey, "this man has been my friend through many a hard time."

"You're a damn fool if'n you put your trust in a bounty hunter," Dylan said.

The professor kept his eyes on Dylan as he said, "I was taken aback by my old friend's switch of allegiances at first. But if you'll let me explain, I can surely put your troubles to ease."

Both Dylan and Danielle stood with their arms crossed, eyeing the professor for a few long moments.

"Well," Danielle snapped. "Go on!"

"Oh," Whiteoak said smugly. "I was just surprised that nobody interrupted me."

Shaking his head, Corey said, "I started taking work as a bounty hunter to get in good with them."

"With who?" Dylan asked. "The law?"

"The law, other bounty hunters, anyone else who might help their kind. Whoever I needed to get in good with to convince them I was to be trusted. Then, once I was on their good side, I was privy to all kinds of things."

Dylan spat out a humorless grunt of a laugh. "The law and bounty hunters ain't some sort of group that all get together and swap stories. It ain't like one can just introduce you to the others and suddenly you're in some kind of inner circle. This asshole is tryin' to pull one over on us!"

"Why would he do that?" Whiteoak asked. "If it was his intention to truly turn on me, Corey could have brought me in several times by now. Besides, I've known him a hell of a lot longer than I've known you."

"Yeah, but you're closer to bein' like me," Dylan said before jabbing a finger at Corey, "than you are to bein' like him."

Danielle stepped forward, reaching out to place a hand on Dylan's arm and lowering it so it was no longer pointing at anyone. "Privy to what sort of things?" she asked.

Corey smirked and nodded at her while tucking the .22 back into the pocket from which it had come. "Finally, someone with the sense to ask the right question. And as far as some of those other things you were saying, you're wrong. There may not be any kind of big, friendly group who meets and swaps secrets among each other, but lawmen and bounty hunters do tend to socialize with their own. Ain't much different than outlaws getting together in the dark corners of shithole saloons so they can swap stories and let each other know where the ripest pickings might be."

"And how the hell would you know anything about that?" Dylan sneered.

Corey had had enough. Rather than keep his distance, he took a few bold steps toward Dylan and glared at him without showing the first bit of fear for the gun that was already in Dylan's hand. "I know because I've killed more than my share of men. I've stolen more money than you've ever known and spilled enough blood to fill your sorry, stinking carcass ten times over."

Frustrated by the effort it took to keep the two men from butting heads, Danielle looked to Whiteoak and asked, "Aren't you going to do something?"

Whiteoak shrugged his shoulders. "Sometimes it's best to just let these things work themselves out."

"All right, then," she said. "That's what we'll do. If you two aren't smart enough or grown enough to talk like men instead of squabbling like a couple of little boys, then let's get it over with."

All three of the men looked at her.

"What do you mean?" Whiteoak inquired.

"All three of you have it out," she replied. Looking to Dylan, she asked, "Can you fight with your wound?"

"Hell, yes, I can," he replied.

"Good," she said. "But I want no guns and no knives. Just beat the bloody hell out of each other until you think you've had enough. Maybe then we can make some progress because all three of you know there's a benefit to working together for at least a little while. Otherwise, none of you would still be here. Am I right?"

Grudgingly, the men nodded their agreement.

"Good. So, all three of you punch each other, kick, bite, scratch, or whatever else it is you feel must be done to get rid of this male bullshit that you all refuse to drop for the sake of our survival."

"Them are some big words for such a little lady," Dylan said.

Danielle rolled her eyes and threw up her hands. "I believe you three know better than to fight each other right now. It's obvious you all have something to say, so let's just say it. Afterwards, we can go our separate ways or we can decide to take further steps."

"Together?" Dylan grunted.

"Yes, together," Danielle told him. "Henry has been dodging bounty hunters for some time now. From what I've heard about Corey Maynard, it must have taken something awfully big to make him join up with the likes of them. And there's obviously something keeping him here," she added while tossing a backhanded wave in Dylan's direction.

The others all looked at each other for a few seconds before one of them broke the silence between them.

"All right," Corey said as he unbuckled his gun belt. "Let's do this."

Dylan displayed a wicked grin and started disarming himself as well. "Oh, yeah. Let's."

"Let's not be hasty!" Whiteoak said before he was unceremoniously punched in the mouth.

Chapter Twenty-Five

It was some time later when Whiteoak staggered into the large tent containing a collection of card tables scattered in front of a battered bar that served drinks as well as food. The man behind that bar wore an apron that was only slightly greasier than the shirt that clung to his flabby body. In one hand, he held a spatula, which he used to push several sausages on a frying pan being warmed on top of a stove. His other hand gripped a bottle of whiskey, which he drank from when he wasn't splashing liquor over the sizzling sausages.

"I'll have some of that, Sidney," Whiteoak said as he approached the bar.

The portly fellow cooking the sausages looked over at him and asked, "Which one, Professor? The sausage or the liquor?"

"Little of both. Trading fisticuffs tends to work up an appetite."

Sidney nodded in appreciation of the

bloody welts and cuts covering Whiteoak's face. "Looks like it was quite a brawl."

"Indeed it was."

"Was what?" Corey asked as he stomped in through the open flap that was the place's front door.

"The professor was telling me about the fight he was in and from the looks of it," Sidney said, "I bet it was quite a damn sight."

"It sure was!" Corey said while picking a spot to stand next to Whiteoak. "Seeing a man get beaten like that will stick with me for a while."

"We were talking about how fighting can work up an appetite." Using the spatula to pick a sausage up from the pan, Sidney added, "Sounds like you know all about it."

Corey's face wasn't unscathed. He'd been given a good amount of cuts and bruises as well but not nearly enough to rival Whiteoak's collection. He leaned against the bar, staring at Whiteoak for several moments before asking, "What have you been telling this man?"

Whiteoak grunted something that couldn't be heard.

"Yeah," Corey said to the man behind the bar. "He's got an appetite, especially after taking one punch to the stomach and puking up everything he ate for the last week!"

"Is that true?" Sidney asked with a wide, anxious smile.

Looking down, Whiteoak brushed away a fleck of dirt from the front of a shirt that was still cool from resting in one of his trunks up until a few minutes ago and replied, "It took more than one punch, I'll have you know. Also, I did a fair amount of damage, myself."

"Sure you did, Professor," Sidney said while waving to a young boy perched upon a stool near the front of the place. Upon seeing the wave, the boy nodded once, hopped down from his stool, and ran outside.

"What was that?" Whiteoak snapped. "What did you do?"

"Take it easy," Sidney said.

Whiteoak slapped his hand down on top of the bar, making a clattering sound that was distinctly not created by flesh against wood. Sure enough, the short barrel of his .38 peeked out from beneath his hand. "I passed easy a long while back," the professor said.

"I was to let Miss Danielle know if you decided to stop by here after you and your friends got things settled. I take it that's what the fistfight was about," Sidney ex-

207

plained. "That's what Mikey's doing right now. He's running off to fetch her and tell her where you are. I thought you didn't mind her being concerned for you, but if I stepped out of line . . ."

"You didn't step out of line," Corey said. "We're all a bit rattled."

Sidney's face, while normally friendly and soft, acquired a few hard edges when he looked at Corey. "I don't know you, mister. Professor, should I be concerned about this here fella?"

Almost grudgingly, Whiteoak said, "No. He and I go back a ways."

"Ah!" Sidney said as he regained his cheerful demeanor. "Explains the fighting, I suppose. If I had a nickel for every time me and my friends have rolled our sleeves up to settle a dispute, I'd be able to set myself up in something a lot fancier than this here tent."

Whiteoak drummed his fingers on top of the bar. With every pass of his tips against the splintered wood, he tapped the surface harder.

Corey motioned for Sid to bring him a drink and the barkeep was all too happy to oblige. After the glass was put in front of him, Corey said, "I thought we'd made peace with what I done."

"The bounty hunting, perhaps," Whiteoak grumbled. "But you didn't have to strike me."

"If memory serves me correct, you kicked me first."

"It wasn't a kick! Children kick. Women kick. I . . . may have hit you first."

"There you go," Corey said while somehow managing to withhold a smirk. He took a drink from his glass, allowed the firewater to trickle down his throat, and then said, "You really should watch who you decide to side with. Whether he saved your bacon once or not, that Dylan Garviss is a tough customer."

"I can handle him."

"Since when have you taken to partnering with killers again?"

"And why are you so concerned about me?" Whiteoak snapped. "You up and left the minute you had a chance."

"We parted ways after things got rough back in Montana," Corey reminded him. "Wasn't that the plan?"

"We were also supposed to meet up again after a while. Or did you forget that part?"

Corey took a deep breath and tipped his glass back again. After that sip of liquor had gone down, he sighed, "Yeah. That was the plan."

"Instead, you decided to tack a star onto your chest and play lawman," Whiteoak sneered.

"I don't wear a badge and I don't call myself no lawman."

"Whatever."

"You need to focus on the real reason I'm here," Corey said.

"And I will," Whiteoak told him. "But first . . . another drink."

CHAPTER TWENTY-SIX

When Danielle arrived at Sid's place, Dylan wasn't far behind her. The outlaw strode past the bar and to the large round table where the other three had already taken their spots. Unlike the others, he seemed to have barely gotten a scratch from the fight.

"Who invited him?" Corey asked.

"You want me to leave?" Dylan replied.

Corey nodded once. "Yeah."

"Well, tough. I'm part'a this, too, whether you like it or not." With that, the outlaw plopped down onto one of the chairs and stayed there.

Clearly aggravated, Danielle asked, "Are you three ready to speak like civilized people now?"

"We are," Corey told her. "That was a great idea you had about getting all that fighting out of our systems. Really cleared the air."

Danielle pressed her fingertips against her

closed eyes while letting out a long sigh. "I didn't expect you all to fight," she said.

"But . . . that's what you said we should do."

"I thought I'd say that so you could all hear how stupid it sounded and would then come to your senses."

All of the others looked at each other quizzically. Since they seemed to be getting along well enough for the moment, Danielle let it rest.

"Now that we're all thinking calmly," Whiteoak said, "no matter how it came about, why don't we get back to discussing business?"

"Thank God," Danielle said.

"There is one man responsible for sending all of these bounty hunters for your scalp," Corey said to Whiteoak.

"Do I know this person?" the professor asked.

"His name's Wilson Auberjohn."

Everyone else at the table watched as Whiteoak pondered that name. Never one to pass up a moment to hold an audience, the professor made the most of it by tapping his chin, furrowing his brow, and doing everything else he could to show how hard he was concentrating on his task. Eventually, after meeting everyone's gaze one by one, he announced, "Doesn't ring a bell."

"Auberjohn made a boatload of cash importing liquor and fabrics from China and such," Corey said. "Then he made triple that amount when he started smuggling illegal stuff back and forth all over the world."

"What does he smuggle?" Danielle asked.

"Name it," Corey told her. "Gold, opium, slaves, doesn't matter."

"It does matter if you want me to help find him."

Now the attention at the table focused on her. Dylan asked, "What the hell can you do to find anyone?"

"I know people," she said. "More importantly, I know Tara Simms and she makes it her business to find out what kind of dirt is under her customers' fingernails."

"Tara runs the cathouse," Whiteoak explained. "She is quite a fount of information. People do like to talk when they're in the company of a pretty woman. And if those women are charged with wheedling whatever information they can out of their clients, that makes for some very interesting stories."

"Tara is what brought Henry to Dugan's Find," Danielle added.

"It's true," Whiteoak admitted. "I needed to know the lay of the land around here and nobody knows it better than Tara."

"But she doesn't tell everything she knows to just anyone," Danielle said.

"Why would she trust you so damn much?" Dylan scoffed.

"She trusts me with her money."

For the men sitting at that table, that spoke volumes. One of them, however, was less impressed than the others.

"What's he to you?" Corey asked skeptically while looking at Dylan.

"What does that matter?" Whiteoak asked with an uneasy laugh. "If someone wishes to help, they should be allowed to do so."

Now Corey shifted his uneasy glare to the professor. "And when did you become so trusting?"

"I don't want to see Henry killed," Danielle said before the professor could speak up. "And I don't want to see people I know get hurt. From what I've heard and seen, it looks like those are the very things that could happen if things get any worse."

Whiteoak straightened his string tie. "That is, if they get worse."

"Do you see them getting any better?"

Whiteoak nervously cleared his throat, allowed his eyes to wander, and then conveniently became distracted by some bit of nothing on the other side of the room.

"So, who the hell is Wilson Jabberjaw?" Dylan asked.

"Wilson Auberjohn," Corey said, "is an importer turned smuggler who kept a good portion of his cash at a certain bank in Kansas. A bank that just so happened to be robbed some time ago by one of the men sitting at this table."

Glancing nervously at Dylan and Danielle, Whiteoak muttered, "I'm not sure what you're referring to."

While all of the others seemed on the verge of laughter, Dylan was the first to break out. "You're so full'a shit," he guffawed. "I've barely known you for a full day and I already know you had something to do with a bank robbery."

"What? How?" Whiteoak sputtered.

"You brag about it," Danielle said.

"I most certainly do not!"

"You do. You brag to me and to any of the other girls around here if you think it'll lift you up a few notches in their eyes."

"Or for free drinks," Corey said. "Don't forget about all those times you spout off in saloons to draw a crowd so one of them'll buy your next drink."

"That's different!" Whiteoak said. "People

215

expect to be regaled with stories while gathered around the watering hole. It's custom!"

"You call it custom," Danielle said. "I call it bragging."

"Whatever anyone calls it," Corey said, "word has been spreading like wildfire ever since you robbed that bank in Kansas."

"You mean you were part of that robbery?" Danielle asked.

Turning to Whiteoak, Corey said, "You see? When you keep your head down and mouth shut, not everyone knows your business."

Whiteoak dismissed that with an aggravated wave. "Those rich men are just going through the motions of coming after me. It's all so they won't look weak in front of their associates. The real story is that they lost some dirty money, which I'm sure they've already earned back a couple times over by now."

"But it's not only about the money," Corey said.

"It's always about the money," Whiteoak replied. "From what you were telling me yesterday, this man has been sending killers after me so all I need to do is avoid them until that same man runs out of steam."

"But it's not just about you," Danielle said.

Whiteoak's eyebrows shot up. "It's not?"

Reaching out to pat his hand, she told the professor, "I know it's difficult for you to grasp, but yes . . . sometimes things that happen in the world affect other people as well." Her tone lost its condescending flair when she added, "Wherever you go, the killers come sniffing around. Before you arrived at this camp, there were men . . . men with guns . . . who asked about a professor driving a painted wagon. They were rough when they asked their questions. We even thought they might shoot someone just to make them talk even though we didn't know anything. I didn't even know you'd be coming and when you did, the men didn't show up for a while. Then, they started coming back."

"Why didn't you tell me?" Whiteoak asked.

"Because it would only make you run again and when you start to act too quickly or are backed against a wall, you tend to make stupid decisions that usually wind up with you almost getting yourself killed."

"Sounds like you two know each other pretty well," Corey said.

For the first time since Corey had known

Henry Whiteoak, the professor actually seemed uncomfortable in his own skin. Whiteoak recovered nicely, however, scratching his head and saying, "It's a long story."

"You want a shorter story?" Danielle asked. "Here's one. Those killers are going to keep coming until they find you. When that happens, there will be more gunfire and more blood spilled. In case you hadn't noticed, folks around here don't need much of a reason to join in on any sort of shooting once it starts. Just about everyone has someone they'd like to kill whether it's for mining rights, some old grudge, or some stupid nonsense one man said to another when he was drunk."

"Or I could lead them away from here," Whiteoak offered. "At least until I come up with something else."

"Like what, Henry?" she asked in a tired voice. "Another swindle? Another fight? When will it stop with you?"

"It won't stop until someone gets lucky and puts a bullet into the professor here," Dylan said. "Seein' as how he kept me from dyin', it seems only fair that I return the favor."

Corey spat out half of a laugh. "Lord Almighty, you might be full of more bullshit than the medicine man over here."

"Just because he has somewhat of a shadowed past," Whiteoak said, "doesn't mean he's always lying."

"The only reason he wants to go after those bounty hunters is because they're after him, too."

Dylan nodded ever so slightly. "I guess there's that, too."

"This is simple," Whiteoak said. "Ever since these bounty hunters have become a problem for me, I've kept moving until I found a place where they haven't caught sight of me yet. Once they do, I move along to the next place. I'll be certain they're following me and those men shouldn't pose much of a threat to this camp any longer."

"It ain't that easy," Corey said. "Things are about to get a whole lot worse for you and this camp. Maybe even for this part of the Badlands."

"How so?"

"You haven't been leading these bounty hunters on one big chase. Well," Corey added, "perhaps you were at the beginning but that's over. Now you're the one that's being led and you took these men right where they wanted to go."

Whiteoak scowled. "What are you talking about? I've barely known where I would end up before . . ."

"Before coming here," Corey said.

"Why?" Dylan asked. "What's here?"

Before the silence at the table could get too uncomfortable, Danielle said, "I am."

"Then I'll take her with me!" Whiteoak offered. "It'll be fun!"

"Auberjohn's got eyes and ears all over the place," Corey explained. "I should know because I was one of 'em for a spell. It didn't take long for me to poke around and sniff out the main group of killers that was being sent out after you."

"If I recall correctly," Whiteoak said, "they were being sent out after both of us."

"There were some comin' after me, but I killed them off," Corey replied as though he was referring to a distasteful meal he'd had several weeks ago. "I killed a bunch of men that were after you, too, but they kept being replaced. After I took some steps to make it look like I disappeared, I put on my Ed Brudaker name and made like I was with one of the men who were sent after me. I collected the bounty and was put onto the bigger hunt."

"You collected a bounty on yourself?" Dylan asked.

Corey nodded.

"Nice," Dylan said through a wry grin.

"You mentioned there was more than money involved with my bounty," Whiteoak reminded his partner. "This Auberjohn fellow is angry with me about something other than losing some of his money at that bank in Kansas?"

"Damn right he is," Corey replied. "You killed his son."

Any trace of smug self-confidence on the professor's face was washed away in an instant. His face paled slightly when he asked, "Who was his son?"

"Davey Auberjohn."

"Doesn't sound familiar."

"I don't guess it would," Corey said. "Davey was only eleven years old. Big for his age, but still pretty young."

Whiteoak shook his head slowly at first, but the motion became almost frantic when he said, "That's not possible. I would never kill a child! That's absurd!"

"That's not what his father thinks."

Whiteoak jumped to his feet with such force that he knocked his chair over behind him. "I won't listen to this rubbish. I've been accused of being a lot of things, but this is . . . this is just . . ." He didn't even have the coherence to finish his sentence before storming away from the table and out of the tent.

CHAPTER TWENTY-SEVEN

Whiteoak walked slowly down the crooked lane that passed for the main street of Dugan's Find. Every so often, he would receive a tip of the hat or casual greeting from someone he passed. While those things were acknowledged by the professor, he didn't offer anything else in return. Soon, he found he wasn't walking alone.

"I should never have taken that bank," Whiteoak said without having to look over to see who walked beside him.

Corey kept pace with him and stuck his hands in his pockets. "You're just now realizing that wasn't the right thing to do? It's been against the law for a good while, you know."

"I've robbed places before," Whiteoak continued with a slow shake of his head. "Even robbed banks before, but there was something different about that one."

"Course there was. That's why you had

to rob it."

"There was so much shooting. So much confusion while I was in that damn town. Sometimes it comes back to me like a few of the tough spots I was in while I served in the Army."

"We seen worse."

"I never killed a child those other times. I knew what I was doing. I wasn't some stupid animal behind a gun."

Corey chuckled. "You ain't never been an animal, stupid or otherwise. And you didn't shoot no child."

"What about Davey Auberjohn?"

"That was an accident."

"How would you know?" Whiteoak stopped and pushed Corey's shoulder so he could square off with him. "Did you know what happened in Kansas?"

"Hell, no, I didn't. Davey Auberjohn wasn't killed by no gun. He got ahold of too much of that serum you used to rob that bank."

"What?"

Corey took a deep breath and reached out to place his hands on Whiteoak's shoulders. "That tonic you used on them folks in Kansas, too much of it got into that boy's mouth and it took him down. I know it's not what you intended . . ."

"It's not possible."

"I know it's a mistake. You would never intend to —"

"No!" Whiteoak snapped as he pulled loose from Corey's grasp. "It's not possible, I tell you! That tonic wasn't lethal! I tested it myself. Tested it *on myself* before ever giving it to anyone else. I know what I'm doing!"

"I know you do, Henry. All I'm saying is —"

"You're saying that I mixed up a tonic the wrong way and killed someone! This is my livelihood, Corey! My profession. My life. You think I would be that irresponsible?"

"Mistakes happen sometimes. Bullets go through walls and hit innocent folks. Crops can get burnt that cause families to starve or farmers to go broke. Every damn thing that happens has its consequences."

"You don't think I know that?" Whiteoak hissed.

"I think you need to be reminded of it."

Now that he'd caught his breath again, Whiteoak looked around to see that a few locals were starting to take interest in his conversation. They may not have known exactly what was being said, but the fire in Whiteoak's voice was easy enough to detect.

Corey nudged him and started walking.

Once Whiteoak fell into step with him, Corey said, "I made it look like some of them bounty hunters killed me. That ruse saved my life and I've got you to thank for it. Remember us doing something along them lines down in Louisiana?"

"Yes," Whiteoak said in a tired voice.

"I learned it from you and that saved my life. You've saved my life plenty of times."

"Just as you've saved mine," Whiteoak said. "That doesn't make it acceptable for me to end the life of an innocent child."

"You remember why you had us make like we was dead while we were in Louisiana that time?"

"Doesn't matter now."

"It does," Corey insisted. "You did it so we didn't have to blast our way outta that predicament. I was all for throwing lead and storming out of that swamp the messy way, but you wouldn't have none of it. You said too much blood would be spilt."

"Mostly I was referring to ours," Whiteoak admitted.

"Bullshit. There were others in that swamp besides us and them men that wanted us dead. I wanted to start a fight and escape in all the confusion, but you said there would be too many bullets flyin' and odds were too good that everyone would wind up dead. Now, between you and me, we knew our odds were better than average to make it out of that fight. Once you saw them young ladies being held by them killers, you had to find another way outta there."

"I went to one of them to try and get them to escape as well," Whiteoak said in a faraway voice. "They were too frightened."

"They was whores," Corey said. "Maybe one or two of 'em had hearts in the right place, but the rest were either unwilling to give up all that stolen cash them killers was payin' them or got their thrills from sharing their bed with wanted men. Either way, they weren't worth us risking our lives to save theirs. That's how I saw it. But not you. Because of you, we went through that elaborate ruse of pretending to be dead, sneakin' around and all that other shit that wound up bein' a whole lot more dangerous than shootin' our way outta that hellhole."

"If you're trying to distract me from events at hand, you've failed."

"I'm not tryin' to distract you, ya goddamn peacock!" Corey said. "I'm tellin' you what kind of man you are since you sometimes forget."

"You think I forget what sort of man I am?"

"Then maybe it just gets lost under all that silk and lace."

Whiteoak couldn't help but look down at the front of his shirt and then his sleeves. "I don't wear lace," he grumbled.

"You're not the sort of man who would harm an innocent," Corey told him, "even if it meant you had a better chance of surviving yourself. What happened in Kansas was an accident, and those come up whether you like it or not."

"This one was of my doing," Whiteoak said.

"But it wasn't your intent and it's not something you should be killed for."

"I can't ignore it."

"I wouldn't expect you to," Corey replied. "We'll see to it that justice gets done for what happened to that boy, but it won't be at the hands of a bunch of bloodthirsty murderers like the ones that Auberjohn put on your trail."

"I should just turn myself in. Where's that U.S. marshal?"

"You're not turning yourself in. Not here, anyhow."

"Why not?"

"Because there's more going on here than one man trying to get vengeance for his boy. If Auberjohn wanted that, he's got a dozen lawmen he could have spoken to that would've been glad to hunt you down legal. Lord knows you've made it plenty easy for them riding in that garish circus tent on wheels."

"What else could be going on?" Whiteoak asked.

"I'm not certain yet. I got wind of it a short while ago but couldn't get any closer unless I wanted to tip my hand when it came to my name not bein' Ed Brudaker. Whatever it is, though, it's got Auberjohn worked up enough to gather a few of the most expensive killers and trackers money can buy. Seeing as how you ain't so hard to find, that strikes me as peculiar."

"Yes, it does."

"And when I tried looking into it further, I got chased off quicker than a randy cowboy from a virgin's bed."

"So you decided to recruit my help," Whiteoak stated.

"I'd hoped to pay you a visit once this whole mess with the bounty hunters was cleared up. I figured it was the least I could do after all we've been through."

"How noble," Whiteoak chuckled. "Especially since your head is on the chopping block right beside mine. How long do you truly believe this ruse of your supposed death will remain intact?"

"Yeah, well, there's that, too."

"Even so, I appreciate it. You could have cut and run, like you've threatened to do so many times."

"Now what kind of partner would I be if I did something like that?" Corey said.

"A smart one. A living one."

"You'd better stop before you actually talk me out of saving your worthless hide again."

CHAPTER TWENTY-EIGHT

It had been more than half an hour since Whiteoak left the saloon with Corey chasing soon after him. Out of respect for the professor's fragile state when he'd left, Danielle had allowed him to go without trying to find him right away. As time ticked by, however, the waiting became increasingly difficult.

"How long are we supposed to sit here?" Dylan asked.

"Until he comes back," she told him.

There were a few quiet moments that came to an end when a group of three miners came into the place ordering drinks for everyone there. Before opening a bottle, Sidney asked for payment and was handed a small pebble of gold. After a quick inspection, Sidney handed it back.

"That's not real," the barkeep announced.

"The hell it ain't!" one of the miners

replied. "I pulled it out of the ground my-self!"

"That doesn't make it real. Why don't you take it over to Winslow? He'll tell you for certain one way or another."

One of the other miners slapped the first one on the back. "You should get one of them machines from Professor Whiteoak! It'll tell you how pure your gold is and you won't have to waste time with no broker or pay a broker's fee!"

"You got one of them machines?" the first miner asked.

"No."

"Aw, fer Christ's sake!" And with that, the miner took his disputed gold along with his friends out through the front door.

"One thing that professor knows," Dylan said, "is how to advertise. I hear more folks talk about him and his tonics or machines around here than anything else."

"Henry is quite the expert when it comes to spouting off about himself," she sighed.

"So . . . it seems like you two are pretty close."

"Is that what you think? After knowing the two of us for about a day, that's what you've come up with?"

"Yeah," Dylan said. "And since you're act-ing like I struck a raw nerve, I'd say I'm right. How long have the two of you been together?"

"We've never been together," she said grudgingly. "Not really."

"He move around too much?"

"No. Actually, he's always been a bit too willing to stop moving for me."

"Aww, that's sweet."

Despite the teasing tone in his voice, Danielle could pick up on some genuine sentiment beneath it. "It's just one of those things that doesn't seem to happen. When he wants to settle down, it's for the wrong reasons. When I want to settle down, it's not the right time. The only time it really seems to work is when we just meet up and enjoy each other's . . ."

The outlaw started chuckling lewdly to himself while waggling his eyebrows.

"Enjoying each other's *company*," she said.

"Sure. That's what you're enjoying."

Shaking her head, Danielle said, "Forget it. I don't even know why I'm telling you any of this."

"Because there's time to kill. You two seem to work well together. At least, you did from what I've seen."

"I suppose we do."

"Have you ever worked with him in his

other job?" Dylan asked. "You know, selling those tonics and whatnot."

Danielle couldn't help but smirk. "Yes. I've helped him with that. Henry wanted a woman to speak on behalf of some beauty cream he'd whipped up out of perfumed cake frosting so he could sell it to a bunch of rich old women."

Dylan laughed loudly and slapped the table. "Did it work?"

She laughed as well as she said, "Actually, yes. It did."

"Perfume and cake frost?"

"That's right. Those old ladies not only smeared it on their faces, but they bought every bit of it that Henry had and swore it made them look younger. He had a few other things for me to do, telling me what a help it was to have a woman working on his behalf."

"So, you were a swindler for a while?" Dylan asked.

"All I did was bring the right men to Henry's shows or demonstrate whatever it was he was selling at the time. We both made a pretty penny."

"You set 'em up and he knocked 'em down. Sounds like a good relationship. I've had a few of them myself. Of course, when things are rollin' pretty good, things tend to get even sweeter."

"They did," she said fondly. "For a while. Then I woke up and decided I no longer wanted to lie for a living and he didn't appreciate me so much when I stopped worshipping the ground he walked on."

Dylan scowled at her. "Is that how it went?"

Shrugging, Danielle said, "Not really as harsh as that made it sound, but close. We didn't see each other for a while until he came riding back into the town where I was living to ask me to do some more work for him. I did and it started all over again."

"Round and round she goes," Dylan mused. "Been there myself. You think this is one of them times when the professor leaves town and doesn't come back until you're sweet on him again?"

"Why would you think that?"

"Because he's been gone a while."

"He was just taken by surprise by that terrible news," she said with almost absolute certainty.

"Do you think he might have killed that kid?"

"Henry may not be a saint, but he's no murderer," she replied. "If he had any hand in something like that, it was a horrible mistake."

"You're damn right it's horrible," Dylan said. "Horrible enough to call down a whole lot of hell onto whoever's responsible. Could make life real miserable for anyone caught in that storm."

"Absolutely."

"If a man cared about a pretty woman, he might wanna get far away before that storm swept her up as well. Especially if there'd already been shots fired on account of it."

"Fine," she said while pushing away from the table and standing up. "I wanted to give him some room to clear his head, but if you insist on checking on him before he decided to come back, that's what we'll do."

Dylan had to move quickly, but he caught up to her soon after she was outside of the tent. "Didn't he make a habit of pulling up stakes and leaving?" he asked in between huffing breaths.

"Yes, but only when there was a good reason."

"This might be one of those times, you know. I mean, if he cares about you at all and there's bounty hunters sniffing him out . . ."

"He wouldn't leave at a time like this when I'd worry about him every second," she said in a rush. "Not after all the good times we've been . . . I mean . . . the times

235

we used to have."

They arrived at the spot where Henry's wagon had been left, only to find the horses missing and every opening on the wooden structure securely locked. After circling around the wagon to inspect it, Danielle let out a measured breath, balled up a fist, and slammed it against the board where his name was painted in large, mystical letters.

CHAPTER TWENTY-NINE

"You're just leaving your wagon?" Corey asked.

Whiteoak rode beside him on one of the horses that had been tied to his wagon. Both animals were breathing heavily after being run for a good, long stretch of trail. Without looking back, Whiteoak said, "Yes. It's all locked up and Danielle will know what to do with it should I be gone for too long."

"If she's the kind of woman to get angry at something like this, you might not have a wagon when you get back."

"She wouldn't do anything drastic."

"You're sure about that? I've known some women to hold some pretty nasty grudges."

"She'll be upset, but not overly so. Even if she was, she wouldn't do any harm to me. At the worst, she'd simply leave my wagon where it was. If that's the case, my locks will hold until I get back."

For a few seconds, the only sounds that

could be heard were the horses' heavy breaths and the crunch of their hooves against the ground. Eventually, Corey said, "She could always burn that wagon to the ground."

"Now, why would you say something like that?"

"I'm just sayin' . . . a woman gets mad enough, some wicked things go through her mind."

"Maybe the sort of women you keep company with, but not my Danielle," Whiteoak insisted.

"Your Danielle? Last time we were working together in Montana, you never even mentioned her."

"We hadn't seen each other for a while."

"And then you decide to come back to pay her a visit," Corey said. "Out of the blue, probably bringing a bunch of flowers or some such nonsense."

"She was happy to see me," Whiteoak said.

"Oh, all right. So long as she doesn't mind being set aside, left behind, and otherwise forgotten for months at a stretch. Come to think of it, plenty of women don't mind that sort of thing at all."

"There have been some difficulties, mainly because of me, but she's left me behind more than once so she could pursue other things."

"Sounds like a delightful arrangement," Corey said in words that dripped sarcasm the way honey dripped from a hungry bear's paw.

"It is," Whiteoak forcefully replied.

"And why didn't you at least tell her where you were going?"

"Because she'd either try to stop me or want to come along."

"Sounds like an awful lot of loyalty from someone who doesn't mind if you don't see each other again."

"What, may I ask, is the purpose of this line of questioning?" Whiteoak asked.

"Just making conversation. We still got a long ride between us and the stagecoach depot at the Nebraska line."

"There's more," Whiteoak said. "I know you well enough to be certain of that. Out with it."

"Well . . . considering everything that's been happening . . . perhaps it's time for you to pack in the circus wagon and settle down before you get killed."

"I'm not the kind to settle down. Even if I was, I doubt any woman worth the effort would have me for long. Danielle has barely tolerated me for a few weeks at a time."

"Doesn't mean it ain't worth a shot." Seeing he wasn't going to get a lot more out of the professor for the moment, Corey shifted his attention back to the trail in front of him and flicked his reins. "Just sayin', is all."

The rest of the day was spent riding south toward a large station where stagecoaches brought hopeful miners into the Badlands and took more despondent ones home after losing everything but the cost of a ticket on fruitless claims and fragile dreams. The ticket office was a small shack that smelled of the stew that had been burnt inside by a clerk who was no longer there.

"Empty," Corey said as he peered in through a small square window and tapped a fingertip upon the glass.

"They'll be back in the morning," Whiteoak said.

"Could be before then."

"No. The morning. Seven o'clock, to be exact."

"How do you know?" Corey asked as he pressed his face against the glass.

"There's a sign on the door. They'll be here in the morning."

"And they won't be any earlier than what it says there," said a short woman who was almost as wide as she was tall. Her face was smooth and friendly, framed by silky strands of black hair. "Might as well get a room for the night," she said while motioning to the only other building in sight apart from the stagecoach station. It was a wide house with a livery beside it. "Rooms are cheap and the beds are soft."

"You run the place?" Corey asked.

"Sure do. Name's Becky."

Whiteoak approached her. "How much to put up our horses while we're gone?"

"You catching the stage to Kansas or Chicago?" she asked.

Corey was wise enough to let Whiteoak barter for prices and was pleased with the end result. They even wound up with their own room, which seemed like a bargain until he got a look at the room itself. Barely larger than a closet, the space they'd rented was just big enough to hold a bed and a chair. Whiteoak shut himself in without another word, leaving Corey to fend for himself until morning.

CHAPTER THIRTY

Corey's eyes snapped open and his hand reflexively jerked toward his gun belt, which was draped over the back of the chair beside his bed. The pistol was cocked and ready to fire before the rest of his brain knew he was awake. Sitting perfectly still, Corey waited a few seconds to let his eyes become accustomed to the dark. While temporarily blind, however, his ears were doing a good job of taking up the slack.

A slight breeze rustled against his window.

Someone outside was having a heated conversation.

Boots were scraping against the floor on the other side of his door.

All of those things hit his senses at once, but it was the latter that brought him all the way out of his sleepy haze.

Corey waited for a few more seconds but no more footsteps could be heard. An unsettling cold found its way into his stomach as though he was about to take one last step off the edge of a cliff. He swung his legs over the side of the narrow bed, doing his best to remain light upon the balls of his feet as he made his way to the door. As he approached it and reached for the handle, he could almost feel the heat of a body waiting for him on the other side.

He pulled the door open, shifting to a sideways stance while pointing his gun forward and flattening himself against the adjacent wall.

Rob McGurn stood outside wearing a patient smile. His hand rested easily on the grip of his holstered pistol. Despite being on the wrong end of Corey's gun barrel, he stepped into the room as though he had an invitation.

"You were supposed to meet up with me yesterday, Ed," McGurn said.

"Things have gotten kinda hairy," Corey replied.

"That why you're traveling with that medicine man now?"

"Whiteoak has his uses, but he ain't deaf. Keep your voice down. He's in the next room."

"That's why I didn't bust in," McGurn replied.

"You didn't knock, either. If I didn't know

243

any better, I'd think you intended on sneaking up on me."

"If I or anyone else could sneak up on you that easily, you'd deserve whatever you got." McGurn made his way to the room's small square window and looked outside. "I'm here now, so why don't you tell me what's on your mind? Last time we met, you were gonna see about tracking down Dylan Garviss or possibly get some news on Henry Whiteoak."

"Do I even have to mention Whiteoak?" Corey asked in a whisper that could barely be heard.

"Not now. Hearing something from you earlier would've gone a long ways to setting my mind at ease."

"What the hell are you worried about? I said I'd track down them two and I'm within spitting distance of one of them right now."

"He's supposed to be in chains," McGurn said. "Whiteoak is a slippery little eel and he's sleeping like a baby in the next room. In fact, you never even had his hands tied when you were riding in here."

A quiet moment crawled by before Corey asked, "How long you been watching me?"

"Long enough to raise some questions. If there hadn't been some men who'd already spoken on behalf of you, I'd have a lot more than just questions."

"Who spoke up for me?"

"I asked around about you like I would any other man who wants to work with me," McGurn said. "Them who've heard of Ed Brudaker told me you weren't ever anything but a bounty hunter. Not a particularly good one, but —"

Corey drove a fist into McGurn's kidney hard enough to knock most of the wind from the other man's lungs. Before McGurn could collect himself, Corey hit him again in exactly the same spot. His other hand grabbed McGurn by the shoulder to jerk him backward and off his balance.

McGurn had already started to reach for his gun, so Corey slapped his hand on top of McGurn's holster to keep the shooting iron from clearing leather. When McGurn looked at him, his eyes showed a fiery rage born from pain both physical and mental. Rather than struggle for the gun that was already being held in check, McGurn slipped his hand out from under Corey's to pull a knife from the scabbard hanging from his belt.

Corey barely managed to hop back before the blade came whistling toward him. Sharpened steel sliced through the air, cutting a path directly toward Corey's neck. It came so close to drawing blood that Corey felt the blade brush against his skin before it was flipped around to come at him again. This time, he brought up both hands to stop McGurn's swing completely. Before he could do anything else, Corey felt the solid thump of an elbow slamming against the side of his head.

"I knew it," McGurn hissed as he snaked one hand around the back of Corey's neck. "Fucking traitor."

McGurn drove his knee up into Corey's gut to soften him up. Because Corey tensed his muscles at the right time, he was able to absorb enough of the blow to keep moving without being impaired. Having been in his share of knife fights himself, Corey had a good idea of what McGurn's next move might be. Even if he was slightly off, straightening up his posture and twisting to the side was a sound strategy.

It turned out that his guess concerning McGurn's tactics was accurate because he came in for a straight stab to the midsection while pulling him closer using the hand he'd wrapped around the back of Corey's neck. McGurn's only mistake was in thinking he'd weakened Corey more than he had by that knee to the stomach. Instead, Corey had enough strength to pull away a few inches, turn his body around, and allow McGurn's knife hand to scrape his shirt instead of impaling his torso. Once the blade had passed him, Corey reached down and over to take hold of McGurn's knife hand and give it a powerful twist in the wrong direction.

Yelping as his hand was forced against the bend of his wrist, McGurn allowed the knife to slip from his fingers and into Corey's waiting hand. The instant he tightened his grip around the knife's handle, Corey brought it up and then drove it straight down into the thick layers of meat at the base of McGurn's neck.

Corey used the deeply imbedded knife to move McGurn toward the bed. He then plucked the knife out and stuck it in between McGurn's ribs where it shredded vital organs and caused the bounty hunter's entire body to stiffen. Keeping hold of the knife, Corey slapped his hand flat against McGurn's mouth to muffle the other man's dying gasps.

McGurn tried to talk with his last few gulps of air. Whether his words were pleas for mercy or a string of hateful obscenities Corey would never know. He wasn't interested in any of those words so long as they didn't make a noise that would carry beyond that room. Once McGurn stopped grunting and thrashing, Corey grabbed a handful of blankets from the bed and mashed them against the bounty hunter's fatal wounds. Blood had sprayed from McGurn's neck to spatter upon the window, which Corey only noticed when he looked outside to see if anyone was coming to check on a disturbance.

As far as Corey could tell, there was nobody outside.

When a set of knuckles rapped lightly against the door, Corey drew his pistol.

"Are you awake?" Whiteoak asked groggily.

"Yeah," Corey replied. "You just woke me up."

"I thought I heard something."

Corey looked back into his room, completely ignoring the body that was lying covered by blankets on his bed. "Nope," he said to Whiteoak.

The professor shrugged and shuffled back to his room.

Chapter Thirty-One

The next morning, Whiteoak was awoken by a loud knock on his door. That was followed by the sound of his door being forced open. Heavy footsteps thumped through his room, which caused him to grab for the pistol kept under his pillow.

"What is wrong with you?" Whiteoak snapped when he saw Corey standing over him. "I could've killed you."

"Yeah," Corey said. "That reminds me of something."

Less than twenty minutes later, the two of them were leaving the hotel by a back door. Corey led the way, carrying one end of a large bundle wrapped in blankets. Whiteoak brought up the rear, carrying the back end of that bundle. It was early enough that the only people outside were the ones working at the platform where stagecoaches picked up or dropped off their passengers. Two men swept the platform while another nailed a new schedule to a wall nearby. They were busy enough to not take much notice of Corey and Whiteoak, who circled away from the platform to keep out of sight.

There were some trees nearby, which was where Corey headed with the bundle. Since he didn't have any other choice, Whiteoak followed. As soon as they got behind the trees, Corey said, "Here's good."

"Good for what?"

Corey started swinging his end of the bundle back and forth, causing Whiteoak to do the same. "On three, toss him," Corey said.

"Right here?"

"One . . ."

"Won't someone find him?" Whiteoak insisted.

"Two . . ."

"But this is insane!"

"Three."

The bundle flew from their hands, landing in the grass in the shadow at the base of one of the biggest trees. Upon landing, one of McGurn's arms slipped free of the blankets as if to grasp at the dirt beneath him.

Whiteoak stared down at the body. "Why didn't you tell me about this?"

"I did," Corey said. "As soon as you woke up."

"No! I mean when it happened," Whiteoak said. "We can't just leave him there. Someone's bound to find him."

"Sure they are, but not until after we're long gone. Look, this is why I didn't say anything until the morning. You would've gotten all worked up and want to plan an elaborate way to get rid of the body or cover it up or bury it somewhere isolated . . ."

"All very logical courses of action," Whiteoak said.

"And unnecessary," Corey added. "I rode with McGurn for a while when I was living as Ed Brudaker. McGurn is one of the bounty hunters in this area who is not only after you, but he's also after that new friend of yours, Dylan Garviss."

"And you're telling me he didn't recognize you?"

"I know how to live without constantly drawing attention to myself. I know how to enter a town without announcing it and leaving so nobody knows I'm gone. I don't paint my name on the side of a wagon and —"

"All right," Whiteoak cut in. "Point taken."

"McGurn came to me last night because he was already suspicious. He was waiting for me to slip up and he already knew that you and I were on friendly terms."

Looking to his friend, Whiteoak asked, "How did you manage to get the drop on him?"

"Because he was cocky and thought he knew exactly what I was gonna do. He also thought he could take me in a fight, which is a lie I'd been letting him believe since the moment we met."

Nodding appreciatively, Whiteoak said, "Feigning weakness until the opportune moment. Sounds like something I might have taught you."

Grudgingly, Corey said, "Maybe."

"So, we're just leaving him here?"

"Our stage arrives in less than an hour. Would you like to dig a hole, fill it in, and hold a proper service in that time or maybe you'd prefer to postpone our journey?"

Whiteoak sighed. "I just don't like the notion of leaving this here where it can be found so easily. Let's at least cover him up."

"All right." Corey walked over to a pile of dirt and started kicking it toward the corpse. Some of it spattered onto the body while most of it simply formed a dirty layer around it. "Better?" he asked.

Shaking his head, Whiteoak removed his coat and draped it over a branch beside him. Rolling up his sleeves, he said, "Show some respect for the dead," before he hunched down and began scraping at the earth with both hands.

Corey moved in beside him to help in digging the shallow grave. "Respect for the dead? For this piece of shit?"

"It's common courtesy. Without it, we're all a bunch of barbarians. Also," Whiteoak added, "the longer this body goes unnoticed, the better it is for us."

"Now that's something that makes some sense."

The two men dug for about half an hour, stopping occasionally to make sure their activity wasn't drawing any spectators. While the number of people on or around the stagecoach platform slowly grew, those people weren't very interested in much of anything that didn't have to do with the platform itself or the new schedules that had recently been posted there. Whenever someone did glance over at the rustling sounds in the trees, Whiteoak or Corey would simply make it look as though they were answering the call of nature. Although some of the looks they got back were more dubious than others, nobody wanted to venture over and see what the two of them were doing for themselves.

The stagecoach to Kansas arrived earlier than scheduled, which suited Whiteoak and Corey fine. It took less time than expected to cover McGurn with a thick layer of dirt and rocks. No marker would show the bounty hunter's final resting place and, in the years to come, his carcass would only feed a few fortunate scavenging animals.

CHAPTER THIRTY-TWO

"So that's it, huh?" Dylan said. "The doc just walks away from you and you take care of his wagon for him?"

Danielle counted out a few dollars from some money she'd taken from her pocket and handed it over to a burly old man wearing suspenders and what looked to be remnants from a suit that had seen at least half a dozen previous owners. The old man's clothes were dark brown and in rough shape but made him look at least a little more dignified than most of the miners staggering in from the hills. Once he had his money, the old man nodded to her. "That'll pay for storage but not any upkeep," he said.

"Don't worry about upkeep," she told him. "All that wagon needs is a roof over its head until Henry gets back. Same for the other horse."

"If he comes back," Dylan grunted.

To that, Danielle merely laughed. "Where

this is," she said while hooking a thumb toward the wagon, "is where Henry will be sooner rather than later. He'd want it out of sight."

"And you know this because yer both such good friends," Dylan scoffed.

"Something like that."

The old man whistled sharply. Instead of a dog responding to the call, two younger chips off of his old block came running to meet him. Both of the boys shared the old man's facial features and even moved with a similar loping motion that had become more pronounced in the old man. "Fetch a couple of horses to move that wagon into the livery," he told his two boys. They hurried away.

"What does any of this matter to you?" Danielle asked the outlaw who remained sulking nearby. "You're healing nicely. You can be on your way anytime you like."

"The doc needs protectin' and I'm just the man to do it."

"First of all, he's not a doctor. Professor, is what he is and even that title is somewhat dubious."

"You call him what you like and I'll call him what I like."

"Fine," Danielle said with an off-handed wave. "Call him whatever you want from wherever you want. I've got things to do."

The two young men returned promptly with one horse each, which they immediately hitched to Whiteoak's wagon.

"You know where the doc went?" Dylan asked.

"His note didn't say."

"Well . . . maybe he'd prefer it if I stayed here to keep an eye on ya."

"I don't need that," Danielle told him. "I can take care of myself and if I need help, I've got other friends right here in camp."

"But can they be trusted?" Dylan asked.

"Trusted? You mean like I'd trust a known outlaw and killer who's probably just out to get on Henry's good side in the hopes of being paid for it?"

"Sure. At least you know I got a stake in keeping you alive. And don't tell me a man who owns all this," he said while motioning toward the wagon, "and dresses in all them fancy clothes won't pay to keep his sweetheart safe."

Danielle shook her head when she heard him refer to her as Whiteoak's sweetheart. She was about to walk away from him altogether when she was stopped by a tentative voice.

"Ma'am?"

Turning back around, Danielle found one

of the younger versions of the liveryman struggling with a lever attached to the side of the wagon's driver's seat. "Do you know anything about this?" the boy asked. Due to the layers of dirt on his face, it was difficult to guess his age as anything more than somewhere in his late teens. The second kid seemed to be only slightly younger than him.

"We can't get this to work," the older kid said.

"Aw, fer Christ's sake," Dylan snarled. "It's a goddamn brake lever! You ain't never worked one of them before?"

Danielle motioned for Dylan to stop and he reluctantly complied, grumbling to himself while making disgusted faces. "Step down from there," she said while approaching the wagon. "Let me see."

While not as critical as Dylan, both of the boys seemed doubtful that she would have any better luck than they did. As soon as their boots hit the ground, they circled around the wagon so as not to catch any more teasing from Dylan.

The fact of the matter was that the lever was anything but simple. Before Danielle climbed up into the driver's seat, she'd already touched two different panels hidden within the grain of the wooden panels of the wagon's frame. Each of those unlocked a portion of the mechanism that held the brake lever in place. Once she was aboard the wagon, she tapped another panel with her foot while also holding a smaller trigger attached to the brake lever itself. The smaller trigger was a brass piece resembling the grip used on a steam engine. After all the other triggers had been released and the handle was gripped along with the brass piece, Danielle was able to pull the lever and release the brake with little effort.

"But I tried that!" the older kid insisted.

"You tried holding that other handle?" Dylan asked.

"Yes!"

"I didn't see you do that, ya damn fool."

Danielle let them bicker as she climbed back down from the wagon. As far as she knew, she was one of the few people who knew how to unlock the brake on Professor Whiteoak's wagon. As far as every other security measure he'd installed, she was certain only the professor himself knew about them all. "Try it now," she said.

The older boy climbed into the driver's seat while the younger one went to the front where the horses had been hitched so he could lead them by the bridle. Sure enough, amid a chorus of laughing taunts from

Dylan, the wagon rolled easily upon its wheels toward the livery where it was to be kept.

"So, what do you say?" Dylan asked.

"About what?"

"About what we were talkin' about! Me staying on to keep an eye on you while the doc's away."

"I already told you and you already went on about how much you need to stay. If you want to stay, that's up to you. I can't force you to leave."

"So . . you think the doc would want me to stay?"

"You mean will Henry be grateful enough to pay you when he returns?"

"Yeah," Dylan said.

"You'll have to ask him yourself. Until then, stay away from me."

When she started to walk away, Danielle was stopped by a rough hand grabbing her arm. She immediately pulled out of Dylan's grasp and followed up with a swing from her other arm. Her fist bounced off his chest without doing anything more than making a dull sound.

"Why won't you let me help you?" Dylan asked. "I owe the doc a debt and I owe you, too! When I offer to keep you safe, you hit me. You know how close you came to hitting the spot where I was stitched up?"

"There's no need for you to be so persistent," she said. "Just listen to what I tell you and leave me alone. You don't owe me or Henry anything. There's enough trouble always sniffing around him and I don't need any more while he's away."

Danielle stormed off. Although Dylan started to follow her, he cursed under his breath and stayed put until she'd marched straight back into the wood-framed tent where Tara Simms conducted her business.

CHAPTER THIRTY-THREE

For the first portion of that day, Danielle expected to see Whiteoak return. It would more than likely be one of his quieter entrances, but she could vividly imagine him skulking into Tara's cathouse and creeping into her room. Her mind drifted off from there to some more delectable fantasies, but she quickly put herself back on track. There was work to be done and the camp was short on women who were as good with numbers as she.

The sun drifted across the sky, marking a hazy trail to the western horizon. As the light faded, so did her hopes of seeing Henry come back so soon. If he hadn't come back yet, he wasn't coming back. At least, not until he completed whatever task he'd set for himself. Trying to figure out Whiteoak's moods and motions was akin to predicting the exact spot a dry leaf would land after being felled from its branch by an autumn wind.

She was closing her ledgers when Tara escorted a man back to her room. Standing up, Danielle cast her eyes away and started to go somewhere else. While Tara didn't impede her progress, she was sure to catch her attention by saying, "Danny, this marshal was asking about you."

She looked up and saw Travis Farell standing, hat in hand, a few steps behind Tara. "What is it, Marshal?" Danielle asked. "I'm sure Miss Simms told you I don't do the same things as the rest of the girls who work here."

"Oh, most definitely, ma'am," Farell said. "I'm not after a whore. I wanted to ask you some questions in regard to your relationship with Professor Whiteoak."

"We're friends. That's all."

"Is there somewhere more private we can talk?"

Knowing how nervous Tara would be if a U.S. marshal was in the same room as her ledgers, Danielle pointed to one of the other rooms nearby. "We can step in there if it's all right."

"Sure," Tara said with a grateful nod. "We're slow right now. Go on ahead."

Farell stepped into the room and looked for a spot to sit. There was only a bed, a stool, and a washbasin there, so he chose the stool. Danielle stepped into the doorway and remained there with her hands clasped in front of her. "I hope you understand if I don't come inside and close the door."

"I don't have any intentions toward you," he assured her, "but I would like some privacy. I am a marshal of these United States if that helps ease your worries."

"It doesn't. We get plenty of lawmen in here and their thoughts always drift to the same place as any other man's. If you want privacy, we can step outside."

The marshal's eyes narrowed and for a moment it seemed he was thinking about pulling Danielle into the room and keeping her there. That moment passed and, instead, he lowered his voice to a growl that even she could barely hear.

"Your friend Henry Whiteoak is wanted for a long list of things," he said.

"Like what? Selling sugar water and passing it off as miracle tonic?"

"Like stealing gold from dozens of men throughout the Dakota Territories. Men who were supposed to be delivering that gold to be deposited in the federal reserves."

"You're saying Henry robbed federal marshals?" she asked skeptically.

Farell took a breath and let it out in a sigh.

"See, this is why I wanted privacy. This matter is potentially embarrassing to some very important people. Several couriers were transporting gold across the country. Where they would be met by other couriers to pick up their shipments."

"You mean gold."

"Yes, but nothing in very large quantities. No more than what could fit in a carpetbag, but still very valuable."

"Sounds like you'd need to worry about those couriers instead of Henry," Danielle pointed out.

"Those men were told they were transporting quantities of bogus minerals."

"Fool's gold?"

"Yes. Exactly."

"Why?" she asked, leaning in closer to him as she became more interested in the marshal's words.

"To keep them from stealing it or, at least, to make it easier for them to transport such a valuable package. Even if a man is honest, he tends to get nervous or otherwise anxious when he's carrying a bunch of gold. But, when he thinks it's not real gold, he relaxes and keeps his mind on the task at hand."

"And they honestly thought they were hired to transport a load of worthless rocks?"

"They were told the false gold was to be used as a decoy for other federal shipments. To be put on trains or stagecoaches that would be sent out along alternate routes while the real shipments went in other directions."

"So, if those were robbed, it wouldn't matter," Danielle offered.

"Precisely. We could also use such shipments to smoke out robbers and gangs that have become particularly troublesome."

"Not a bad idea, really."

"It's not and it's an idea that will be put into action sometime very soon. For all I know, it may already be in place."

"You mean you don't even know?" she asked.

The marshal gave her a short, humorless laugh. "There aren't many men in the government who know every last thing going on. We only know what we need to know and that suits me fine. What I know is that this particular shipment of gold contained the genuine article."

"You're certain?"

"Yes," Farell told her. "Otherwise, my superiors wouldn't be so upset that so much of it has gone missing."

"You think Henry stole this shipment?"

"That one shipment was split up among

at least a dozen couriers. The whole batch wasn't taken, but enough of it went missing that something obviously happened to it before they arrived at their destinations."

"So, they completed their jobs?"

"Yes," Farell said. "It turned out that a small percentage of their gold was replaced by fool's gold. The amount was small enough to border on inconsequential, but when it's all added up, it comes to a small fortune."

"You think Henry had something to do with this?" Danielle asked.

"Yes. His medicine show was present at several spots along many of these couriers' routes. He is also showing a new device that is supposed to separate real gold from that of the fraudulent variety. All of this seems like too big of a coincidence to me. Since Whiteoak is also wanted for stealing from some other important men, he seems like a very likely suspect."

"But you couldn't prove it. Is that why you're telling me about all of this?"

"I know you're familiar enough with Whiteoak to be of some use to me in this regard. I've visited several other towns and camps that the professor has visited recently and you're the only one in all of them who seems to have a genuinely close relationship with him."

Shaking her head, Danielle muttered, "Shows how much you know."

"I do know about that, so don't try to convince me otherwise," the marshal said with absolute conviction. "I'm giving you this one chance to help me willingly."

"Or what? You'll force me to help you unwillingly?"

"No, but you'll be dragged into this mess in some other manner other than as someone who cooperated with me to see it through."

"Threatening me isn't such a good idea," Danielle warned. "Especially since you've already told me all about this supposedly secret plan by the government to use all that fool's gold."

Marshal Farell shrugged. "Go ahead and tell whoever you want about it. The couriers have already completed their routes. That's how we know some of the gold was replaced. And if word spreads about government shipments being loaded with false gold, that will deter robbers, anyway, which was the whole idea. Even if you somehow manage to sink everything I've tried to accomplish, it'll only take me off the job so someone else can do it. Replacing me won't exactly ruin my superiors' day."

Growing more impatient, Danielle asked, "Then what the hell do you want from me?"

"I want you to help me bring in Henry Whiteoak as quickly and easily as possible. As you may or may not already know, I've tried to catch him more than once and he's slipped away every time."

"Then you must be real slow or blind because that wagon doesn't move too quickly and it's real hard to miss."

"Simply catching him isn't the problem," Farell explained. "I need to catch him in a way that proves he's guilty. I need a confession. I need to see him with some of that federal gold in his possession. I need to know how he found out who those couriers were and what they were transporting. I also need to know who he's working with and if he may have an informant in the government."

Danielle winced as she said, "That could be real tricky. Henry is more careful than any robber or lawman and he's damn sure a whole lot smarter."

"So you know what he's been up to?"

"I've known him for a long while, but he's never told me anything like this."

"I'm sure you could find out more if you went about it the right way."

Shaking her head, Danielle replied, "You

can wipe that smirk off your face and take that smug tone from your voice. I'll never be a whore again. Not for you, not for the government, not for any man."

"I wasn't suggesting —"

"The hell you weren't!"

Marshal Farell rolled his eyes and approached her. "You wouldn't have to do anything I'm certain you haven't already done. Just put him in a good frame of mind, get him to drop his guard, and then steer the conversation a certain way. Women have been doing that sort of thing ever since Eve damned this whole world to hell."

Danielle stood her ground, refusing to be intimidated into taking so much as a single step away from him. Crossing her arms defiantly, she stared him in the eyes and asked, "Are we through here?"

"Yeah," the lawman said with plain disgust. "For now." He then shoved past her and left the room to stomp toward the front door.

She stepped outside as well and was soon met by Tara who asked, "What was that all about?"

"Just another asshole lawman thinking he can get whatever he wants."

CHAPTER THIRTY-FOUR

Danielle waited for a while before leaving Tara's cathouse. The only person she talked to was Tara herself and Quince, one of the young men who worked there. After she talked to Quince, she didn't hear back from him for some time. So, Danielle waited.

Her conversation with Tara was short.

"Why was that marshal here?" Tara asked.

"He had some questions about Henry," Danielle told her.

"What kind of questions?"

"Doesn't matter. He's a government lawman so he can rot in hell for all I care."

Tara smirked and rubbed Danielle's shoulder. "The way you talk, someone could mistake you for an outlaw or at least someone who spent most of her time in the shadows."

"They'd be right."

"Shadows, maybe. Outlaw? Nah. You've just been around long enough to have your eyes opened. Anyone who doesn't see this world as a slop hole filled with liars and fools just wasn't paying attention."

"That sounds like someone I know."

Tara's light touch on Danielle's shoulder became a loose grip. "I hope you didn't get that someone into any trouble."

"Henry calls plenty of trouble down onto himself. He doesn't need my help. Besides, I've never been a help to lawmen like that marshal and I won't start now."

"Good girl."

Hours passed and the night grew dark. Danielle kept herself busy with simple tasks like straightening her small room and mending some clothes for herself and a few of the working girls who couldn't afford to visit the cart owned by a tailor who claimed to be from New York City. She was admiring a hem she'd raised when Quince snuck into her room.

Danielle was startled by Quince's entrance but not surprised. After all, Quince was known for his sneaking. When she looked at the boy, she saw a familiar dirty face with sunken features and shy eyes that didn't want to return her gaze. "Did you find anything?" she asked.

"No, ma'am."

"You checked the livery?"

"Yes, ma'am."

"What about the marshal? Was he lurking about?"

"Yes, ma'am, but he ain't around no more. He went to sleep."

"Where?"

"In a bed," Quince replied. "With a woman. Like the same way that men go to bed with the women here."

Quince may have been stealthy, but his skills didn't extend to his vocabulary. Talking to Quince was like yanking nails out of rusted iron plates, which was why not a lot of folks talked to Quince. Softening her tone, Danielle asked, "Where's the bed he's sleeping in, hon?"

"Swan Hotel."

"What about the deputy?"

"Ain't seen him at all," Quince replied.

"So it's all clear?"

"Yes, ma'am. Like I said before. I didn't find nobody outside the last time I checked. That's why I came to you."

Rather than point out the flaws in his choice of words, Danielle patted the young man's cheek and handed him the money she'd offered to pay him when she'd sent him out on his errand. Quince accepted the money respectfully and left the room like a wisp of cloud being blown across the sky.

Danielle slipped a shawl over her shoulders and tucked a Derringer pistol into one of the folds of her dress. She then made her way out of Tara's place through a back door that led into an alley that was mostly used to dump drunks who'd gotten out of line with one of the girls. It was a cool night and getting colder with every step she took along the crooked, rutted path. Although her head remained angled downward, her eyes never stopped moving. Flicking back and forth, they glanced from one shadow to another, studying every face she saw, all as she continued walking.

She was ready to divert her path at any moment to circle out of sight and back around again if she thought she was being followed. But it seemed that Quince had truly earned his pay because there was nobody out that night to give her cause for alarm. Even so, she circled around a few times, anyway. Even when she arrived at the livery and ducked inside, she kept her movements quick and quiet.

Danielle stood completely still as the darkness wrapped around her. Without the stars or occasional flickering torch to provide some amount of light, there was absolute black on all sides. Her eyes eventually got used to the visual desolation and were able to pick out a few shapes that she already knew were there. She'd been to the livery plenty of times and knew that a lantern was kept hanging on a hook within arm's reach of the front door. She got to it with a small amount of fumbling, found a box of matches stashed against the wall nearby, and struck one against the closest plank.

When she'd first arrived in Dugan's Find, she'd worked for the liveryman in much the same capacity as she now worked for Tara. Everyone had books to balance and being handy with numbers had always served Danielle well. For the first couple of weeks, she'd slept in that same livery. Not only did that give her a working knowledge of the place, but it made her nose immune to the smells that drifted from the piles of hay-covered horse shit all the way up to the rotten beams in the ceiling.

As soon as the lantern's wick was ignited, Danielle twisted the knob to keep the flame dim. Compared to the inky nothingness from before, even the small bit of illumination allowed her to see more than well enough to find what she was after. Of course, once the tarp was pulled off of Whiteoak's wagon, it would have been hard to miss under any circumstances.

She approached the wagon carefully,

reaching out to touch it as though she was afraid it might suddenly catch fire if she and the lantern got too close. When her hand brushed against the finely sanded wood, it lingered as though it had found an old friend. Within seconds, she pulled her hand away and circled to the front of the wagon with renewed purpose.

Every panel on the wagon was locked tight. Every little drawer and compartment used for storage and Whiteoak's demonstrations was latched and sealed to keep their contents away from prying eyes. Danielle went to several of the panels, touching them without attempting to open a single one. Shaking her head, she went to the door at the back of the wagon and reached out to run her fingers along its frame.

"Whatever it is you hold most dear," she said quietly to herself, "you'll keep it inside."

She kicked the wooden slats folded at the bottom of the frame causing them to come loose and drop into a set of steps leading to the narrow door. After setting the lantern down on the ground at the bottom of those steps, she climbed to the second one and once again reached out for the doorframe. Her left hand found a spot at the upper edge of the frame moments before her right hand settled on that side of the frame right around its vertical midway point. Danielle closed her eyes to concentrate, feeling for spots with three fingers on each hand. A smile drifted across her face when her fingers settled into the proper spot and small sections of the doorframe moved slightly inward.

"Damn thing," she said while hopping on the step. For Whiteoak or anyone else closer to his weight, the switch in the stair bracket would have been tripped by standing on the correct step. Since she was quite a few pounds lighter, Danielle needed to try a little harder. After a few more short jumps, she felt the panels in the doorframe slide inward even more and she was able to start the arduous process of unlocking the wagon's rear door without a key. She knew the steps to be taken, but it still took her a few tries to get the job done.

Holding the door open, she reached down to collect the lantern and take it with her as she stepped inside. It had been a while since she'd last entered that wagon and it was even more cramped than she recalled. After two steps into the wooden box, she started to feel more like she was in a coffin packed with bottles and vials of all shapes and sizes. Everywhere she looked, there were small drawers and various chemist tools hanging from hooks. The smell of chemicals drifted into her nose, making her feel leery about having the lantern in there. Danielle knew Whiteoak needed a lantern when he was in there, but she also didn't want to risk putting a flame in the wrong spot so she went up in smoke with the rest of the wagon. Relieved to find an empty hook in the ceiling, she hung the lantern there and turned her gaze downward.

The floorboards of the wagon were slightly smaller and narrower than what one might usually expect, but nothing so out of the ordinary as to look suspicious. "Okay," she sighed while stretching her hands down to the floor and extending her fingers, "let's see if I can remember how this goes."

At first, her fingers merely scraped along the boards without doing anything other than drawing little lines in the dust. With a bit of persistence, however, she got one of the boards to slide about half an inch. She licked her fingertips for better traction and got to work once more. When the second board moved, she smiled and found her rhythm.

Knowing the ideal pressure to use when pushing the boards was key. After that, the boards moved fairly easily. The trick was knowing where the boards needed to end up. When Whiteoak had showed her the sliding boards a few years ago, it had been to assure her that he could watch out for some money they'd both come into after completing a job together. That was back when they were a lot more than just partners and he was probably also trying to impress her with his ingenuity. Although she would never tell him, it had worked.

The boards in the floor worked much like an old Oriental puzzle box, which was where Whiteoak had gotten the idea. She couldn't remember the name of the fellow he'd claimed had actually built the puzzle into his floor, but it was just as likely that he'd been making that name up, anyway. The important thing was that she'd watched him very closely when he'd opened that puzzle. Unfortunately, her memory must have faded a bit because she couldn't solve it on the first, second, or even third try.

"There we go," she said victoriously on her fourth attempt. Once solved, the puzzle allowed her to pull open a section of the floor. The trio of narrow slats swung up on greased hinges to reveal a little compartment below.

Tentatively, Danielle reached into the compartment to retrieve one of the three leather pouches that were stored in there.

Even before she opened it, she had a pretty good idea of what was inside by feeling the weight of it in her hand. The pouch was sealed with a simple drawstring, which she pulled open so she could look at its contents.

"Henry, Henry," she whispered as she examined the sparkling gold ingots. "I hope this isn't what I think it is."

One by one, she examined the rest of the pouches only to find they each contained similar amounts of gold. There was always the possibility that the gold came from any number of sources or was nothing more than profit that he'd collected from all of his travels. The single most damning piece of evidence against him, however, was what was stamped on the pouches themselves: *Property of United States Treasury.*

CHAPTER THIRTY-FIVE

The ride to Barbrady, Kansas, would have taken several days to complete via stagecoach. Fortunately, there was a train depot along the way to shave some time off of the trip even if a train ticket was an added expense. By the time Whiteoak arrived in Kansas, he already felt he'd been gone for too long. But there was still a ways to travel and he needed to rent a horse to get there. Corey got a horse as well, insisting on accompanying Whiteoak all the way to his destination.

Once the long journey was finally behind them, Whiteoak pulled back on his reins so he could take a lingering look at the horizon in front of him. It was a hot afternoon and the sun blazed down at them like an angry lord trying to burn its subjects. There was something special about different kinds of heat. The differences only became clear to those who'd traveled enough to feel them on their skin. Kansas had a dry, intense heat that seemed especially suited to baking flesh right off of bone. Because there wasn't much of anything to stand in its way, the wind gained more than enough strength to cool Whiteoak off a bit while also threatening to steal the hat from his head.

"Not much of a place, is it?" Corey asked.

Both he and Whiteoak were looking at the town that was about a mile away. Their horses stirred beneath them, scratching the ground with their hooves as though they were even more bored with the scenery than Corey.

Whiteoak nodded slowly, lost in thought. "It's not," he said, "but it's been quite a thorn in my side."

"A thorn in your side?" Corey chuckled. "You robbed them, right? It wasn't the other way around?"

"True," Whiteoak admitted with a smirk. "And they sure didn't have much of a sense of humor about it."

"I've never been here, but even I heard about the bank in Barbrady. It was supposed to hold a mother lode of cash, but it was guarded by half the town."

Whiteoak nodded as though he was fondly remembering a summer romance.

"There were a few gangs that tried to bust

into that bank," Corey continued, "and they got shot to pieces by a mob."

"The old men who live there would all take their rifles to the upper floors of the buildings near the bank or along the street," Whiteoak said. "With the advantage of high ground, they'd shoot down at any robbers or outlaws, blasting the living hell out of the entire street. A good recipe for a bloodbath."

"You say that like you miss the place."

"I say that as a man who survived the gauntlet," Whiteoak declared. "One of the few to not only live to tell the tale but come away with the spoils."

"And a price on yer head," Corey added. "Don't forget that part."

One of Whiteoak's eyebrows danced upward in a bemused fashion. "A small price to pay to live such a fine story."

"What happened to the old men with the rifles after you left? They restock the bank and try again?"

"I don't rightly know. Perhaps. That's not why we're here." With that, Whiteoak turned his eyes toward a spot on the outskirts of town. It was a small patch of ground that was covered in lush green grass and markers arranged in neat rows. Whiteoak snapped his reins and steered toward the cemetery with Corey following alongside him.

Even with them taking a wider, more circular route to steer clear of the town itself, it didn't take long to arrive at the gate at the cemetery's entrance. The fence surrounding it was made of rusted iron that formed a thin barrier less than three feet high. More of a way to separate the cemetery from the surrounding land, the fence was simple with only a few artistic embellishments near the gate. Simple curls in upward pointed spikes gave them a smoky appearance while also creating a few sharp deterrents to anyone who might want to hop over the fence at its lowest point.

Upon reaching the gate, Whiteoak dismounted and tied his horse to a hitching post just off the trail. Corey followed suit and then approached the gate. After taking hold of the thin iron bars, he said, "They're locked."

Whiteoak removed his coat and hung it on one of the pointed fence spikes before casually rolling up his sleeves. When he saw the professor start walking around the fence, Corey asked, "Where are you going?"

"Inside," was the professor's reply.

"We can wait until tomorrow. It'll probably be open by then."

"I came too far to wait."

"But . . . breaking into a cemetery? Isn't

that . . . kinda gruesome?"

"No," Whiteoak said once he'd found a spot along the fence line that suited him best, "it's just impatient." With that, he took hold of the top of the fence and vaulted over in a mildly impressive show of agility. He stumbled a bit upon landing on the other side of the fence but played it off well.

Corey walked over to the spot where Whiteoak had jumped the fence. Nervously glancing toward the nearby town, he asked, "Ain't this a bad idea? You said yerself that these old men tend to guard what they got pretty tightly."

"That was the bank."

"I know, but defiling their graveyard might be frowned upon, too, you know."

Snapping his head around to look over his shoulder, Whiteoak said, "I'm not defiling anything! You know why I wanted to come here and I sure as hell didn't twist your arm to accompany me."

"No need to get yer dander up," Corey groused as he jumped over the fence. "I told you I'd come with you so you could visit this place and not get buried in it. All I'm sayin' is that you shouldn't push yer luck."

If Whiteoak was listening, he gave no indication. He'd started making his way up and down the rows of tombstones, glancing at each in turn before moving to another row to see what it had to offer.

Corey followed behind, spending most of his time looking at where he was stepping instead of what was written on any of the stones. "I hate places like this," he grumbled. "Always seems like I'm gonna step on a body. Hell, we are stepping on bodies. Every step. You ever see a body that's been buried for a while? They melt down to mush and get soaked up by the dirt and worms. Even the dust that gets on our clothes in a place like this could be some dead asshole."

"They weren't made for you to enjoy."

"I know, which is why I don't come to 'em unless I have to."

"This is far from pleasurable for me, you know," Whiteoak said. "In fact, I wish there wasn't any reason for me to come to this town at . . ."

Corey didn't need to ask why Whiteoak had stopped talking. When he looked up again, he saw the professor standing in front of a small marker near the end of one of the back rows. Most of the other markers were elaborately carved and obviously expensive, but this one was a simple cross with a few words chiseled into its smooth face.

Davey Auberjohn
Beloved Son
Gone Too Soon

Whiteoak stared down at the marker intently. His hands were clasped in front of him and his feet were planted shoulder-width apart. After a few quiet moments, it seemed he wouldn't move before all of those stone markers got up and walked away.

"I know you didn't mean to hurt no kid," Corey said.

"You don't know anything."

More than once during the ride from the Dakotas, Corey had broached the subject of what had taken place in Barbrady. While Whiteoak was always more than willing to discuss the robbery, he wasn't eager to delve any deeper than that. Rather than try to force more of an explanation from him now, Corey settled with, "I know you well enough to be certain you could never intentionally hurt no kid."

Whiteoak silently gnawed on the inside of his cheek, chewing on whatever words he wanted to say before swallowing them down. Through a clenched jaw, he said, "Doesn't matter what I intended, does it? Here he is. You know, part of me actually thought I wouldn't find a grave with that boy's name on it. That it was some vicious lie to further taint my name. But it's no lie. Seems I've tainted my own name beyond all reprieve."

"This here," Corey said while pointing at the little cross, "is a tragedy. But that don't make it your tragedy."

"How do you figure?"

"Because bad things happen. Sometimes they happen on purpose. Sometimes they happen for no reason at all. You ever think about Independence Day or New Year's Eve?"

Whiteoak blinked a few times before looking over at Corey as though he'd just awoken from a deep sleep. "What does that have to do with anything?"

"Any of them holidays where folks go out and shoot their guns in the air, whoopin' and hollerin' makin' a bunch of noise to celebrate."

"All right."

"A friend of mine . . . though he wasn't a very good friend . . . got killed because of all that merrymakin'. It was the middle of the night on New Year's Eve and all the people in town were makin' merry and drinkin' and whatnot. Well ol' Sanchez . . . that's my friend . . . he suddenly jerks to one side and drops to his knees. Blood's pourin' from his head and eyes, he's twitchin', it was a hell of a sight."

"Jesus," Whiteoak said. "What happened?"

"Nobody around him was shootin' at that moment and nobody had a reason to hate Sanchez. We took him to the doc, but it was already too late. He was dead as Abraham Lincoln by then. But the doc did some diggin' to see what the hell happened and he pulled out a bullet from the top of Sanchez's head. Well, in it actually. Near as we could figure, all of them shots that were fired a short while before Sanchez dropped sent a bunch of lead into the air. Once it came up, it had to come down. Doc said he's seen a few cows get hurt that way, but it's pretty damn rare. Sanchez bein' hit like that was a one in a million fluke. My point is, if you could find the poor bastard who fired that particular shot into the air, would you call him a murderer?"

Whiteoak cringed. "No, but it's hardly the same thing. What I did was intentional."

"You didn't mean to hurt nobody permanently, right?"

"Of course I didn't!"

"So, near as you could tell, it was a fluke. That's what I'm tellin' you, Henry. Maybe not as big of a fluke as a New Year's bullet comin' down into Sanchez's skull, but a fluke all the same. Neither you nor that idiot who shot his gun in the air to make some noise meant to kill anyone."

"I appreciate the thought, but . . ." Whiteoak snapped his head up and looked toward the front of the cemetery.

Corey did the same and both men saw the man standing at the gate that was now wide open. He was slightly less than average height and had a thick build with slightly stooped shoulders. He wore dark pants and a white, sweat-stained shirt with the sleeves rolled up almost to his elbows. He carried a hunting rifle in his hands but not aimed at either of the two men visiting the small headstone.

Both Corey and Whiteoak had drawn their pistols, but Corey was first to speak. "We ain't here for trouble," he said.

The man at the gate held his rifle in one hand by the barrel and stretched both arms out to his sides. "Me, neither! I'm just the undertaker."

"Sorry for trespassing," Whiteoak said while lowering his gun. "I wanted to pay my respects."

"Paying them to little Davey Auberjohn?" the undertaker asked.

"That's right."

"Well I couldn't help but overhear some

of what you were saying when I arrived. If you're looking for a fluke death, you should look somewhere else. When Davey Auberjohn died, it wasn't no fluke. I know that much for certain."

CHAPTER THIRTY-SIX

The undertaker's office was sparsely furnished and clean. Most of the main room was taken up by a large table and several kitchen cabinets. As soon as he was inside, the undertaker placed his rifle on a rack above the door and proceeded to fill a trio of glasses using a clay jug. While the stuff from the jug looked like water, it had the potent smell of moonshine.

"Brewed it myself," the undertaker said proudly as he took one of the glasses for himself. After taking a sip and letting out a hearty exhale, he stretched a hand out to both of his guests. "Name's Clive, by the way. Clive Beam."

"Henry Whiteoak," said the professor. "And that's Corey Maynard."

"Henry Whiteoak?" Beam said. "As in, Professor Henry Whiteoak?"

"That's right."

"You're the one that robbed the bank a

while back! I thought it was you!" Beam exclaimed. "I seen one of your shows but couldn't stay for the whole thing. Do you remember me?"

"Can't say as I do," Whiteoak said.

Beam shrugged and took another drink. "I don't really get to town very much, even though it's just over yonder. Only ride in for supplies and the occasional visit to Miss Trish's cathouse."

"Why is that?" Corey asked.

"Because Miss Trish has these girls there that'll —"

"No," Corey said quickly. "Why don't you go to town very often?"

"Oh, well, most folks who live there isn't nothin' but a bunch of stuck-up old-timers who think they're better than any man who gets his hands dirty for a livin'. Bunch'a crooked businessmen and rich folks squattin' on their money like a hen on an egg. They don't have no use for me unless they need someone put in the ground or if they have some other job they don't wanna do, so to hell with 'em."

Although Whiteoak was quick to take a seat as well as the drink that had been offered to him, Corey wasn't so easygoing. He stood between the table and the front door with his hand hanging low where it

293

was close to his holster in the event he needed to arm himself. As much as he studied Beam, however, he couldn't find a reason to feel threatened. Making his way to the table, he took the remaining glass and sniffed its contents.

"I hope you'll forgive my friend," Whiteoak said. "He's the suspicious type."

"Can't say as I blame him," Beam said. "Especially considering he's traveling with a man who's as well known as the professor here. After what you did, Mister Whiteoak, I'm surprised to see you anywhere close to Barbrady again. Don't you have men out to bring you down?"

"Plenty of them, I'm afraid," Whiteoak replied. "Sometimes, the safest course of action is the one that is least expected. Coming back to Kansas, I surmised, would be quite unexpected."

"Because it's stupid," Corey grunted.

"Your friend has a point," Beam said. "Have you been in Kansas all this time?"

"No," Whiteoak told him. "I've been a lot of places. More recently, the Dakota Territories."

"Christ almighty," Corey groaned.

"It doesn't do any harm to say I was in the Dakotas," Whiteoak retorted. "It's a large piece of land."

Paying little mind to the two men's bickering, Beam asked, "You came all this way just to visit a grave?"

"I did."

"Can I ask why?"

"I would think it was obvious," Whiteoak said in a somber tone. "I was responsible for the poor child's untimely death. While I've been forced to send plenty of men to their graves for various reasons, I've never taken the life of a child. It's a terrible thing and the least I could do was come back here to pay my respects."

"And," Corey added, "to make sure there was a grave at all."

Whiteoak lowered his head but his partner kept his held high.

"You didn't think there was a grave?" Beam asked.

"I heard about the kid from some asshole bounty hunters," Corey explained. "Having that sort of accusation went a long way in making things worse where the professor was concerned and I've seen men do a whole lot less just to motivate men to do what they want."

Beam poured himself some more moonshine. "There is a child buried beneath that stone," he said. "I know because I put him there myself."

"Then what were you saying before about Davey Auberjohn?"

"What I said was that his death wasn't some fluke."

"So, you think I intended to kill him with my serum?" Whiteoak asked.

"Not hardly," Beam replied. "I was working as an apprentice to the town's former undertaker when you robbed that bank. Both of us thought we'd get a whole lot of work after that robbery since a good portion of the town was filled with a bunch of bodies lyin' in the street or in their homes. But then they started waking up. Some of them had aching heads, but ain't none of them was dead."

Whiteoak leaned forward. "Are you certain of that?"

Beam nodded. "Real certain."

"Then what about Davey Auberjohn?"

"That boy was shot."

Whiteoak pushed his glass aside so he could place both hands flat upon the table and lean forward. "How could you know that?"

"Because," Beam said simply, "I was the one who dressed him for his burial. And don't ask me if I'm sure about how he died because the sight of a child that's been shot in the chest ain't something anyone could likely forget."

"Who would shoot a child?" Corey asked.

"Someone who, if they ain't burning in hell right now, surely will be when their time comes."

"Didn't you tell anyone about this?" Whiteoak asked.

"Not right away," Beam explained. "Mostly because it didn't seem like something I had to tell anyone about. Someone brings me a kid who's been shot to death, you don't exactly think you need to mention that the poor little guy's been shot."

"So that story about him being poisoned by Henry's tonic," Corey said. "That was a lie?"

"A big one," Beam said.

"Who would start saying such a thing?" Whiteoak asked.

"Probably the same man who wanted it kept quiet about how that boy died."

"Who told you to keep it quiet?" Corey asked.

"The former undertaker of Barbrady. He came back one night, spooked as hell, and made me swear I didn't know anything about what happened to that boy. Far as anyone knew, he was the one who handled the preparation and burial and he was sworn to secrecy about the bullet wound."

Beam had to pause long enough to take another long pull from his moonshine. After setting the glass down again, he had enough wind in his sails to continue. "When he came back from town that night, he was white as a ghost. Asked me if I talked to anyone about the kid and when I said I hadn't, he made me swear I never would. He said he was threatened to keep it quiet and nobody could say a damn thing about it to anyone."

"Where is he now?" Whiteoak asked. "Maybe he can shed some light on a few things."

"I'm sure he could," Beam replied. "Including what the Pearly Gates look like. He was killed about a day and a half after I had that conversation I just mentioned. Buried him myself."

"Who killed him?" Corey asked.

"Not sure, but I imagine it's the same person who killed the kid."

"Did you go to the law?"

To that, Beam merely laughed and then took another drink. "The law and those rich old bastards are the same damn thing around here."

"To that, I can certainly attest," Whiteoak said.

Corey slammed his fist down on the table.

"Then leave, dammit! Go find someone else who'll listen!"

"The former undertaker, rest his soul, left me the business," Beam said. "It's thriving. These old fellas die on a regular basis and they got plenty of money to do their funerals up right. Besides, all of them assholes in town are in each other's business and they all got secrets of their own. I hear rumors and I barely even talk to anyone." Shaking his head, he added, "And nothing I do or say or tell to anyone else will bring that poor kid back. I have been keeping my eyes open, though. I been waiting and watching to see if anyone came along who was interested in that grave. Even the family of that poor boy don't come around, so I figured whoever did might know something about it or at least might wanna know what happened. That child deserves folks who care about him to know the truth."

"We are certainly interested in that grave," Whiteoak said. "Very interested, indeed."

CHAPTER THIRTY-SEVEN

"Here," Danielle said as she opened the livery doors. "You wanted to see what Henry was hiding? Go and find out for yourself."

The U.S. marshal and his deputy stood in the doorway, looking at the brightly colored wagon as if they thought it might jump at them like a giant, uncaged beast. "I tried to get a look in that wagon but couldn't get it unlocked," Farell said.

"I have the key," Danielle replied. "Shall I open the door for you?"

"And you give me permission to search inside?"

"Yes."

"Can you give such permission?" the deputy asked.

The younger man was silenced by an impatient wave. "She's in current possession of the wagon. She was entrusted with it, so she can give permission. Besides, all I really needed was someone to unlock the damn thing. Go on, miss."

Having already gone through the process of unlocking the door, using the key was mostly for show. Danielle only had a copy of the key because Henry had given it to her as a dramatic display of how much he trusted her. He'd called it the key to his heart before handing it over with a crooked smile and a glint in his eye. To his credit, the gesture had been rewarded by Danielle later that same night those months ago.

Now, she handed the key over to Marshal Farell. It fit into the lock and released the latch to allow the door to swing open. Once that was done, the lawman moved the door back and forth and then looked down at the key in his hand. "Funny," he said softly. "That door seemed a lot sturdier when I tried to open it before."

"Henry bought a very strong lock," Danielle said.

"I'll say," Matt grumbled. "Withstood a whole lot of kicking without —"

"It's open now," Farell snapped. "Let's do what needs to be done so we can finally see if this Whiteoak person is the man we're after."

Dylan was there as well but kept his distance thus far. As the lawmen approached the wagon, however, he inched closer as his hand drifted to his holster. Discreetly, Danielle placed her hand on his arm and pushed it away from the gun hanging at his hip. Allowing himself to be denied his weapon, Dylan took a few more steps toward the wagon and asked, "What the hell is it you're hoping to find in there?"

"Evidence," Farell said.

"If you're so certain the doc's guilty, why didn't you bring him in or string him up?"

"Because that's not how the law works, sir," replied the marshal.

Placing herself between Dylan and the wagon, Danielle crossed her arms obstinately and said, "They're not after Henry. They just want the gold. Like every other greedy asshole who comes through this camp."

Dylan forgot about his pistol for a moment so he could put both hands on his knees as laughter wracked his entire body.

"It's not that funny," Matt said as he perched with one foot on the lowest step leading up to the wagon's back door.

"She called you guys greedy assholes!" Dylan said. "That's pretty damn funny to me!"

Matt's brow furrowed as he looked back and forth between Dylan and Danielle. The more times his eyes bounced back and forth between them, the angrier he got. Before he could vent some of the steam building inside him, Marshal Farell reached out from within the wagon to catch his attention with a sharp punch to the shoulder.

"Keep an eye on them and don't be distracted," the marshal said.

"They were provoking me," Matt said.

"And if they keep provoking, you can shackle them to a tree or something. Until then, stand guard and don't let them come inside this wagon."

"What if they try to come in?"

Fixing his eyes squarely on Dylan, the marshal replied, "Then shoot them where they stand."

Matt liked the sound of that. Wearing a smug grin, he hooked his thumbs over his gun belt where his hand was only one lethal thought away from drawing iron.

Dylan didn't reach for his pistol as he made his way to where Danielle was standing. He turned his back on the wagon so he could loom over her and keep their voices from drifting toward the lawmen when he whispered, "Did the doc tell you to do this?"

"No," she said. "He would never tell me to do this. That's why these men were so eager to take me up on my offer when I told them I would."

"So they didn't force you?"

She shook her head slightly. "No. They've been poking around here, talking to anyone who bought anything from Henry, looking for some piece of dirt to use against him. They're after this gold, so I'm going to let them try and find it. They've already tried getting into that wagon more than once, I'm sure. After they finally get inside to take a look around, they'll have the answers they were after and will leave this camp for a while."

"I think the doc knows how to deal with law dogs like these two," Dylan sneered.

"He does, but they keep coming around. By now, getting an unimpeded look inside that wagon is the mother lode for all the lawmen and bounty hunters on Henry's trail. When he's here, he can fast-talk them, trick them, or just run away. When he's gone, these two marshals get to see what they want without him here to pull any tricks."

"Kinda like peeking at a gambler's cards," Dylan mused.

"Yes," Danielle sighed. "Something like that."

Dylan turned to face the wagon again while standing close to Danielle. Gritting his teeth, he shook his head warily. "I don't think the doc would want them in there."

"He'll have a fit when he finds out."

"You're gonna tell him?"

"There's no way to hide it," she said. "That wagon is Henry's entire world. It's what he holds most dear. He guards it with his life and when he's gone, he takes steps to keep it safe."

"Seemed pretty easy to get inside," Dylan said.

"Only because I made it look easy. Trust me, there's a lot more to getting that door open than turning a key. If you don't know what you're doing, you can shoot that thing with a cannon without getting what you want. It's made to either stay shut or destroy whatever it is he wants to keep hidden. Very impressive construction, actually."

As if to emphasize the reason for Whiteoak's precautions, sounds of shattering glass, splintering wood, and spilt liquid drifted out from the wagon. The first few things that were broken seemed accidental. The next few were destroyed with more force, making it seem like anything but a misstep.

"This is a good thing," Danielle said more to herself than Dylan. "Henry would never allow it, but it had to be done. Otherwise, these lawmen would just keep coming."

"Doing it for his own good, right?" Dylan offered.

"That's right."

"Yeah. That's what my pa said when he was beating the hell outta me with a switch."

The next time she heard a crash come from inside the wagon, Danielle winced even harder.

"So," Dylan said as he leaned in close enough to her to whisper almost incoherently, "did the doc steal that gold or not?"

"How should I know?" Danielle flatly replied.

"You know a lot about him. I'd wager he would've mentioned it to you or you could at least figure it out on your own."

She said nothing to that.

"Do you know what'll happen if they find anything useful in there?" Dylan asked.

"They'll feel justified in grabbing Henry the next time they see him."

"Or gunning him down on the spot."

"They haven't found any gold so far," she said. "That's why men like him keep trying to find Henry or get a peek inside that wagon. The ones who want to try and kill him don't fare too well, either. Once these two get to have their way, they'll be out of excuses to come after Henry like they have."

"The bounty hunters won't stop," Dylan pointed out.

"Bounty hunters are nothing more than almost-deputized killers. Henry can handle them."

"Maybe, but you can shoot a bounty hunter without too much repercussion. A lawman, on the other hand, ain't so simple."

"Lawmen need good cause to do what they do. Otherwise, there's hell to pay. Some lawmen don't care about that, but it's not such a problem killing them. Real lawmen need to sniff around for a while to get their cause. And when they sink their teeth in, they've got the strength of the law and government behind them. Hopefully, this will keep any lawmen from sinking their teeth into Henry for a while."

Dylan looked over at her with a hint of cautious trepidation in his eyes. "Sounds like you know a bit on this subject."

"I've learned a lot in the time I've spent with Henry Whiteoak," she said. "Some of it, I'd as soon forget."

Chapter Thirty-Eight

When Whiteoak entered Barbrady, he was a different man than the last time. He drove no wagon. There was no fanfare. There was no waving to bystanders or shouting out his greetings. There were only three men on horseback, one of which was known and the other two carrying their heads angled down-ward.

Whiteoak had removed his string tie, unbuttoned his top two shirt buttons, and wore a duster that he'd packed among the few things he'd brought on the journey. Before climbing into his saddle back at the cemetery, he'd slapped his hat against the ground to give it a dustier, more battered appearance. For most men, it wouldn't have been much of a disguise. For him, however, it was almost enough to fool one of his best friends.

Every couple of seconds, Corey looked over at him and blinked in disbelief. "Can't rightly say I've ever seen you look so common," he told the professor.

"Common?" Whiteoak snorted. "I can't rightly say I've ever aspired to that unimpressive title. At least nobody seems to be recognizing me."

"Except for that fella over there. The one drawing his pistol."

Whiteoak snapped his head around to look in every direction. He saw nothing but the street and a few locals shuffling about their business. When he turned back to face Corey, he saw a wide smirk on his face. "Very funny," Whiteoak said before settling back into his disguise.

"This may not be such a great idea," Beam said from slightly behind the other two. For most of the ride into town, the undertaker had been fairly quiet. Now when he spoke, his voice was taut and nervous.

"I know it's not a good idea," Whiteoak said. "But I want to look this man in the eyes and tell him I had no part in killing his son."

"He'll probably try to shoot you," Beam warned.

"I already told him that when he first wanted to come out here," Corey said. "Didn't do any good then and it won't do any good now."

"Don't go that way," Beam said.

"But you told me Auberjohn lived up this street," Whiteoak said.

"He does, but you can't go there."

"I came all this way to —"

"I know why you came here," Beam snapped. "Just follow me, dammit." Without waiting for further discussion, Beam steered his horse back to the corner they'd just passed.

Whiteoak stayed where he was for a second, unsure as to whether or not he should follow the undertaker. Looking over to Corey only allowed him to see a half-hearted shrug from the other man.

"Might as well," Corey grunted. "He took us this far and I doubt that Auberjohn asshole's goin' anywhere."

Sometimes, the simplest logic was the toughest to dispute. Whiteoak followed the undertaker to a row of cabins near the western border of town. There were a few children playing outside one of them, which brought a weary smile to Whiteoak's face.

"You know them kids?" Corey asked.

"No. It's just good to see young faces in this town."

Settling into his saddle with a grunt, Corey said, "I don't like kids. Too damn noisy."

"There were barely a handful of young ones to be found the last time I was here. Maybe something is changing around here."

"Or maybe some local idiot got drunk and found his wife in an agreeable mood," Corey countered. "What difference does it make?"

Whiteoak wasn't about to argue with his partner on the matter. It was good enough for him to watch the children play for a few moments until he got close enough to be noticed when he waved at them. The children froze for a second and then scattered like birds that had been flushed from some bushes. They disappeared almost immediately, leaving the street still and eerily quiet once again.

Beam dismounted and tied his horse to a post outside a cabin that was next to the last in line. He kept his head down and his steps swift as he pushed open his door and stepped inside. Before Corey and Whiteoak could get their reins tied to the same post, the undertaker poked his head out and hissed, "Come on and get in here!" before disappearing again.

Both Corey and Whiteoak had their hands near their holsters as they entered the cabin. What they found inside may have been a mess, but it wasn't particularly dangerous.

A narrow cot was in one corner, covered by some rumpled blankets. The opposite corner had a small stove and some cabinets containing dishes and food. Whiteoak could tell that much because most of the cabinet's little doors hung open. A short square table was situated against a battered roll-top desk, which was where Beam went as soon as he saw he was no longer alone inside the place.

"I didn't give this to you right away," Beam explained while sifting through a stack of papers, "because I wasn't quite sure about your intentions. But I can tell you mean business. I mean, why the hell else would you of all people come back to Barbrady? Right?"

"Does this have something to do with that grave I visited?" Whiteoak asked.

"It's got everything to do with that grave."

Whiteoak waited for a few more seconds but didn't get another word from Beam. Instead, the undertaker continued rifling through his papers while grunting incoherently to himself. Eventually, Whiteoak stepped forward to grab Beam's upper arm and spin him around to face him.

"I've traveled a long way and it's taken me a long time to get here," Whiteoak said. "Therefore, I am not in the mood for vague riddles or meaningless tasks."

"Coming back here took a lot of balls," Beam said without struggling to break free of Whiteoak's grasp.

"Yes, I suppose it did," the professor replied.

"The fact that you're here at all tells me a lot. Frankly, I was like everyone else in thinking you would never show your face here again."

"I thought the same thing," Corey said.

"But you did come back and it was to visit the Auberjohn child's grave," Beam continued. "There haven't been many folks to visit that grave at all, outside of the boy's mother."

"His mother is here?" Whiteoak asked.

"Not anymore," Beam said. "She died last spring."

Whiteoak's expression softened as he blinked and looked down as though he'd forgotten he was holding on to the undertaker's arm. "Oh," he said while releasing Beam. "That's a shame."

"Not even Auberjohn himself comes to that grave," Beam said. "And this is why."

Beam had found what he'd been searching for within the papers. It was a piece of paper, the size of one that would be used to write a letter, neatly folded into thirds. Parts of it were stained a dark crimson from blood that had soaked into the paper and dried.

"What is that?" Whiteoak asked.

"It was tucked into Davey Auberjohn's waistband, under his shirt. I found it there when I was redressing the poor lad for his final rest. Most likely, it's what got him killed."

Whiteoak took the paper from Beam, unfolded it, and started to read. The more words he saw, the faster his eyes soaked up what was written on the page until he reached the end.

"What?" Corey asked as Whiteoak turned the page over to see if anything was on the back. "What is it?"

"Who wrote this?" Whiteoak asked.

"Isn't it obvious?" Beam replied.

"When was it written?"

"Can't say for certain."

Growing angry as he reached the end of his patience, Corey growled, "Will someone tell me what the hell you're talking about?"

Rather than say anything, Whiteoak handed over the paper.

Corey held it in both hands, straining his eyes to get a look at the words that had been scrawled in large, blocky letters onto the paper. It didn't take him long before he grew as silent as the other two men. Looking up, he saw Whiteoak staring back at him with silent rage boiling in his eyes.

"Jesus," Corey said. "You say you found this on the Auberjohn kid when he died?"

Beam nodded.

"And you don't think his father knew it was there?"

Beam's jaw tensed as he shook his head again. "The boy was brought to us by a few of Auberjohn's workers. We were told to get him into a coffin and in the ground as soon as possible. One of those same men came back shortly after to ask if the job was done. The former undertaker, the man who trained me, told him he'd cleaned the boy up and changed his clothes. It wasn't long after that when the old man was killed."

"The old undertaker, you mean?" Whiteoak asked.

"That's right."

"After the old man was buried, that same fella came back to pay me a visit," Beam continued. "Asked if I'd helped in getting the kid ready for his funeral. After the awkwardness of the two funerals I'd put together, I didn't want to see Auberjohn or any of his men again so I told him I hadn't done anything more than dig a hole and fill it in once the boy had been put into the ground. That was good enough, I suppose, because I didn't hear from any of them again."

Taking the letter away from Corey, Whiteoak held it in front of Beam's face and said, "You didn't see fit to show this to anyone else?"

"Who would I show it to?" Beam replied.

"The law! The rest of the boy's family!" Suddenly enveloped by rage, Whiteoak lunged forward to grab the undertaker by the front of his shirt. "Dammit, telling anyone or doing anything would have been preferable to waiting around for me to show up in this damned town again!"

Either unwilling or unable to break the professor's grip, Beam said, "The law is indebted in one way or another to the rich old geezers in this town, which means they're practically good for nothing unless it's in them old men's interest. And the boy don't have no more family. Just his pa, and you read what that son of a bitch was up to."

"How'd you know I'd come back?" Whiteoak asked.

"I didn't. I was hoping someone might come along who could do something with what I had to say. It had to be someone able to stand up to men like Auberjohn and his men and it had to be someone with the conviction to see it through once the fight was started. Looks to me like that someone's you."

"And what if I never came along?" Whiteoak asked.

"Then I guess I'd come up with something. I tried to look into this myself," Beam said in a tired voice. "But Auberjohn hired on more gunmen to protect his interests since the bank was hit. For all I know it's too late to do much of anything at all. Even if it ain't, I can't fight and I can't shoot much of anything. Folks don't even listen to what I have to say, anyhow. Even if they did, they all have known Wilson Auberjohn a hell of a lot longer than they've known me and see him as one of the town's most generous souls. He helps anyone he can around here. Ain't nobody's gonna believe a cross word against him. At least, not when it's me doing the talking."

"You think anyone would listen to me?" Whiteoak scoffed.

"Talk ain't what's needed, mister."

Chapter Thirty-Nine

Normally, Whiteoak liked to set himself up in a town when he first arrived in one. There were things that needed to be done and some that he wanted to do, all of which had become so ingrained in his routine that they bordered on ritual. This time, his first several hours in Barbrady were as quiet as his initial arrival. The longer he went without stretching his legs with a walk up and down the main street or picking a spot at the bar in the most popular saloon, the more Whiteoak sank into his chair.

Positioned with his back to a wall, Whiteoak hunched over a small round table in a saloon that was barely large enough to contain a proper bar. Apart from him, Corey, the barkeep, and one filthy drunk, the place was empty. At one time, an hour or two ago, someone had wandered into the place to buy a bottle and promptly leave.

"Can I have some more of that?" Corey

asked, nodding toward the bottle of whiskey sitting in front of the professor.

Whiteoak mulled over his decision before nudging the bottle across the table.

Corey took it and poured some firewater into his glass. After lifting the drink to his lips, he sipped it and set it down again. "You think we should be out in the open like this?"

"Nobody knows I'm here," Whiteoak said. "They don't recognize me."

"Beam recognized you."

"He was watching for someone. Nobody comes in here other than that barkeep and he's about three blinks away from falling asleep."

"Didn't you tell me about a barkeep in this town who bought all of that tonic you made to sweeten up cheap whiskey?"

"This isn't him," Whiteoak said.

"Then maybe you can tell me what you've got in mind."

Whiteoak reached for his shirt pocket where the folded letter Beam had given him was kept. Rather than take it out, he pressed it against his chest and winced as though it burned him all the way down to his heart. "I want to go to Auberjohn's place and put an end to this."

"We don't even know if what's in that letter . . ." Corey stopped when he saw the burning look in Whiteoak's eye. Cautiously, he said, "We don't even know if it's true."

"There's one good way to find out."

"I wouldn't call what you've got in mind good."

After taking a pull from his whiskey, Whiteoak said, "You don't know what I'm thinking."

"I've known you for a long time," Corey said. "We've stirred up plenty of shit together and one of the things I can always count on is that you've got at least a dozen ideas rattling around in that head of yours at any given time. Right now, though, there's only one and I can tell it ain't a good one."

"There's no time for plans tonight."

"Then what are we doin' sitting here?"

Whiteoak held up his bottle of whiskey and poured some into his glass. "Preparing."

CHAPTER FORTY

It was deep into the night before Whiteoak decided to venture away from the little place where he'd been drinking. In that time, he and Corey played some cards and drank some coffee to try and sober up a bit. The bitter brew didn't go far in counteracting all the whiskey they'd drunk, but it helped steady their steps when they eventually saddled up their horses and rode out to Wilson Auberjohn's place.

The house was one of the large ones in Barbrady, even considering that the town was mostly populated by rich old coots. The front half of the structure looked out onto the town's largest strip of shops while the back side of it faced a wide expanse of empty Kansas prairie, Whiteoak and Corey stuck to the shadows as they approached one of the two smaller buildings apart from the house. One of those was a stable and the other was a livery that was barely large enough to contain a single wagon.

"You check that one," Whiteoak said as he pointed toward the stable. "I'll go into the other one."

Corey glanced back and forth between the main house and the two smaller structures. He could see two men posted at either side of the house, one of which carried a shotgun. "They're trying to protect something," he whispered.

"I know. That's why we're here."

"What I mean is there's probably more men than what we can see outright. It wouldn't be wise to . . ."

But Whiteoak had already started walking toward the livery, seemingly unconcerned with drawing attention.

"Hey!" shouted one of the men near the house. "Who's that?"

Whiteoak kept walking toward the livery. When he was close enough to reach the door, he tried it only to find it was locked.

"Get away from there!" the man at the house demanded. By now, his voice had drawn the notice of the man posted at the other end of the house as well as a third who ran around from the front porch.

Whiteoak brought his knee up close to his chest and snapped his foot straight out. Even though his heel pounded squarely against the door near the handle, there wasn't enough muscle behind it to break the latch. Rather than try again, he drew his .38 from its holster and fired twice into the door.

The three men from the house broke into a run, shouting to each other while firing into the night sky. One or two of the shots were aimed toward the intruders, but none of them came close enough to cause much concern.

"See anything in there?" Corey asked as he placed one hand flat against the wall behind him and dropped to one knee.

"Not yet," was Whiteoak's curt reply.

"Well don't take too long. It's about to get hot here."

"Let it."

Gritting his teeth, Corey knew there wasn't much use in trying to argue with the professor. Once he had his mind set on something, he was going to see it through whether he had much help or not. Since he'd come this far and wasn't about to abandon his friend, Corey thumbed back the hammer of his pistol and took aim.

After firing a few wild shots at the livery, the three men from the house spread out and stopped wasting their ammunition. The next shot came from a rifle, which hissed dangerously close to Corey's cheek. That rifleman was put at the top of Corey's list of priorities and immediately found himself in the gunman's sights. Corey squeezed his trigger once and when he saw the rifleman drop, he guessed he'd hit his target. The rifleman had either been grazed or merely frightened because he clambered to his feet right away and fired back.

Inside the livery, Whiteoak barely took any notice of the hell that was raging nearby. He busied himself with lighting a nearby lantern and using his feet to sweep away the loose hay scattered on the floor. With such little space inside the livery, it didn't take long for him to uncover a square hatch set into the floor. The panel was about the size of a kitchen tabletop and was kept shut by three separate locks. Whiteoak wasted no time in blasting the locks with his .38. The iron devices were so sturdy, however, that he needed to reload his pistol to deliver the final bullet that allowed the panel to open. Reaching down, Whiteoak grabbed hold of an edge and lifted the panel. It swung on a set of hinges, slamming against the floor on its way down.

"Hello?" Whiteoak said.

Gunshots ripped through the night outside the livery, making it hard for him to hear much of anything. Whiteoak grabbed the lantern and held it above the dark opening in the floor. The pungent stench of human excrement and rotten meat drifted up from the hole. Once some of the lantern's light trickled down, the source of those smells was clear enough to spot. At least half a dozen men and women were tied up, gagged, and wedged into the cramped space under the floor like sacks of flour being stored for winter. Only two of them looked up at Whiteoak. Another two averted their eyes and the remaining prisoners hadn't moved for quite some time.

Whiteoak dropped down into the festering hole as quickly as he could without stepping on any of its inhabitants. After holstering his pistol, he reached down to his right boot where he kept a slender knife in a leather scabbard. The blade flashed out from its home to slice through the ropes of a young black man whose face was mostly covered in scraggly whiskers.

"Who are you, mister?" the prisoner asked once his gag had been removed.

"Doesn't matter," Whiteoak replied. "Take this," he said while slapping the knife into the prisoner's trembling hand, "and free the others."

For a moment, the man didn't seem to

know what to do with his newfound freedom. Very quickly, however, he nodded and started cutting the bonds of the prisoner closest to him.

"How many others are there?" Whiteoak asked.

"Just these here."

"Are there more holes like this?"

"No," the prisoner said. "Not that I know about."

"All right, then. Once it's clear, all of you need to get the hell out of here as fast as your legs can carry you."

"All right. Wait!" the prisoner said as Whiteoak started hoisting himself out of the pit. "I gotta know your name. I owe you my life."

"You don't owe me anything," Whiteoak told him. "If you want to thank someone, thank Davey Auberjohn." Whiteoak then finished climbing out of the pit and drew his gun.

CHAPTER FORTY-ONE

Corey knew his bullet would hit pay dirt the moment he pulled the trigger. Sometimes it was like that. Things lined up and a man could feel in his bones that he'd done something right. The three men from the house were making their way to the livery, closing the distance between them and the intruders while also lessening the chances that they would miss on their next shots. When Corey took his charmed shot, he sent one of the riflemen straight to his back. That left two more men who were suddenly not so anxious to continue the fight as they'd been a few moments ago.

"That's enough!" shouted someone from the vicinity of the house.

Although both of the remaining gunmen stopped firing, Corey sent one more chunk of lead through the air. His bullet clipped the arm of one man, knocking him back several steps amid a stream of pained obscenities.

The man who'd called for the cease-fire stepped into view, coming around from the front of the house with another man walking beside him. One of the men wore dark pants and a bleached white shirt while the other was dressed in a simple manner like the three men who'd been guarding the house when Corey and Whiteoak had arrived. As he took a few more steps, a stray bit of light from the moon glinted off the pistol already in the well-dressed man's hand.

"If you're looking to steal horses," the man in black and white announced, "you won't find any in there. I suggest you throw down your guns and give up before this gets any worse."

"You're a slave trader!" Whiteoak said as he strode over to stand next to Corey. "I don't see how things could get any worse than that."

As the well-dressed man kept walking, he motioned for his remaining guards to stay where they were. "And what would make you come here in the middle of the night to toss around wild accusations like that?" he asked.

Whiteoak carried the lantern in his left hand, which he swung around to shine its light on the livery. Standing inside the doorway were the filthy men and women who'd been held under the floor and were now too frightened to take another step. "They're all the reason I need!" Whiteoak said.

"I see," the man replied. "You're trespassing on my property, stealing even more of my property. I can shoot you where you stand."

"Let's bring in the law to settle this dispute over your property," Whiteoak said, spitting the last word out distastefully.

"The law only comes to me when they're called; and when I call them, they come with guns blazing. Sure you want to buck those odds?"

Corey leaned close enough for Whiteoak to hear him when he whispered, "Might be best to get out of here while we still can. You got what you came for, right?"

"Not just yet," Whiteoak snarled. In a booming voice, he said, "You're Wilson Auberjohn, I take it?"

The well-dressed man took another bold step forward. "I am. And who might you be?"

"Come here and we can discuss that."

Auberjohn had a short conversation with his men before walking toward the livery.

"I'm bringing one of my men with me," he said. "You two will drop your guns and step inside that livery. First hint of any violence and the two of you will be gunned down. Understand?"

Whiteoak let his pistol fall from his hand where it hit the dirt near his feet, prompting Corey to do the same.

"I'm not an idiot," Auberjohn said. "Kick those guns toward me so my men can collect them."

Shrugging, Whiteoak said, "It was worth a try," before using his foot to send his .38 skidding across the ground away from the livery.

"You sure about this?" Corey asked in a measured tone. "I reckon we can still get away from this place if we take 'em by surprise."

"I agree, but the time for surprise isn't right now," Whiteoak said.

"If you say so." Corey grudgingly kicked his weapon as well, much to the pleasure of the elder Auberjohn.

When he was close enough to see inside the livery, Auberjohn shifted his demeanor to become vicious and imposing. "Get back into your damn hole!" he snarled.

The prisoners obeyed for the most part, except for the one who'd been the only among them to speak thus far. "There's dead in there," he said. "They reek of disease and worse."

"I'll have it cleaned out later. For now, do what I told you."

The prisoners retreated into the shadows deeper inside the livery, which brought a contented smile to Auberjohn's face. "So," he said, "what brings you men here?" Suddenly, his eyes widened. "I'll be damned! It's Professor Whiteoak. You've got balls the size of boulders to step foot in Kansas, not to mention this town, again."

"I came to have a word with you," Whiteoak said.

"About them bounty hunters, I presume?"

"No. About your son."

Auberjohn's eyes narrowed into seething slits. "What about him?"

"Why are you spreading lies about me being the cause of his death?" Whiteoak asked.

"They're not lies," Auberjohn replied. "If you hadn't run like a damn coward after looting this town's bank, you would have known as much."

"I have sources that tell me otherwise."

"Like who?"

"Like," Whiteoak replied while slowly reaching for his breast pocket, "your son."

Although the anger in Auberjohn's eyes

was growing in intensity, he didn't make a move to stop Whiteoak from taking the folded paper from his pocket. When he saw that the paper was indeed what Whiteoak had been after, Auberjohn asked, "What's that?"

"A letter," Whiteoak told him, "that tells about the poor, sick people that were being held under the floor in the livery. It describes sick, dying people who were dragged in and out of this livery where they were handed over to men who came at night to cart them away in wagons."

"Who wrote that?"

"Davey."

Auberjohn's anger spiked into seething rage when he said, "Don't you speak that name to me."

"But that's who wrote this letter. See for yourself," Whiteoak said as he extended his hand.

Reluctant at first, Auberjohn was quickly overcome by curiosity and he stomped toward Whiteoak. All of the gunmen behind him tensed and brought their guns up ready to fire if they saw one move they didn't like. But Whiteoak wasn't a fool and he wasn't going to give an excuse for the firing squad in front of him to pull their triggers.

Auberjohn took the letter with resentful

skepticism etched into his features. His expression changed dramatically the moment he saw the neat, blocky lettering written onto the paper he held. His eyes darted back and forth, taking in each word multiple times before reaching the end and starting at the top again.

"Your son was a smart boy," Whiteoak said quietly. "He was too young to know exactly what was happening, but he described a slave ring well enough for anyone to recognize it. He also knew it was wrong, that's for certain."

"I kept what I was doing hidden from him," Auberjohn said, mostly to himself. "He couldn't have seen all of this."

"He had a window in his room, I'm sure. He saw things. He must have heard talk as well."

Shaking his head, Auberjohn said, "He writes about seeing the hatch in the floor. Hearing people coughing, hacking, and dying down below. I never saw him go anywhere near the livery. I never allowed it."

"Come now," Whiteoak said. "Tell me honestly that, as a boy, you never snuck out of your room and fled your home for a short while to partake in some small adventure. And tell me that the most enticing places to have those adventures were the very spots you were warned to never go."

Despite the understanding that was beginning to show on Auberjohn's face, the man shook his head as though he was fighting for his next breath. "I told him to stay away from this place, but he wouldn't listen. I told him not to come out when the buyers came to pick up their merchandise, but he insisted on sneaking around to look."

"You caught him, didn't you?" Whiteoak pressed. "You caught him one too many times and you had to punish him."

Auberjohn held the letter in both hands, staring at the familiar handwriting with dry, cold eyes. "Davey saw me disciplining one of the . . . some of the merchandise. He screamed for me to stop whipping her, came running out to holler and cry at me in front of one of my best clients. I sent him to his room without supper and when I came up to have a talk with him, Davey called me a monster. My own son called me a monster."

"That must have been tough to hear," Whiteoak said.

But Auberjohn wasn't listening. He was too far into his own thoughts for his words to be anything but a singular dialogue. "He *judged* me."

The venom dripping from those words was enough to wipe away the attempts at sympathy Whiteoak was trying to convey. The hatred in Auberjohn's voice was startling, even to the ears of someone who'd heard and seen more than enough of mankind's ugliness to turn his stomach.

"That little bastard had the gall to judge *me*," Auberjohn seethed. "He said I had to confess my sins to the town preacher and when I told him how ridiculous that was, he said I had to tell the sheriff about the people I was whipping and keeping under the livery. I tried to tell him about how business worked, about how money is made, but he didn't listen."

"He was just a boy," Corey said.

Slowly, Auberjohn cast his eyes upward to look at the men in front of him. "He was too much like his smart-mouth, judgmental bitch of a mother. When he looked at me with his cunt mother's eyes and threatened to go to the law if I didn't, I had to teach him a lesson in real power. Even when I put a bullet into him, he still wouldn't take back what he'd said to me. He would have truly turned me over to the law. Me, his blood. He would have talked to anyone he could about my affairs until someone heard that might be able to do some damage."

"So you killed him?" Corey asked through gritted teeth.

"He . . . didn't leave me a choice."

"Wouldn't any other choice be preferable to murdering an innocent child?" Whiteoak asked.

"There was no other way to keep the business afloat. I do have other family to consider. Do you have any idea how much rich men are willing to pay for slaves? Men to labor in mines or fields, women to appease every appetite. It has always been a lucrative trade, but after the War Between the States the profits have tripled. Quadrupled!"

"I didn't know all of that," Whiteoak replied. "And it sickens me that I do now."

"But why?" Auberjohn sighed. "Why would Davey write this letter?"

"Did you read the entire thing?" Whiteoak asked. "At the end, it states very clearly that he was writing that letter to his aunt in Missouri in hopes that she might come and take him away before possibly trying to tell you what a mistake you were making in harming those people you were treating like so much cattle."

When Auberjohn looked at the professor, he studied Whiteoak very carefully. The longer he stared, the more perplexed he became. "How did you get this? Did Davey send it to you?"

"It was stuck in the boy's clothes," Corey

spat. "You might've found it if you hadn't been in such a damn hurry to put the body underground."

"That boy saw what was happening here," Whiteoak said. "He knew it was wrong. I imagine he loved his pa but didn't know how to make you stop what you were doing. He wrote this letter and was going to mail it when he came to you to give you one last chance to do the right thing."

Auberjohn shook his head as his hands gripped the letter tightly. His fingertips poked through the paper and once he'd done the initial damage, he kept ripping. "You couldn't know all of that! You had to be sent by someone else!"

"I read what was in the letter," Whiteoak said. "The words used by the boy don't just describe his intent. They show his feelings. What I didn't read, I surmised."

"Yeah, you're real goddamn smart," Auberjohn growled. "You've always got an angle, though. What's your angle here? You think you can blackmail me? Threaten to expose my business if I don't cut you in?"

"I came back here to see how I might atone for what I'd done. But I didn't have anything to do with that boy's death. You decided to tack it onto my already impressive list of crimes so you could be rid of it.

And since you're the one supplying part of the reward, you steered the bounty hunters that have been sent after me. You and others in this dreadful town have lawmen in your pocket as well, which means you can feed rumors into the mill and watch them become accepted as fact. It all becomes one giant whitewash with me in the middle of it, allowing you to do whatever the hell you please."

"Now you think you can judge me?" Auberjohn sneered. "What makes you any better than all the other thieves and killers who deserve to be hunted by the bounty hunters and posses of this world?"

"Oh, I'm not better than any of them. I do deserve to be hunted, which is why I've all but accepted my role as prey. I am a thief and I am quite the artist when it comes to deceit. That's why I can spot a con when I see one. What you're doing is all one giant diversion to misdirect the eyes of the law or competitors or whoever else you don't want sniffing around your affairs."

"Davey was my son!"

"And I'm sure you feel badly about killing him, but that doesn't mean you'd volunteer yourself to pay the price for what you did."

"You should've been strung up for that, you bastard," Corey said.

Ignoring the rage boiling inside of Corey, Auberjohn kept his eyes fixed on Whiteoak when he said, "Whoever sent you here made a mistake. There's nothing to show a judge that would put a man like me in jail. I *own* judges! I *own* lawmen! You don't even know the full extent of my business affairs!"

"That's one good thing about being someone in my very expensive boots," Whiteoak said with a grin. "I don't need enough evidence to convince a judge. All I need is enough to convince me. And, between that letter and what you've told me, it is quite convincing."

"All right," Auberjohn said through a thick veneer of calm. "You stumbled back into town and learned a thing or two. If you were going to leave this place alive, you might have something. As it is . . ."

Whiteoak snapped his hand forward to shake loose the small wedge-shaped knife secreted there. Flicking his wrist like the end of a whip, he sent the knife through the air and into the throat of Wilson Auberjohn.

Having plenty of experience in following the professor's lead, Corey threw himself at the gunman who'd followed Auberjohn into the livery. The gunman was quick enough to fire a shot, but his bullet merely scraped along Corey's back as Corey leaned forward to drive his shoulder into the gunman's midsection.

Bracing himself with a strong stance and a muscular frame, the gunman kept himself from being shoved to the floor. After absorbing a few chopping blows from Corey, he raised his pistol to take a downward chop of his own. Before he could drop the hammering attack onto Corey's neck or face, the gun was plucked from his hand. The gunman shoved Corey back and wheeled around to face the man who'd disarmed him, immediately snapping a sharp jab into Whiteoak's chin.

Whiteoak staggered back, doing his best to get a proper grip on the gun he'd taken. His fingers slipped into place around the weapon, cocking the hammer back and then squeezing the trigger. His first shot caught the gunman in the meaty muscle under his arm. The second one carved a messy hole into his chest, turning his heart into quivering pulp.

The gunman tried to take another step toward Whiteoak but dropped to his knees. He tried to take a breath but could only flop forward into a heap.

Bullets began ripping through the front of the livery as the remaining gunmen outside opened fire. Whiteoak and Corey scooped up whatever weapons they could find on the fresh bodies lying nearby before seeking refuge behind a short stack of hay bales.

"Just like Carson City, right?" Whiteoak said excitedly.

"You mean Carson Springs?" Corey corrected.

"No, it was Carson City where we —"

A few shots hissed dangerously close to Whiteoak's head, forcing him to crouch down even further. "Perhaps we should discuss this later," he said. "After we put those other hired guns down."

Holding the gun that had once belonged to Auberjohn, Corey said, "Now that sounds like a damn good plan."

CHAPTER FORTY-TWO

The first barrage of gunfire ripped into the livery like a deadly storm. It was short-lived, however, since there were only a small handful of men doing the shooting and they were forced to reload once the barrage had concluded. Before they could replace half the rounds in their pistols, Corey and Whiteoak exploded from the livery with guns blazing. Their first few shots were intended to keep the hired gunmen off their guard long enough for them to reach a better spot from which to fight. Once they were outside the livery, Corey and Whiteoak could line up their targets with relative ease.

The gunmen stood in a row, positioned to cover the livery but lacking any cover from an attack. They were caught on open ground in the middle of reloading. What followed in the next couple of seconds was just short of a slaughter. Corey sent one man to hell with a pair of shots that drilled into the gunman's chest. Whiteoak fired three shots at another hired killer, intent on hitting him in the head. His first two missed, but the third caught the gunman in the temple, spinning him around and killing him before he dropped.

Thunder from the gunshots rolled through the darkness, giving Corey and Whiteoak enough time to retrieve their guns, which had been tossed away only a few minutes before. Voices could be heard in the distance, prompting both men to glance toward the house.

"Sounds like we'll have some more company," Corey said. "How many killers do you think are on Auberjohn's payroll?"

"He didn't have much reason to surround himself with gunmen," Whiteoak replied. "Not in this town."

A few figures emerged from the house, some of which carried shotguns or simple tools like shovels or pitchforks.

"They look like workers to me," Whiteoak said.

"Leave them to us," said a scratchy voice from the livery.

Whiteoak turned to find the prisoners stepping out of the small building brandishing makeshift weapons of their own. "You're weak," the professor said. "You need to rest."

"We do," the prisoner replied. "But we also know these parts well enough to get away. We'll make it. You've done enough. You need to go before the others come."

"What others?" Corey asked.

"There have been other voices," the prisoner said. "Folks who come around to feed us or the like. There were only a few who carried guns. I think you got most of them."

"At least let us make sure you're all right."

"You're the medicine man, right?"

"I suppose so," Whiteoak replied.

"I heard them talking about you and how you robbed this town's bank. We might be safer on our own than with you."

"And I think we'll all be safer once we get outta here," Corey said. "Those others may not be killers, but they're getting curious. The longer we wait, the more time they'll have to screw up the courage to take a run at us."

"Good point. I see some horses over there."

When Whiteoak and the others headed for the stable, the people near the house shouted at them and fired a few reluctant shots in the air. Answering voices came from elsewhere in town, but Whiteoak didn't stay there long enough to see who was shouting. He and Corey retrieved their own horses and rounded up a few more so they and the prisoners could escape into the night. As the town started to come awake, there was only one spot in the area that Whiteoak thought might offer some bit of refuge.

"Sorry about this," he said to Beam when the undertaker answered the frantic knocking on his door. "I didn't know where else to go."

Glancing past Whiteoak and Corey, the undertaker looked at the tired, dirty faces of the prisoners behind them. "Who are they?"

"Remember the slaves Davey talked about in his letter?" Whiteoak asked.

"Yes."

"Here they are."

"So . . . Davey was speaking the truth," Beam said.

"And murder is illegal," Corey grunted as he started ushering the freed slaves into the undertaker's home, "but that don't stop people from killing folks. So long as there's shitty work to be done or filthy desires to be sated, there'll be reason for men to own slaves."

"I suppose so, but what do you expect me to do with them?"

Once everyone was inside, Whiteoak checked the street and shut the door. "There's nobody following us now, but there soon will be. I imagine people heard gunshots."

"I heard the shots from here," Beam said. "I'd say the Committee is probably forming as we speak."

"Committee?" Corey asked. "You mean them old-timers who line up in the second-floor windows to fire down at the street?"

"That's the one," Whiteoak replied. "I've had plenty of run-ins with them before and don't wish to repeat the experience. We need to go."

Beam already had his coat on and was hurrying to the back of his house. "That's right, you do. All of you."

"I was thinking we could leave in the morning," Whiteoak said. "These good people are weak. They need to rest."

One of the men from beneath Auberjohn's livery reached out to place a hand on the professor's shoulder. "We are hungry, but we don't need rest. All we've been doing is resting and if we got the chance to run, we're ready to take it."

Whiteoak looked at the dirty faces gathered around him and saw nothing but anxious readiness in their eyes.

"It might be best to go right now," Corey said. "That Committee or the law are probably still tryin' to figure out what happened at the Auberjohn place. Plus, we got the cover of night on our side."

"I've got food," Beam added. "You're welcome to it. As much as you need."

"Are you sure about that?" Whiteoak asked. "I'm not certain if or when I'll be able to repay you."

Shaking his head, Beam smiled. "I've been sitting on that letter, waiting for someone to give it to. It needed to be someone who'd understand it, know what to do about it, and have the gumption to do it. That's you two and you both came through even better than I could've imagined. That wickedness Mister Auberjohn was committing is done and he's paid for killing that poor, defenseless child. At least . . . I assume he was the one who killed him."

"He was," Whiteoak said. "No doubt about it."

Beam sighed. "I had a lot of time to stew about that letter and that bullet wound in Davey's body and that's all I could come up with that made any sense. Glad I was right. Well . . . not glad. You know what I mean."

"You mentioned food?" asked one of the

freed slaves who hadn't spoken until this moment. All Whiteoak could tell for certain was that the slave was a man. Color and even ethnic background was difficult to discern through the layers of dirt and grime caking his face. In that respect, he resembled the others who'd been found beneath the Auberjohn livery.

"There's some bacon, jerked beef, and canned fruit and beans over there," Beam said while pointing to his kitchen cupboard. "Take all you want."

As the slaves rushed to the cupboard, Whiteoak pressed his hand against Beam's, passing him a small roll of folded bills. "Here's some money," he said. "It's not much."

"I couldn't," Beam protested.

"Take it," Whiteoak said. "I won't hear otherwise."

Corey stood at one of the windows looking out to the street. "And don't tell a soul we were here," he warned. "Or where we're headed."

"You won't know where we're headed," Whiteoak added in a gentler tone. "As for the rest, do what you will. I'm not about to threaten a man who's done so much."

"No need for threats," the undertaker countered. "I set you on the road to the Auberjohn place. Doesn't make any sense for me to double-cross you afterwards."

"I suppose that's it, then," Whiteoak said. "We should go while there's plenty of darkness to cover our tracks."

Beam offered to draw a map of the surrounding area or describe some good routes to take, but Whiteoak politely refused. Having been there already for a major heist, he'd scouted the terrain more than enough and his memory was up to the task of seeing him through a night's ride. Within minutes, he and Corey and their group of freed prisoners were getting ready to leave.

The horses were saddled; bags were found near the stalls and loaded with the food that had been taken. By the time they all rode out, sounds of activity could be heard from the direction of the Auberjohn place. Whiteoak and Corey led the prisoners away from town in a silent procession until shadows were thick on all sides around them. As soon as their eyes adjusted to the dark, they quickened their pace and left Barbrady behind them for good.

After less than an hour of tense, cautious riding, the prisoner who'd done most of the talking thus far brought his horse to a stop.

"What're you doin'?" Corey snapped. "We got a ways to go before we can rest."

"Not resting," the prisoner replied. "We should split off from here. We'll travel faster on our own."

"Do you know the way?"

"Yes," the dirty man replied. "I've ridden through Kansas front and back several times. There's a friend who owns a farm —"

"Fine," Corey said, uninterested in the details. "You wanna strike out on yer own? Go on ahead."

After Corey continued along the path that had been chosen earlier, Whiteoak stayed behind to get another look at the men who'd been freed. He didn't know their names. He didn't know if they had families. He didn't know where they were from or where they were going. All of those unknowns came together inside him like several small holes converging into a gaping, empty pit.

Either sensing the professor's uncertainty or reading it on his face, the spokesman among the freed slaves said, "Just go, friend. You've already done so much."

"No, I . . ."

"You came from nowhere to answer our prayers," the slave chuckled. "It's more than we ever hoped we'd get. Thank you. Thank you so much. I'll think of you and that blessed child for the rest of my days."

All of the other dirty faces nodded in unison, mirroring their spokesman's sentiment.

"Good luck," was all Whiteoak could think to say to them. There was still lots of ground to cover, so that would have to be enough.

Chapter Forty-Three

The ride through Kansas was long and tedious. Not much was said between Corey and Whiteoak, simply because they were tired throughout the entire journey. Every step of the way, they were expecting to confront a posse or more bounty hunters looking to string them up for any number of offenses. They only rode on the main trails for short stretches of time, covering most of their ground on broken trails and all but forgotten paths across vast expanses of flat prairie. They didn't even risk using the same train station that had been their entry point into Kansas for fear of being spotted by a set of eyes searching for them.

Along the way, they paid for food and supplies in a fashion that was very familiar to both men. They stole. Corey snatched whatever he could at any small store he could find and Whiteoak used his rambling voice to distract various unsuspecting souls while his deft fingers picked their pockets. They didn't get much that way, but it was enough to see them to the northern Kansas border where a fairly large train station was situated within a town that still smelled of freshly cut lumber.

Whiteoak tugged at the edges of his coat, rumpling them instead of straightening with the intent of looking as little like himself as possible. While the common eye might not have picked up on much of a difference before and after the rumpling, Whiteoak felt changed enough to take on a slightly different posture and gait as he walked up to the ticket booth.

"Good afternoon," he said to the teller behind the small counter.

Fresh-faced and young, the clerk looked almost as new as the rest of the town. He gave Whiteoak a crisp nod and smile as he asked, "Where you headed, mister?"

"The Dakotas."

"We have a train leaving in two days for a station not too far from Deadwood."

"Anything sooner?"

After consulting with his schedule, the clerk said, "Only if you want to take a less direct route. There's one heading into Nebraska and then back through the state again before dropping you off at a connecting one heading north. That'll get you into the Dakota Territories, but it will take longer than if you waited for the one that's —"

"I'll take that one," Whiteoak said. "Two tickets, please."

The clerk shrugged and started filling out the paperwork.

Whiteoak glanced around for any suspicious looks being cast in his direction or any sinister figures waiting to pick him off. While he didn't see any immediate threats, he did spot something that caught his attention. Hanging from a corkboard near the ticket counter were several crude maps showing train routes, lists of arrivals and departures, and a bundle of reward notices advertising the prices being offered for various unsavory characters in the area. Whiteoak rustled through those out of habit, checking to see if he could spot any familiar names listed alongside the poorly drawn visages of the nefarious faces. More recently, he had started looking for his own name on those papers. After all, it was good to know if a higher price had been put on his head to stoke the fire already raging around him.

"What's this?" he asked while tapping one of the notices at the front of the collection.

Glancing up only momentarily, the clerk replied, "That one's no good any longer."

"Has it been cashed in?"

"Either that or canceled. How much luggage will you be taking with you to the Dakotas?"

There were other questions as well, along with payment to be arranged. Whiteoak handed over the last of his money to cover the expense, knowing he would recoup the loss once the horses were sold. "Mind if I take this with me?" he asked while still holding on to the notice he'd spotted.

"Go ahead. I've got a few more around here somewhere."

Whiteoak tore off the page and went outside. Corey stood nearby, holding the reins to both horses in his hand. "You get the tickets or will we still be needing these?" he asked.

"Look," Whiteoak said, presenting the paper he'd taken.

Corey squinted at the reward notice. "It's one of yours. And mine, according to the small print. I'm just an accomplice, huh? Misspelled my name again."

"No! Look at the fresh ink across the middle of the page."

"Repealed? What's that mean?"

"It means the reward's been canceled!" Since he wasn't getting the reaction he wanted from Corey, Whiteoak held the reward notice in both hands in front of him as if it was Holy Scripture. "The reward's been called off. There's no more money being offered. Since Auberjohn was the man putting up the funds for it and he's no longer with us, there's no more reward money! That means no more bounty hunters! For God's sake, you spent time as a bounty hunter. Aren't you familiar with this sort of thing?"

Blinking at the paper as though he thought the ink might shift into new words entirely, Corey explained, "I wasn't a bounty hunter for long and I sure as hell never saw any reward get canceled. That . . ." His expression shifted into pure joy. The lines around his wide grin were deep enough to cause cracks in the layers of trail dust that had collected on his cheeks over the last several days. "That's great!"

"Word sure travels fast."

"There's telegraph wires hooked into that ticket office," Corey pointed out. "Word was sent out from Barbrady probably as soon as that asshole Auberjohn was found dead. Last thing anyone wants is to have a bunch of bounty hunters trying to collect a reward that nobody's gonna pay."

Whiteoak nodded enthusiastically for several seconds before his expression dimmed a bit. "Of course, there's still a few smaller rewards that have been floating around out there in regard to some earlier jobs of mine."

"Yeah," Corey said in a sobering tone. "I got a few of them with my name on 'em, too."

"And we probably won't want to announce who we are in these parts anytime soon. In case there are some others who might have a problem with the money that was lost in that bank."

"And them bounty hunters I fooled will probably put together who I am sooner or later. I should probably steer clear of them as well."

"Right. Good point. I suppose lawmen don't exactly need a reward, either." Whiteoak glanced around nervously. He lowered his voice considerably when he said, "There's a train leaving today that will get us back to the Dakota Territories on a rather indirect route. I got the tickets."

"Good. Sooner the better. I'll sell these horses."

Whiteoak looked once more at the reward notice in his hands. He folded it neatly and tucked it away into a pocket.

CHAPTER FORTY-FOUR

Danielle sat in her little office, balancing Tara's books while trying to ignore the sounds of men rutting with other girls in nearby rooms. Her figures were off by a few dollars on the ledger she'd been studying for the past several hours, which would normally nag at her like a little unscratchable itch in the back of her mind. On this day, however, she decided it was close enough and slammed the ledger shut.

It had been just under three weeks since she'd last seen Henry Whiteoak or Corey Maynard. Dylan showed up every now and then to check up on her, but he had other reasons for visiting Dugan's Find apart from making certain she was doing all right. More often than not, the outlaw remained in the hills tending to his own affairs. He was never keen to tell her what those affairs might be and she didn't care enough to ask.

It was darker than she'd expected when

she stepped outside of Tara's tent. Although it felt somewhat comforting to be locked away in her room with only a few lanterns to keep her company, time tended to slip by without her noticing. Danielle looked up and found a few bright stars in the sky above her. As her eyes grew accustomed to the night, more stars appeared like friendly neighbors poking their heads out to say hello.

She walked through camp, keeping her head down low enough to avoid human contact while making sure her eyes were at the right level to spot any potential trouble coming her way. As always, the only trouble in camp was the usual sort. Cowboys still got drunk and wild. Assholes still screamed and shot their guns off sometimes. Miners still scrapped for every bit of gold they could see. None of it concerned her. At least, it hadn't for some time. Even so, considering where she was headed, Danielle knew she couldn't afford to let her guard down.

Rather than walk a straight path to the camp's perimeter, she took a curving route that allowed her to see if there was anyone trying to follow her. There were no lurkers in the shadows but going through those practiced sets of motions brought her closer to the one who'd taught them to her. A tired smile drifted onto her face as she savored the memories that drifted through her mind and, before long, she was outside of Dugan's Find.

The path from there was well known to her and there was no need to take extra measures to ensure she wasn't followed. There were more than enough dry branches, gnarled shrubs, and fallen leaves at or near foot level to make noise should anyone come along. Danielle walked to a spot far enough from camp for the torch light to dim, but not so far that she couldn't hear the occasional shout or disturbance from the nearby settlement. Ahead, a large shadow loomed, silent and unmoving. She approached it while reaching a hand out as if to pat the side of a passing beast.

"It's still there," came a voice from behind her. "Bravo."

Danielle spun around, fumbling for the little holster strapped around her calf. Once her hands found the Derringer kept near the top of her boot, she drew the pistol and held it in front of her. "Step out where I can see you!" she demanded.

Whiteoak moved out from behind a tree, holding his hands up high.

"You nearly scared the hell out of me," she said.

"Nearly?" Whiteoak chuckled. "I couldn't help myself. It was a childish prank, to be sure, but surely not one worthy of a firing squad."

Slowly, almost reluctantly, Danielle lowered her Derringer. "How long have you been back?" she asked.

"A few days."

"A few days? Why didn't you find me sooner?"

"I hung back to watch for any bounty hunters that might be waiting for my return. I didn't see any, so I decided it was safe to enter town. Why is my wagon out here instead of tucked inside a stable?"

"It's been quiet," Danielle said. "Mostly because folks think you're gone. Kind of hard to do if your wagon is still where everyone can see it. Feels strange, considering everything that happened."

"Not really," Whiteoak said as he stepped closer to her. "Corey and I managed to snuff out the price on my head at the source. Well, the largest price, anyway. Bounty hunters are professionals, after all. Without a reward, there's no reason for them to come after me."

"I'm sure some of them have reasons to kill you other than money."

Whiteoak was close enough to her now to

reach out and place his hands on her waist.

"What about you?" he whispered. "Do you want to kill me?"

"Sometimes."

"I suppose I've earned that." He smiled and added, "You learned a lot from a man you'd like to shoot. I saw how you snaked your way through town, watching for tails and looking out for suspicious faces."

"You were following me for that long?"

"Indeed."

"Then I suppose I wasn't as good as I thought," she said.

"You're very good," Whiteoak told her while easing his hands around to clasp at the small of her back. "I'm just the best."

Danielle pulled back and when he wouldn't unlock his hands, she leaned away from him and thumped both fists against his chest. The pelting blows weren't hard enough to break her loose and she didn't continue trying. Scowling into his eyes, she said, "I kept an eye on this damn wagon of yours for nearly a month!"

"Barely a flicker of time in the scheme of things."

"I didn't hear anything from you!"

"I didn't think you were overly concerned."

Lowering her head, Danielle spoke in a

much softer voice when she admitted, "I was worried sick about you."

Whiteoak wrapped his arms all the way around her and pulled her close. He nestled his face into her soft, curly hair and replied, "I know."

After several long, blissful seconds, she asked, "What happened in Kansas?"

"I'll tell you everything later. All right?"

When Danielle looked up again, she placed her hands on his face and said, "You didn't kill that boy."

Whiteoak's eyes widened a bit. "How do you know?"

"Because I know you, Henry. You may be a liar, a cheat, a swindler, and untrustworthy, but you're too careful to do something like that. You're a good man."

"After all that, I'm a good man?" Whiteoak chuckled.

She nodded. "You are and . . . I . . ."

"Yes?"

"I missed you."

With that, she pulled his face closer and kissed him. Their lips remained pressed together until they each had to take a breath. Almost immediately, they came together again with more passion and intensity than before. Whiteoak eased back and stepped around to stand beside her.

Draping an arm around her, he gazed at his wagon parked nearby and announced, "There's something I've been meaning to do."

CHAPTER FORTY-FIVE

It didn't take long for the fire to spread.

A few well-placed splashes of kerosene followed by the touch of a torch here and there was all that was needed to set the garishly painted wagon ablaze. Before one drop of kerosene had been spilled, Whiteoak had gone inside to fetch a few things and when he returned, he got the flames going without a moment's hesitation. Now, standing beside Danielle and a short stack of his possessions, all that remained was for the professor to watch what had been his entire world burn to a cinder.

"I'll admit," Danielle said in hushed reverence, "this wasn't what I was expecting."

"There's plenty of time for what you were expecting a little later," Whiteoak chided while wrapping her in his arms and kissing her cheek.

She playfully swatted him and twisted around to face the fire without breaking his hold on her. "When did you decide to do this?" she asked.

"As soon as I heard about the Auberjohn boy."

"But you told me about what happened while you were away," she said, referring to the detailed account Whiteoak had given her while preparing the fire. "You didn't have anything to do with his death."

"I know. When I first thought about this drastic course of action, it was out of guilt. Then it became something else. That wagon was my home and prosperity for years until it became a part of me. The part of me that wanted to be seen no matter how dangerous it was or who was looking to find me. It was the voice that screamed everything running through my head at the world, good or bad."

"Screaming how amazing you think you are," Danielle pointed out.

Whiteoak shrugged. "Also, how stupid I thought most others could be. Perhaps it was a challenge for someone to call me on some of my exaggerations."

"I called you on them. All the time."

"Which is why I wanted you here with me when I made this shift in my life. Everything must shift. Change is inevitable and necessary. It's destructive and painful. It's also freeing. Very, very freeing."

She shook her head and leaned back against Whiteoak's chest. "You're burning this wagon because it seems like the last possible thing you *should* do. You like to spit in the face of common sense just to prove you can get away with it."

"Seems like a good reason to me."

Suddenly, the fire blazed and flared as glass within the wagon shattered and its contents were summarily destroyed.

Danielle straightened up as her muscles tensed. "Perhaps we should have moved that wagon farther away from camp. What if the flames spread?"

"They won't," Whiteoak assured her. "Just watch."

Slowly, Danielle settled against him. She wasn't completely at ease, but she wasn't about to go anywhere.

"I rigged specific chemicals to be set within the floorboards in the event I ever had to destroy my beauty over there," he explained. "They burn quite hot and very fast. Should be quite the spectacle."

"Coming from you, that must be something to see."

They didn't have to wait long. At first, the fire began to reach out and up as different chemicals and concoctions were set alight to turn the flames into a variety of bright colors. Pale blue, dark red, bright orange, and even a few flashes of green lit up the night as the wooden box was consumed.

"That's incredible," Danielle sighed.

"Just wait."

At first, there was a moment of silence. That was followed by a rush of air that swept in toward the wagon as a massive fireball was unleashed. Something inside the wagon had been touched by the flame, much like a bundle of dynamite is touched by a crackling fuse. There was a dull thump. Heat washed over them.

Silence.

Danielle hadn't realized she'd closed her eyes until she pried them open again. The first thing she saw was Whiteoak standing right where she'd last seen him, gazing with wide eyes at the smoldering pile of charred wood in front of them. The wagon was gone. In its place was a twisted heap of wood, metal bands, and several small fires nipping at the whole mass with all the intensity of a few cooking fires.

"What happened?" Danielle gasped. "I thought we were going to . . ."

"Die?" Whiteoak said. "Not hardly. The science is solid. There's a practice among some firefighters to put out a fire with an even bigger one. Since fire feeds on air, hence blowing on a spark to get it to burn, a large fire would eat up all the necessary air being used by the smaller fire."

"But, doesn't that still leave the large fire?"

"The package I created was intended to flare out in a spectacular flame like a huge puff of smoke. In the process, it consumed the smaller fire before evaporating itself." Shaking his head, he mused, "Always wondered if that truly would work."

"We could have stood a bit farther away," she pointed out. "In case it hadn't worked."

"What? And miss the show?"

Coming from anyone else, that statement would have been maddening in its arrogant recklessness. Coming from Professor Henry Whiteoak, it seemed about right.

Still looking at the flames, Whiteoak put his arm around Danielle and held her close. Then he whispered, "I looked for the gold and didn't find anything but a mess. Looked as though some filthy bandits ransacked the poor girl."

"Gold?"

"Yes. The gold I kept in a compartment inside that wagon. The compartment that only you and I know how to unlock."

"Oh, that gold. I gave most of it to that U.S. marshal."

Whiteoak tensed but didn't take his eyes away from the charred remains in front of him. "Can I ask why you would do such a thing?"

"Actually, I gave some of it to Dylan, also."

"Well, he earned it by keeping an eye on you. He did keep an eye on you, right?"

"Oh, yes," Danielle replied. "He watched over me until I sent the marshal after him."

Whiteoak's arm slid off of her and he slowly turned to face her. "Explain that to me because I couldn't have possibly heard that correctly."

"It was both of our idea," she said. "The marshal paid me a visit, telling me about some scheme you had where you were stealing gold or fool's gold from government shipments."

Rolling his eyes, Whiteoak let out a haggard sigh. "I barely took a fraction of that gold and it was handed over to me by the idiots who were driving those shipments from place to place!"

"But you still stole it?"

"You saw my presentation with the Mineralogical Purity Detector, didn't you?"

"Yes."

"Same thing, exactly. All I needed to do was put myself in a position where the best possible audience could hear my explanation and see the demonstration," Whiteoak said. "Standard practice for any salesman."

"But not every salesman targets government shipments," Danielle pointed out.

"True, but did that marshal tell you those gold shipments were merely being used as a diversion tactic?"

"He explained that the fool's gold would be used as bait to keep real government funds from being stolen or tracked. It sounded like a necessary precaution and, frankly, an idea you might have come up with if you were in their position."

Whiteoak stopped short before answering. He thought about what he'd heard, tapped his chin, and grinned. "I suppose I might have come up with an idea like that. Instead, I came up with this one. I showed those couriers my purity detector and they were very interested. You know why?"

"I'm sure you're aching to tell me."

"It's because they wanted a quick and easy way to know if they were carrying shipments of real or false gold so they could take it for themselves."

"You know they meant to rob that gold?" Danielle asked skeptically.

"What else does one do with gold besides hoard or spend it?" he scoffed. "Look, I'd heard about these shipments by sheer chance. I found myself in a spot . . ." Upon seeing the stern gaze from Danielle, Whiteoak quickly added, "I put myself in a spot where I might meet up with some of these couriers. Not only were they of suspect character, but they affiliated themselves with some very unsavory men known as thieves and smugglers themselves. And before you ask, yes, I knew those unsavory men after having worked with them myself."

"Good God, Henry."

"You want to hear this or not?"

She crossed her arms and raised an eyebrow like a schoolmarm listening to one of her rowdiest students.

"If those couriers meant to just do their job," Whiteoak continued, "none of them would have taken more than a passing interest in what I was selling. As it was, I only had to find two couriers before I got my first real prospect."

"How did you find those couriers?"

"Rumors circulate. Thieves talk amongst themselves. The whole crux of this government plan was to set bait to trap robbers. Wouldn't do much good if those robbers could never find the bait."

She rolled her eyes. "Guess it pays to think like a thief," Danielle sighed.

"Sometimes more than others," he replied.

"Anyway, all I had to do was set up shop along some of the major routes and play up my purification detector. Once it was shown to work, word spread and the couriers came to me. They were always the men with the freshly cast gold coins and small bars that had been cast to make them easy to transport. They went into my detector and fool's gold always came out. Simple bait and switch. One never goes wrong with the classics."

"So, they bring gold to test and you switched it out for the fakes."

"Exactly. Same switch every time. They would invariably approach me after a demonstration, asking to buy a machine, and I would talk them into merely testing whatever gold they had for a small fee."

"How could you convince them to do that?" Danielle asked.

To that, Whiteoak merely grinned as though he was posing for a statue being carved to honor the greatest salesman of all time.

"Right," she replied dryly. "I almost forgot."

"A few of the men who approached me wanted only the machine, but I would raise the price to such a degree that they wouldn't take it. The ones I was after didn't want to carry around something like a piece of equipment designed to test the purity of gold. That would only implicate them if they were caught."

"You came up with all of this on your own?"

"Over the course of some time, yes," Whiteoak said. "The hard part was in figuring out where some of those couriers would be at what time."

"How did you do that?"

Whiteoak shrugged as the fires dwindled down to crackling flickers. "Bribed a crooked politician at a fort used as a stopping point for federal couriers. Been doing that for years and it finally paid off."

"Weren't some of those couriers carrying fool's gold?"

"Sure, but it didn't matter. I took enough of it to make the enterprise worthwhile. The real gold was locked safely away and the fool's gold was used for future demonstrations."

"All that time spent planning," she mused. "All that effort to figure out what to do, where to go, when to act. All that money used to bribe and put together this entire venture. Surely there was danger involved."

"Not really. I allowed the couriers to think I suspected nothing. After all, there's no law against testing gold."

"Even so, wouldn't it be easier just to put your efforts into your inventions? You have real talent, Henry!"

"Thrill of the hunt, I suppose. Not the same as being fed your supper on a silver platter."

"What about that purity detector?" she asked hopefully. "That obviously works, so you could . . ." She sighed again and watched the dying fire. "It doesn't work, does it?"

"No."

"What about the demonstrations?"

"You know those folks at the beginning of my show?" he asked. "The ones who I swear I've never met who bring some gold trinket or little nugget to be tested?"

"Yes."

"I knew them."

After a few seconds filled only with the quiet crackle of dwindling flames, Danielle asked, "That's it?"

"Yes. I made arrangements and paid them ahead of time to follow a script I gave them and go along with me for the rest. Simple, really. So simple that most people refuse to believe that's all there is. Ask any magician and he'll tell you a similar story in regard to how some illusion works."

"So your purification device is . . . just a box?"

"It's quite a fancy box," Whiteoak teased. "But, yes. It's a sham. Much like me." He allowed his head to droop a little. He clenched his jaw and looked away from the fire for the first time since it had started. "I'm glad you turned me and Dylan over to the marshals. Lord knows we both deserve it."

"You might deserve some jail time," Danielle told him, "but I'd say you more than made up for it with the good you've done."

"And what good is that?"

Danielle stepped in front of him so she could look into his eyes as she said, "You make real medicines, too, you know. You sell them to folks in need. Your tonics may sometimes be bubbly water with sugar flavoring, but they make people feel better. I've seen you step in and take someone's side because nobody else would."

"I've killed men, Danielle."

"You've killed those who meant to kill you. Those who'd already killed others. You're not a murdering dog. You're a good man in here," she said while placing her hand flat against his chest. "Maybe not an honest man, but you're good. Look at what you did when you heard about the Auberjohn boy. You went out there to set things right as best you could."

"Things could have gone wrong," he said. "I take so many chances, gamble on so many things, something's bound to go wrong."

"Is that why you did this?" she asked while motioning toward the charred pile of wagon parts and scorched chemicals.

"Partly. Mostly . . . I'm just selfish."

She laughed quietly. "You think burning up your livelihood is *selfish*?"

"There still may be men out to find me," Whiteoak told her. "There's plenty out there who have a bone to pick with me or might try to exact some form of payback for money they lost. That wagon was always a way for folks to find me and, for a long while, I was all right with that. I figured, when it comes time for me to pay for things I'd done, I'm willing to pay. That time comes for every man, after all."

"It does. That all seems so exciting. Tracking government money, stealing it, hiding it."

"Makes for a good story," Whiteoak admitted. "Living through it was rather dull. Just a lot of asking questions, paying bribes, and putting on the same shows I normally do. Took a while for me to acquire that gold.

Now perhaps you can tell me why you gave it away."

"I was hoping you'd forget to come back around to that part."

Whiteoak didn't laugh at her awkward joke and instead waited patiently for her to talk again.

After taking a breath, Danielle said, "Those marshals were closing in on you. They'd already searched the wagon."

"They never would've found the gold."

"But they wouldn't stop looking. I wasn't even certain you'd done what they were accusing you of, but had to see for myself. I knew where you'd hide so much gold if you did steal it, so I went to see for myself. I took what I found and showed it to Dylan to see what I should do."

"You trusted that scoundrel with my gold?"

"You trusted him with me! I thought that made him trustworthy!"

Biting his tongue, Whiteoak motioned for her to continue.

"I wanted to find a way to get the gold back to those marshals without them knowing where it came from," she said. "Once they had their gold, they'd go away. That's what I thought."

"Doesn't work that way with federal

men," Whiteoak groaned.

"That's what Dylan said. It was his idea for me to take some of the gold to Marshal Farell and say I'd found it in Dylan's saddlebags. Dylan would take some more of it and ride into the Badlands, spending some here and there to keep the marshals on his trail."

"Why would he do that just to protect me?" Whiteoak asked.

"Because you saved his life. People truly do owe you for some of the good you've done, no matter how pessimistic you may be," she said, poking Whiteoak's chest for emphasis. "I took it to the marshals and told them about Dylan. Farell wanted to search your wagon one more time and I helped him do it. He didn't find much and rode off to help his deputy hunt down Dylan."

"If they find him, it won't be pretty," Whiteoak warned.

"I know, but Dylan insisted. If I didn't help with the ruse, he would've done it himself. Those federal men wanted to find their gold thief and Dylan arranged for them to find one. Now they're not looking for you."

"So, no more marshals and no more bounty hunters."

"Isn't that what you wanted?"

Whiteoak looked away from her and to the smoking pile of malodorous junk. "I was thinking it's time for me to stop making it so easy for my enemies to find me. Perhaps I've paid what I owe and can fade away for a while."

"I can't say I've ever heard you talk like this, Henry."

"Like I said before, I'm being selfish here. Right now, I want to have some peace and quiet so I can find somewhere to live where two folks can just enjoy each other's company beside a roaring fire."

Both of them had to laugh at that. When they were through laughing, Danielle nestled against him and said, "I've never heard you like this, Henry. You seem . . . lighter."

"It's time for a change. Once someone truly embraces that, the world doesn't seem so heavy."

"Would I be correct in thinking I'm the other person whose company you'd like to keep beside the fire?"

"You would."

"Is this the fire?" she asked.

"No. Well . . . one of them. The first of many," Whiteoak said. "How's that for a proposition?"

"I haven't heard a proposition yet."

Clearing his throat, Whiteoak said, "I

intend on starting fresh somewhere else. New life, new home, new everything. Would you come with me?"

"I will."

Scowling dramatically, Whiteoak asked, "The next time I acquire a fortune, are you going to hand it all over to outlaws and lawmen again?"

"I never said I handed it *all* over."

Whiteoak's face exploded into a smile that was brighter than the multicolored flames that had sent his chemicals skyward in a stinking cloud. Some of the folks from camp were making their way to the clearing to investigate the lights and fire, but the professor only had eyes for the woman right in front of him. He took her in his arms, whispered in her ear, and kissed her passionately on the lips.

That night, the Badlands lost a medicine man and Henry Whiteoak became richer than he ever could have dreamed.

ABOUT THE AUTHOR

Marcus Galloway is the author of several western series including *The Man from Boot Hill* and *The Accomplice.* He currently lives in West Virginia.

The employees of Thorndike Press hope you have enjoyed this Large Print book. All our Thorndike, Wheeler, and Kennebec Large Print titles are designed for easy reading, and all our books are made to last. Other Thorndike Press Large Print books are available at your library, through selected bookstores, or directly from us.

For information about titles, please call:
  (800) 223-1244

or visit our Web site at:
  http://gale.com/thorndike

To share your comments, please write:
  Publisher
  Thorndike Press
  10 Water St., Suite 310
  Waterville, ME 04901